A ROMANTIC FANTASY ADVENTURE

MIGHTIER THAN MAGIC

G. S. KENNEY

Copyright

Praise for Mightier Than Magic

I s love mightier than magic? Wow, I am astounded by this book. Blending fantasy and fairytale with an epic world-building experience, *Mightier Than Magic* will make you a believer. Once I started reading, I couldn't stop. Fantasy readers rejoice, your new binge-read adventure awaits you...

A classic fairytale retold in glorious fashion. The characters are so well written, they leap from the pages and into your heart...

I am a die-hard fantasy reader. *Mightier Than Magic* ranks as one of the top reads of the year. Trust me, you'll want to read this book. Highly recommend!

My Rating: 5+ stars
— N. N. Light's Book Heaven

Contents

1. A fortuitous introduction   1

2. The topic of magic is broached   15

3. The queen sets a ransom price   31

4. Alaric proposes a union   50

5. Alaric makes his wishes known   62

6. Katie comes up with a plan   76

7. Katie performs a serious magic   91

8. A new beginning   100

9. Too much, too fast   113

10. A worthwhile mystery   126

11. A mystery in a cavern   142

12. In Larippia   148

13. Katie gets to know Rom   164

14. Return to Darimbia   175

15. A reintroduction   187

16. The fighting intensifies   199

17. Katie learns more magic   210

18. The truth will out   226

19. The oathstone has its way   244

20. The end of the beginning   254

Saving Aran   268

Acknowledgments   276

CHAPTER ONE

A fortuitous introduction

M ouse slipped into the kitchen and inched along the wall, holding her skirts so that they wouldn't rustle.

"Hello, Princess Mouse," said the first assistant cook. He was a young man, no older than her own eighteen years, with curly blond hair and freckles. He turned from the fruit he'd been cutting and gave her a slight bow and an amused smile, revealing uneven teeth.

Mouse found him frightening. All the people in the castle were. They talked about her behind her back. They laughed at her when they thought she wasn't looking. Worst of all, they reported everything she did to her mother, who was always critical of her. Mouse remembered her manners, though, and stood a bit straighter as she returned his greeting.

The young cook went back to his task, that amused smile still on his face.

Mouse redoubled her hold on her skirts and moved as soundlessly as she could along the wall behind the backs of half a dozen people hard at work. Their chopping set up an arrhythmic clatter, a percussive backdrop to sizzling and boiling sounds from the massive stoves and the chatter of the cooks. She edged past the cooking area with its savory aromas of fresh meat and onions, garlic and herbs, and crept up a steep flight of stairs into the staging area.

Tables sagged with dirty dishes littered with bones and half-eaten vegetables and meats waiting to be tossed to the dogs. Other tables were piled with courses still waiting to be served—decorated cakes and pies that had been completed by the pastry chefs earlier in the day, and platters of artfully arranged cheeses and fruits.

A screen between the kitchen staging area and the banqueting hall hid the dirty work involved in the preparation and clean-up of the feast from the nobles dining beyond. Shouts and laughter emerged from the hall, loud and raucous over the clanking of dishes and cutlery. The noise hit Mouse like a barrage of arrows, sending her heart into overdrive.

She reassured herself that she could do this. For all its rich fabric, silk that whispered softly when she moved, her gray dress was almost the exact shade of the stone walls, making it easy for Mouse to creep invisibly around the perimeter of the room.

No, this would be easy. All she wanted was a glimpse of the exotic stranger whom her mother had taken prisoner, a hint that might allow her to dream of someplace faraway with lots of sunshine and fresh air, where perhaps people would be less critical of her many failings.

It probably wouldn't even be necessary to enter the large hall with its pennants and tapestries, its gaily clad nobles and hovering wait staff, its disharmonious noises. Perhaps she could see the man from right here. She hunched down low and leaned forward to look around the screen.

Some twenty-five people sat at the elongated U-shaped table, with her mother in the middle of the narrow far end at the table's head. Queen Claudia wore an elaborately embroidered green satin gown. In her cleavage glistened a large solitaire diamond, a family heirloom. Two young men sat next to her, one on either side. The brilliant red of the one man's costume vied with the bold orange of the other, colors so vivid their faces seemed washed out, their hair the color of old straw. From their age and positions of honor to the queen's right and left, they must be the princes Enrico and Ferdo from Bonaveria, come to court her sisters. And yes, next to each sat one of her sisters. Jocasta, the eldest, wearing a sapphire blue gown embroidered with sapphire beads, sat next to the one in red, and next to the orange-clad prince sat Mercuria, second oldest, giggling at whatever he was saying. She wore an emerald gown a slightly darker shade than her mother's and as richly embroidered as her sister's. Everyone said the two princes from Bonaveria were the most eligible men around. And indeed, Mouse's two sisters were trying very hard to please.

Down the rows of both arms of the table sat all the usual courtiers, from ancient Lord Ned of Desseldown to young Lord Tobey Byron who recently inherited Connoway, the richest estate in the land. Lord Tobey was buck-toothed and a bit slow witted, and he brayed when he laughed. Especially when she was angry, the queen had already told Mouse she was considering marrying Mouse to him.

For her part, Mouse wanted to escape her mother's castle so badly that sometimes her stomach cramped with the ache of it. But she wasn't desperate enough to marry Lord Tobey. Better to stay out of her mother's sight. Better just to disappear.

But where was—?

There he was, the captured king Mouse hoped to catch a glimpse of, right at the very end of the banquet table closest to her. Her mother had brought her prisoner to this dinner to show him off to her court.

He sat in profile to the screen where Mouse hid, his head turned slightly away as he looked down the long table. His dark hair was long and curly and looked a bit unkempt for a king. At least, for the kings she'd read about in her romance novels. But of course, as a prisoner, he wouldn't have the valet and other servants he was probably used to. Or maybe they didn't have servants over there in Westland the way the gentry did here. Mouse could just see the edge of a neatly trimmed dark beard, a prominent nose, a sculpted cheekbone. A good-looking man, and his clothing—sent by the king's brother under truce—was exotic enough to suit her notion of what a foreign monarch would wear. A vest-like garment of white silk covered in delicate rainbow-colored embroidery and thread-of-gold showed off his strongly muscled arms. With gilded buttons along the chest, it fell loose across his legs, revealing slim-fitting dark blue pants that gave a hint of the well-formed legs inside.

Mouse smiled. Indeed, he was attractive enough to claim a place in her dreams.

She'd heard that he'd sworn not to attempt escape or try to harm anyone here, and that her mother referred to him as her guest, not her prisoner. But the man was bound. A thin band chained his left hand to his chair, long enough only to allow him to manipulate his cutlery. But he wasn't eating. He rested his chin on his hand, his body sagging as if with the weight of a great sorrow.

With a rush of empathy, Mouse realized that he probably wanted to escape even more than she did. Poor man! She wished she could see more of his face. She inched out farther past the edge of the screen.

Something whacked her shoulder with frightening force.

"Ow!" She whirled around, frightened.

Her cry was drowned in the clatter of a falling metal tray and the crash of breaking dishes. A serving boy tumbled to the floor after his tray. Mouse reached out her hand to him in case he needed help, but he scrambled quickly to his feet and began loading broken fragments onto the tray.

The banquet hall fell silent, and every face turned toward Mouse. Her face burned; it must be redder than the strawberries all over the floor. She wished she could vanish. Or just die on the spot.

"Mouse!" The queen's voice was coated in ice. "Come here."

Alaric's thoughts kept returning to the problem of how to free himself.

He had no regrets about his attempt to rescue Marco and the two other Darimbian resistance fighters from Claudia's encampment where they'd been held prisoner. He didn't want to lose any of his fighters, especially not his younger brother Marco. They were good men, all of them. Alaric loved Marco, and the people of Darimbia loved him too. While Marco was free, the fight for Darimbia would continue, perhaps even escalate. He still believed he had made the right decision. Assembling enough fighters to face the queen's army would have taken a week or more, and by that time, the prisoners would have likely been dead.

No, the rescue had had to be undertaken immediately, and Alaric was the only one who could do magic, and therefore the only one with any hope of getting safely in and out of the camp.

Only he hadn't managed to get safely out.

He glanced at the forged-iron chain that ran from a cuff on his left wrist to a thicker-than-decorative circle in the framing of his heavy metal chair. He tried to imagine escaping this castle with the chair in tow. Dragging it behind him? Lifting it onto his shoulder? Alaric smiled grimly.

No, there was no escaping. He'd given his word in exchange for his life, and his word was good.

With little notice, Alaric had been ordered to clean up and dress, and then ordered to attend the queen and thirty nobles of the realm at dinner. No doubt she was gloating about making him her prisoner, and there was nothing he could do about it.

He took the opportunity to observe his enemy and the nobles of her court. He would not have chosen this imprisonment as a way of getting to know Queen Claudia, but it had been instructive. She sat at the head of the table, of course, where he had a clear view. She was beautiful in a cold way, her red hair elaborately adorned with feathers and diamonds, her spine stiff, her expression betraying no emotion. Her pale green gown revealed an enticing amount of cleavage, show-casing an ostentatiously showy diamond of several dozen carats.

The conversation at the head of the table was inaudible from his seat, but he could see the queen was doing most of the talking. To either side of her sat a young man, one dressed in bright red, the other in orange, both looking for all the world like overdressed tropical birds listening intently to her words. At first, Alaric thought they might be vying to become her lovers, or perhaps already were. But on the other side of each man sat one of Claudia's three daughters, with the third daughter right next to the second. All three practically hung on the young men as the men focused on the queen. These must be suitors for the daughters then, the young princes from Bonaveria whose names Alaric didn't know, but whose security arrangements he had overheard the guards discussing.

Like their mother, the queen's daughters were beautiful. Alaric had learned their names and descriptions from the reports of his spy, a Darimbian who worked at the palace as a gardener's assistant and saw them coming and going often enough. Now he matched faces to the names. Next to the red-clad prince was Jocasta, the eldest, in a gown of royal blue that set off her deep blue eyes and the highlights in her raven hair. On the other side of the queen next to the orange-clad prince sat Mercuria, second oldest, giggling at whatever he was saying. She wore an emerald gown that matched her emerald eyes and emphasized hair as bright red as her mother's. Next to her was the youngest daughter, Stefania, fair-skinned and blond, in a deep pink dress set with pearls. Yes, all three were trying very hard to please.

"Don't you think so, Your Majesty?" asked the elderly woman sitting next to Alaric.

He hadn't heard a word she'd just said. The lady had been talking nonstop since she sat down, rattling on about trivialities of her life that were obviously as fascinating to her as they were tedious to him. "I beg your pardon, Madam," he said. "I didn't quite catch that."

She drew a deep breath. "Well. I was saying how the fashions today seem to favor the young women over the old. One should not be forced to wear clothing that shows off a girlish waist, not after a certain age, don't you agree?"

"Oh, indeed, Madam. But you, of course, look ravishing." She was wearing a high-collared, loose-fitting dress richly decorated with pearls and sequins. Its pale gray color nearly matched her hair. The dowager countess Matilda, from the far northern province of Nostrium, as far from Darimbia as was possible to be, and still be one of Queen Claudia's subjects. It was a clever seating plan. The countess would be worthless as a source of information for him, and a constant drain on his attention. He nodded his acknowledgment, though, and gave her a warm smile.

"But I say, the young have always wanted to show off, haven't they? I remember, when I was a girl—"

The sudden clatter of a falling metal tray and crash of breaking dishes silenced all conversation. Alaric turned to see a serving boy tumbled on the floor, splattered with cream, surrounded by shards of china, rolling strawberries, and ruined cake. Nearby sprawled a rather nondescript-looking young woman with long light-brown hair, her clothing too rich to belong to a servant, yet too plain for this gaudy company.

"Mouse!" The queen's voice was frigid with suppressed anger. "Come here."

The young woman—Mouse, was it? Certainly an unusual name—stood awkwardly. "Yes, Mother." She walked up the center of the table's U to face the queen.

Mother? Alaric straightened, studying her. Could it be that Queen Claudia had a fourth daughter, one his spy had never seen, or had not seen fit to mention? True, his spy worked out-of-doors, but he had seen the other princesses coming and going. Why not this one? And why had she not been invited to the feast? Could this daughter be an outcast in her own family? If so, that was something Alaric might find useful, if he could make contact with her.

"You told my page you were too sick to attend the feast tonight," the queen said.

"Yes, Mother."

"And now you're obviously feeling better. Unfortunately, you've missed most of the dinner, but perhaps you've come to entertain us.

Is that so, Mouse?" The queen's voice dripped with a cloying, false sweetness, inviting ridicule. A few people around the table tittered.

The poor girl looked like she would be sick. She twisted her skirt in her hands. "N-no, Mother. I'm sorry. I'll—I'll go now."

"No, you will not. Since you have inserted yourself into the banquet, you may as well make yourself useful. Why don't you sing something for us? And stop bunching up your skirt like that. They'll never be able to iron out those wrinkles. Stand up straight."

A few more of the queen's guests joined in the laughter.

Mouse stood straighter, her face now red. She rubbed her hand over her skirt as if trying to straighten it. "What—what shall I sing?" Her voice was so choked she was hardly audible. She looked like she might be about to cry.

"You'll never sing a decent tune if you don't speak up." The queen turned to the young prince at her right. "She actually has a decent singing voice."

"If we could only hear her," added Jocasta, the eldest daughter. The prince next to her gave a laugh, and he was joined by others around the table.

The queen smiled.

Why would a mother humiliate her daughter like that in front of all her guests? Alaric's hands clenched in fists, anger rising like heat in his chest. Whatever this performance was going to be, he didn't want the girl to be subjected to it. He didn't want to be subjected to it himself.

"What did you say? Really, child, you must learn to speak up."

But instead of speaking louder, the young woman burst into tears. "M-mother—"

Queen Claudia looked around the room. "What am I to do with a child like this?" It was a rhetorical question, drawing a few additional titters from the guests. "The burden I bear."

That was it. He'd had enough. Alaric stood abruptly, his chain clattering against the chair as he drew it back. All eyes turned toward him. The queen looked surprised, and well she should be. Whether or not this unexpected fourth daughter would ever prove useful to him, he was determined that Claudia would not have her way in this painful little game. He picked up the heavy chair and carried it down the center of the table toward the queen and her timid daughter. He nodded at Mouse, attempting a harmless smile.

Then he turned toward the queen. "Your Majesty, if I may. Please allow me to propose an entertainment that is likely to be far more amusing than this young girl's singing. Perhaps she is still unwell. May I suggest instead a drinking song?"

There was a smattering of applause and a few cheers, and one or two people called for the waiters to refill their glasses.

The queen's eyes were green ice as she leaned toward her prisoner. "And are you proposing to lead it, sir?"

He bowed his head. "Indeed, Your Majesty. With your permission. I propose a fine, rousing Tainish drinking song." He leaned toward Mouse and spoke quietly, barely audible over the renewed cheers. "Leave as unobtrusively as you can."

The look on her face was one of pure relief. She nodded acknowledgment and took a small step away.

Alaric set down his chair. He stood next to it and gestured toward the waiter behind the queen. "A glass of wine for me, please."

As the waiter brought him the wine, Mouse took another two steps away.

"Now, we're going to start out slow and easy, but the song gets faster with every verse, and every verse gets longer. I'll sing first, and then you all sing the same thing back. We end with a loud, 'Here's to the company,' and anyone who couldn't keep up has to take a drink. Are you ready?"

There were more cheers, and Queen Claudia allowed her glass to be filled, accepting the change in direction as if it had been her idea from the start.

Alaric smiled grimly as Mouse slipped quietly behind the screen at the back of the banquet room. He began singing.

Mouse's acute embarrassment over the debacle in the dining room did not fade overnight. She wished she could forget the whole thing. More to the point, she wished her mother could forget it, but no, here she was, summoned by the queen, no doubt about to receive a stern talking-to.

The sentry who stood watch outside the queen's chambers nodded as Mouse approached. "Princess," he said courteously, dipping a slight bow.

Mouse recognized the sentry. He was new in the palace and close to her own age. He'd given her a hand when she'd tripped on the uneven pavement of the courtyard last week and—unlike the other soldiers nearby—hadn't laughed at her. Instead, he'd introduced himself. Name was . . . Oh, why couldn't she even do something as simple as remembering a name? She blushed but managed a smile and a friendly, "Good morning."

"The queen awaits you," he said, with a hint of a smile. He opened the door and stood aside.

The queen's sitting room was carpeted in elaborate patterns of red, yellow, and blue, and heavy drapes hung beside the windows. Sunlight streamed into the room. Mouse took two small steps forward, her courage running out just past the threshold.

Her mother sat by the fireplace. She closed the book she had been reading and looked up. "Oh, for heaven's sake, come in," she said. "Sit." She patted the arm of the chair next to hers.

Mouse obeyed. Her shoulder still ached from last night's fall, but she remembered to keep her spine straight and folded her hands in her lap. "Good morning, Mother." She chewed on her lower lip.

The queen didn't waste any time on pleasantries. "What did you think you were doing in the banquet hall last night?"

"I . . ." Mouse looked down. She wished she'd never entered the banquet hall, never tried to get a glimpse of the stranger. "It was an accident, that's all. I wasn't trying to attract any attention."

Her mother scoffed. "You never try to attract any attention, Mouse." She scoffed. "Mouse—that's the problem. I expect any daughter of mine to be more assertive. Stronger."

Mouse looked down, clutching the arm of her chair. What a disappointment she must be. Her mother was so strong and proud and beautiful, and wielded her power like a broadsword, never caring who got harmed by the edge. Whereas she, Mouse, was the very opposite of all those things. "I'm sorry," she whispered.

The queen patted Mouse's hand. "This may surprise you," she said, "but I understand how difficult it is for you. I was also a shy child, but I hardened up when I became queen. I had to." Her expression grew rigid, suggesting memories too painful to contemplate. "And you must harden up, too."

Mouse tried to picture her mother as a shy child, but she couldn't. "How . . . How did you do it?"

Her mother sat up straighter. "Listen, Mouse. People will walk all over you if you let them. My father, for example—he constantly bullied my mother and me." Her face clouded.

She talks about her father, but never about mine. Mouse wondered about her father. Her sisters teased her about him. They used all kinds of innuendos—*A commoner*, they said, *probably a scoundrel*—but they didn't know any more than she did. And her mother had avoided her questions with determination, finally forbidding her to bring up the topic again. Mouse no longer dared to ask.

"My mother was queen, of course," Mouse's mother continued, "but he had to have his way in everything. He . . . It's common knowledge that he beat her. And she drank. They both did. He said that she died when she fell down the stairs, but the servants saw it, so I know what really happened."

Mouse had heard this story before, a tale the servants whispered in all its terrible detail. Still, her breath came faster, and her heart pounded. She wanted to cover her ears, but she didn't dare.

"So that's why I became queen when I was the same age you are now, just eighteen," her mother continued. "I had to get tough fast, or my father would have . . ." She gave an exaggerated shiver. "' a cruel world, so you must learn to be ruthless. And to do what must be done, before they do it to you."

"But I thought you said your father died right after your mother, right?"

Her mother looked away, then back. She straightened her hair. "Yes, he . . . had an accident and died." She sat more stiffly. "But enough of this idle chatter. We're talking about you. King Alaric did you a favor last night. He put himself in an awkward spot to do it. I want you to get over your shyness and go thank him. It'll be good practice for you."

"Please, Mother, no. I never wanted to talk with him, only to see what he looked like. I overheard some of the guards saying he's a barbarian, and I thought—"

"You will go thank him," her mother interrupted, dismissing Mouse's words with a wave of her hand. "Engage in conversation. See if he needs anything." She smiled at Mouse, but the smile never reached her eyes. "Learn to talk with strangers. It's not that hard."

Mouse's throat felt suddenly tight. She was sure she was about to burst into tears. "But, Mother, I can't—"

"That's an order. Really, child, it's for your own good." She reached out, took hold of Mouse's arm, and squeezed it so hard it hurt. "But if he does anything the least bit inappropriate, you tell me. That's an order too."

Mouse's jaw was tense with the effort not to cry. She nodded mutely.

"If he does," the queen said, "I'll kill the man."

CHAPTER TWO

The topic of magic is broached

There was a sharp rap on Alaric's door. The guard.

"Yes?"

"A visitor, Your Majesty. Will you see her?"

Who would visit him? The queen? No, surely not. She wouldn't visit him in this tiny tower room she had given him. If she wanted to see him, she'd make him come to her.

A mystery, then. Good. Something to alleviate the boredom. "Yes, of course. Send her in."

The door opened tentatively, and only wide enough for a wisp of a girl to peer in from the threshold. She gripped the edge of the door so tightly that her knuckles were white. She'd probably bolt if he frowned at her. Hadn't he seen her before? He tried to make his expression pleasant.

"Leave the door open," the guard warned.

"Yes, sergeant," the girl said almost inaudibly. She nudged the door open a bit wider and took a small step. Now he recognized her—the girl from the banquet hall last night. She'd called the queen *Mother*, but she didn't act like the other princesses. She wasn't much to look at either, all shrunk into herself, maybe fifteen years old. The cut of her clothing suggested nobility, but the costly fabric was dyed an unassuming shade of dull brown, a color that nearly matched her long, straight hair.

Her eyes were pretty, though, somewhere between green and brown, with long, arched brows. Her generous mouth promised a hint of more boldness than all the rest of her put together. This was a surprise, and an enticing one. Alaric smiled.

The girl relaxed. Slightly.

"Your Majesty." Her voice barely carried across the small room. "My mother the queen has asked me to visit you. To thank you. In person . . . for last night. And to . . . to see if you need . . . anything."

"What, you?" He'd meant that it seemed strange to send a princess on such an errand, when a servant might do. But the instant the words escaped his mouth, he realized it was the wrong thing to say.

The girl's cheeks flushed pink. She shrank against the door jamb and wrapped her chest in her arms. The protective gesture accentuated her womanly shape.

Alaric couldn't help but notice, and his own face flushed with embarrassment. He raised his estimate of her age. She must be seventeen or eighteen, almost as old as he was, and he'd implied . . . "I'm sorry." He couldn't remember the last time he'd apologized to anyone. "I didn't mean that the way it must have sounded. I only meant that if the queen is your mother, you would be an unlikely serving maid."

He offered his best smile, well aware that sometimes people trembled when he smiled. And with reason. He hoped that now he would appear welcoming rather than frightening. "Please," he said, rising and motioning to the chair, which he held for her as if she were a lady being seated for dinner.

"No, thank you," she said. "There's only the one chair, and I wouldn't . . . I couldn't make you stand while I . . ."

The room he'd been given was clean enough, and light streamed through its narrow window. But it was tiny and pressed in too closely. There was only the one chair, a narrow bed pushed against the wall, and a small table barely wide enough to hold two books side by side. "I can sit on the bed," he said, then felt his face grow hot. The bed. Not a piece of furniture that should have been on display to this visitor, and he was sorry to have mentioned it. He cursed the room for its meagerness and himself for a fool.

But his guest appeared not to notice the implications. "Oh. Yes, of course."

He held the chair as she sat, and then settled his tall frame onto the low bed. He avoided watching her too directly—her worried face, her hunched figure—as she fidgeted with her hands.

He waited.

"That was very kind, Your Majesty, what you did last night," she said at last. She nibbled at a thumbnail, watching him from the corner of her eyes.

She was not as plain as she'd first appeared. Her skin was porcelain and clear, her face heart-shaped and perfectly proportioned. Though her nails were bitten to the quick, she had long, delicate fingers. But why so timid? And why had she not been invited to the dinner?

"Please, call me Alaric." He spoke as gently as he could. "What's your name?"

She hunched inward a little more and again wrapped her arms around herself. "Mouse." Her voice was only a hair's breadth above a whisper.

"Mouse? It's . . . an unusual name."

"That's just what people call me."

He could understand why. But he said, "Is that what you want *me* to call you?"

She didn't answer.

"What's your real name?" He attempted the friendliest expression he could muster. He was afraid this timid young woman might bolt like a deer scenting a wolf. He didn't want her to bolt. He could use an ally, even one as unlikely as her, in Queen Claudia's hostile court.

"Alicia Aurelia Katrina Emilia." She raised her chin and straightened a little.

This time his smile was genuine—amusement at the string of names that stretched longer than his room was wide. "And how would you like me to call you, Alicia Aurelia Katrina Emilia? If I needed a glass of water and I had to ask you for it, I might die of thirst before I'd quite gotten all that out."

She smiled shyly back at him. Fear still hovered around her eyes, but her face lit up. "Katie," she said. "Call me Katie."

Alaric's heart catapulted. In the instant of her smile, she was radiant. She'd been wearing an expression of fear and worry so deep-seated that it masked her beauty. "And remember, you may call me Alaric. Please."

Here was a person who was extremely competent at projecting her insignificance. He wondered if magic was involved.

People said it took magic to detect magic. But he wasn't using any magic now, couldn't use it no matter how much he might want to. His hand went to his neck, where he could feel a metal collar about an inch wide and a quarter of an inch thick. There was barely room to slip two fingertips between it and his neck. It was a torque made of wild gold and ensorcelled by the queen. She'd placed it around his neck while he lay unconscious, overextended from the magical exertion he'd needed in order to free his brother and the others. The torque would tighten and strangle him if he tried even the least amount of magic.

Still, by whatever means, he was generally quite good at seeing through an illusion. Yet he'd almost fallen for the illusion Katie projected. How did she do that?

No doubt he was going stir-crazy, alone in this tiny room, but the warmth he felt toward Katie was undeniable. He wanted to know her better. Somehow, he was sure, she was going to be important to him. He couldn't see how, but he'd learned to pay attention to his intuition. He wanted to see her again, and often.

Her smile vanished, and the worried look returned. "I—I just wanted to thank you. You were very kind, but now I really have to go." She stood.

Alaric stood, too. "I've been locked in here for three days . . . Katie." The name tasted round and full on his lips, like ripe peaches. "If your offer of help still stands, I think that maybe what I need most right now is company. Would you be willing to come and visit a tired, old prisoner for an hour or so every day? Just to chat? I'll ask the guard if they might arrange, what do you like? Tea?"

Katie blushed. The color on her cheeks was far more becoming than the nondescript brown of her dress. "Oh, Alaric, you're not old. You're barely more than . . . You're very . . ." Her voice trailed to nothing, leaving him wondering how he looked to her eyes. She changed the subject. "Anyway, I don't suppose you'll be here long. They'll ransom you, or . . . something."

Something. He'd come willingly as a prisoner, not that he'd had any real choice in the matter. But he'd managed to negotiate a two-week truce in return for his promise not to escape or to harm any of the queen's people. If he failed to reach an agreement with the queen on a mutually acceptable end to the war within that time, the queen would have him killed. Or his people would attack, and many would die. Maybe both. He wanted very much to prevent these outcomes and to find a workable solution for both parties, one that didn't involve unnecessary death. There was a chance he could do that, while he was here in person. But meanwhile, he turned his attention back to Katie.

"Come, Katie. Visit me more, even if it's just a brief time. Would you?"

She hunched inward, as if preparing for a blow. "Why? Why would you want to talk with *me*?"

Once, when he was barely more than a boy, Alaric had camped on a ridge in his country's wilderness. He'd watched a small band of wild horses in a meadow below and over an entire day had crept close to them. He had his eye on a yearling colt that was in the process of working loose from the band. Its mother already had a newborn foal at her teat, and the stallion wouldn't let the yearling colt get close to her or any of the other mares. Alaric practiced on the yearling the sideways approach of bonding, now moving with the animal, now away, rewarding it with an apple or a carrot when it followed. By the end of a week, he walked out of the wilderness, the colt prancing at his side.

"I'd like to get to know you better. Is that so strange?"

Katie stared at the floor, the color on her face deepening and rising to the roots of her hair. "Most people don't spend time with me if they don't have to. But my mother wishes—"

"—that you see if I need anything. And what I need is company."

"But what on earth would we talk about?"

This was going to make the yearling horse look like child's play.

The next morning, Katie came again to visit Alaric, as she'd promised. Under the guard's watchful eyes, she knocked on the prisoner's door. Her heart was pounding, but she refused to appear nervous in front of the soldier. She straightened her back and lifted her chin.

"Enter," came Alaric's voice from within.

Katie nodded to the guard, and he opened the door.

Alaric stood up as she paused in the doorway. He was unusually tall and held himself regally straight. Even without a diadem or other adornment he was kingly, exuding a kind of self-confidence she found a bit frightening. He had washed his black hair and, yes, trimmed his beard. His face was lean and hard with a prominent nose and pale gray eyes. He watched her as intently as a bird of prey. Katie's heart skipped a beat, and her breath caught. He was fearsome.

Then he smiled, and the impression of fierceness vanished. "Katie. Come in."

She did.

He'd promised to talk about anything she wished. It was the first time anyone had expressed an interest in her wishes, but when she said she liked to read, he'd asked her to bring some of her favorite books, and she had complied, clutching a book tightly under her arm.

He seated her again in the chair and sat on the bed, adjusting his long legs. "What would you like to talk about today, Katie?"

She wanted to know more about him, but felt afraid to ask. She looked down, away from him. "I . . . don't know." She glanced up to see him smiling gently at her. He lifted a questioning eyebrow.

Somehow, she found her voice and her nerve, both at the same time. "I was wondering how . . ."

He nodded. "Go on."

"I thought kings were supposed to be well protected, so . . ."

"So you were wondering how they managed to capture me, eh?"

She looked away, blushing, and managed to say, "If you don't mind talking about it." Her voice barely came out in a whisper.

"Not at all." He drew in a deep breath and let it out in an audible sigh. "I was trying to rescue my bro—some of my men from your mother's army camp where they were being held. My military leaders were against my going into the camp alone, but I overruled them. I was the only one with any magic, so I was the only one who had a chance of getting the three of them out without any bloodshed. I snuck into the camp alone. So you see, this"—he gestured around the room—"is really my own fault. I ran into some difficulties freeing them, more than I expected. It turned out the chains that bound them were ensorcelled. It took a lot of effort to undo that spell, so much that when I had finished, I passed out. When I came to, your mother had made me prisoner." He looked away, the expression on his face so sad that Katie thought her heart might break.

He clapped his hands on his thighs and sat straighter, adopting a resolute expression. "But enough about that. At least my men got away safely. Let's move on to a cheerier topic. Tell me about the book you brought."

He was as good as his word. During the hour that followed, Katie read to Alaric from one of her favorite historical romance stories. He listened attentively and occasionally added details about the historical period in the book. He seemed to know a lot. Katie envied him that. She wished she knew more, but had never been given the opportunity to study, had never even been more than a few hours' ride from her mother's castle.

"How do you know so much?" she asked.

"I read a lot, like you." He smiled.

Katie liked his smile; he seemed much kinder when he smiled and not nearly as scary. She was beginning to think he might actually become a friend. Katie had no friends in her mother's castle. She'd read about friends, of course, and she'd seen friendships in the castle, particularly among the servants. She herself had had a friend when she was a child—Posie, a little girl her own age, the daughter of one of the cleaning staff. But when Katie was twelve, her sister Jocasta had whispered something in her mother's ear, and the next day Posie and Posie's mother were gone. Katie never found out where. Her sisters certainly weren't her friends. They couldn't be trusted. She'd seen them turn on one another even when they pretended to be friendly. And they never even bothered to pretend to be friendly with her. No, not her sisters, and after Posie left, her mother had made it clear enough that friendship with the servants was unseemly. Katie resolved to figure out ways to make Alaric smile more.

"But you know so much more than I do."

"I'm a bit older than you, Katie."

He didn't look much older, maybe five years, maybe six. No older than her sisters. "Not by much."

His smile broadened. "Well, maybe I've just had more time for reading. Also, I think maybe I read more widely than you."

"More widely? Like what?"

"I've studied quite a bit of history. I also study philosophy and science, military strategy and magic."

Of course. Magic. Her great deficiency and abiding shame. It was always about magic—magic and her lack of it.

He leaned forward and studied her with concern. "What's the matter?"

She bit her lip and brought the book closer to her face, avoiding his gaze. She wished she could disappear. "Nothing."

"Katie," he said gently, "put the book down."

She clutched the book more tightly, stifling the urge to cry.

"Please."

His concern made her feel worse. This was too stupid, too embarrassing for words. If only she had the tiniest little fingernail's bit of magic! She forced herself to lower the book and meet his gaze, hoping her tears didn't show.

"I would like to think we're friends," he said.

Her heart leapt. Yes, friends! But no, slow down. How could they be friends already? They hardly knew each other.

He sounded friendly enough, though, his voice low and gentle. "Friends can talk with friends when something's the matter."

Katie nodded. The lump in her throat squeezed her voice to a whisper. "Yes, Your Majesty."

"Alaric," he said gently. "Call me Alaric. Remember?" He took the book from her hands. It slipped through her unresisting fingers, like silk.

She stared at his hands with their long, elegant fingers, and then forced herself to look away and meet his quicksilver gray eyes filled with concern. What an idiot she was. Whether he was, or would be, her friend, he was the one person in the entire castle who was kind to her. She didn't want him to fret over her, on top of his other and far bigger problems.

She let out a ragged breath and relaxed a little. "Alaric." The name tasted fresh and musical in her mouth, like the water of a mountain stream dancing over its boulders. The name of a person who had called himself her friend. She repeated the name and smiled at him.

"That's better." He returned her smile. "Now tell me, what's the problem?"

Now that she'd worried him, she owed him an explanation. "It's . . . I don't have any magic. I'm the only one in my family that doesn't. When I was a child, my sisters would play pranks on me with their magic. I always assumed I'd come into my own magic after I grew up, and then I'd be like them. But it never happened." Her mother had called her a misfit, the runt of the litter, and her sisters had gleefully picked up that refrain.

"I don't have any magic either, so we're two of a kind," he said. His hand moved toward his throat. "But we can still read about it."

She watched his hand moving around his neck, for all the world as if some object were bound there, something he was trying to loosen. "It's different with you. You're a sorcerer who just happens . . . for the moment . . . to be . . ." Her voice trailed off. "What are you doing?"

"You can't see it, can you?"

She shook her head.

Alaric stood and went to the tiny looking glass that hung next to the window. He peered into it, rubbing his fingers over the invisible thing circling his neck. "I can see it in my reflection, and I can certainly feel it. After I was captured, your mother made me her prisoner, binding me with this torque. I'd need magic to unlock it, but when I try to use magic—any magic at all—the torque constricts around my throat. I'd die before I could summon enough magic to loosen it. A neat little bit of wizardry, this."

Katie ached for magic of her own. Now she tried to imagine having had magic all her life and then losing it. "That's terrible. I wish I could help you."

"Thank you." There was that glowing smile again. "You're a kind person. And kindness, you know, can be mightier than magic."

Katie sighed. "At least I don't know what I'm missing."

"No." He drew the word out long and thoughtfully as if tasting it for the first time. "And yet quite likely you do have the capability."

It was as if her ribcage had dissolved and there was nothing to hold her heart in place. She stared at him. "How . . . Without magic, how could you possibly know that?"

"It's just a guess, but one based on scientific reasoning, which in many ways is also mightier than magic. All the women of your line are capable of magic. Your mother, your sisters, and also your grandmothers and their mothers, as far back as the records go. Even if your father was not . . . ah, perhaps not the same father as your sisters', even if your father had no magic at all, the matriarchal line is pure enough that you would have the capability." He frowned. "What about your father, Katie? What do you know about him?"

Was he referring to those nasty rumors of her low birth? As if being without magic wasn't bad enough. She folded her arms across her chest. "Nothing. Well, once when I was very little, my mother told me he was a powerful prince of a distant kingdom, but she refused to ever say anything about him after that. After a while I realized she'd probably just made that up. I don't know anything about him, really." She sighed. "I wish I did."

He took her hand. "I wouldn't be surprised if what she said is true, and you have magical ability from both sides of your family."

"How could you possibly know that?"

"It's just a hunch, really, but I trust my instincts a lot."

"Well, but here I am." Katie withdrew her hand from his, stood, flounced out her skirt, and gave him a mock curtsy. "As unmagical as this book I was just reading to you. Explain *that*, then." She dared him with her eyes.

He stared at her with such intensity that she shrank away, and he said, "I intend to."

The next day, Katie went to the castle library and found the book that Alaric had requested. It was a small book, bound in worn black leather and covered in dust, its gilt-edged pages so old and thin that the corners sometimes crumbled under her light touch.

How had she ever let Alaric talk her into this? Only yesterday, Katie had refused to talk about magic, and yet he had coaxed her into not only finding the book but also reading it to him. She sighed and continued. "The efficacy of a spell is more directly proportional to the magician's act of will than to his innate magical ability." She glanced up at Alaric. His eyes were closed as he leaned back against the wall, listening. He seemed tired and drawn today, as old as the book she was reading from. "What does that mean?"

Alaric opened his eyes, pale gray, assessing, unreadable. "It means that the power of will is mightier than magic."

"Everything is, according to you." Katie put the book down and counted on her fingers. "The power of scientific reason. The power of kindness. And now the power of will. I suppose you think you are consoling me."

"Not at all. I am merely telling the truth as I see it."

"From which I may take some consolation—as you see it?" She glared at him sharply, defying him to say no.

He didn't. He inclined his head in acknowledgment. "You may, if you wish."

"Well, I don't."

"No, of course not. But you may have your magic back some day, Katie."

"I never had any magic to have *back*, as you say."

To her surprise, Alaric didn't contradict her. Instead, he stood up. He circled the narrow confines of his room, once, twice, three times as she watched, his left hand picking absently at the edges of the invisible torque. As he circled he studied her with unblinking hawk's eyes. "Intuition is also more powerful than magic, Katie, and mine is strong in this matter. I would stake my life on it," he said quietly.

She could almost believe that in some way he already had. She shivered.

When she left Alaric, Katie returned to her room. She peered out from her doorway, right, left, and then right and left again. A wall of cold, dressed stone interrupted here and there by doorways and lamp holders faced an arched colonnade that let out onto a garden courtyard. The granite pavers of the colonnade glistened a pale, flecked gray, clean as a recent scrubbing could make them, unmarked by footprints or dust. No one was in sight. She quietly closed and locked her door.

Her room was not a grand one like her mother's, a room so sizable that a person hardly noticed the large, curtained bed at the far end, with walls so ornamented in gold leaf and mirrors that the room seemed to go on and on forever. No, Katie occupied the least of the royal chambers, small but adequate. The tapestries that warmed the walls were old ones and worn, cast-off remnants that were left over after the redecoration of other, more important rooms. But she loved them all the same, for each one contained a faded story that Katie told herself many a night as she wiped away the tears of the day and prepared for sleep.

From deep between the two mattresses on her bed, she took out an iron key attached to a frayed pink ribbon. She removed a pile of comforters from the top of a maple chest and fitted the key into the lock.

Opened, the chest filled the air with the scent of fresh cedar wood. Katie rummaged through its contents, a jumble of scarves and shawls, mittens and hats for cold weather, until she found what she was looking for.

From the chest, Katie withdrew a ragged cloth doll with a delicate porcelain face. One arm had been ripped off once and sewed back with a child's rough stitches. The dress was torn, its bright colors faded, and its lace altogether missing in places. The doll's once-blond hair was now an indistinct brown and matted beyond combing. Scratches marred the porcelain, but by some miracle had left the bright blue eyes and ruby lips untouched.

"Hello, Mouse," the doll said.

Katie gave the doll a hug, and then sat down on the floor by the chest. She cradled the doll in her arms. "Hello, Dolly. Did you sleep well?"

"Shh. Keep your voice down. Of course I did. I always do. And how was your day?" The doll spoke in a tiny voice much like Katie's own, but a pitch or two higher, and she had a slight lisp.

Katie dropped her voice almost to a whisper, but even so it was full of her high spirits. "Wonderful! I went to the library and got some books for Alaric, and he was so happy. I just love it when he smiles at me like that, like I'm someone special to him. He showed me some books on history and . . ." She faltered. "And magic."

The doll's eyes narrowed, and the scratches on her porcelain face arranged themselves into a frown. "I don't trust that Alaric."

Katie held the doll out at arm's length. "How can you say that? You've never even met him!"

"Shh!" the doll warned. "I don't want to meet him, either. He's a stranger, Mouse. Strangers are dangerous. Who knows what he's up to?"

"He's not *up to* anything!"

"Shh!"

Katie lowered her voice. "Maybe he's just lonely, but I think he really does like me all the same." She felt a warm glow inside, thinking of the friendly way he looked at her. "And he won't hurt me. He can't. He's a prisoner and he doesn't have any magic."

"Not *now*," the doll conceded. "I guess it's all right for you to keep visiting him if you want—for *now*. It's just that I worry about you."

Katie gave the doll a wholehearted hug. "Thank you. That means so much to me."

A long, friendly silence fell between them, and then Katie spoke with some hesitation. "Dolly . . . Alaric thinks I do have some magic, somehow. Do you think that could be true?"

"No." The doll spoke with authority. "Not a chance."

CHAPTER THREE

The queen sets a ransom price

Alaric strode into the queen's audience hall, his dislike of the woman lengthening his stride so that the two soldiers who escorted him half-ran to keep up with him. The room was large, and sunlight streaming through the high windows did little to illuminate the lower level of the chamber. His footsteps echoed from the walls and floor, cold marble set in sweeping patterns of red, green, white, and black. A slight trace of expensive perfume was all that remained of whatever gathering Queen Claudia had recently hosted here, but no one was present now save the queen, seated as still as a statue of ice on her throne, and behind her in the shadows, four soldiers.

He schooled his face to careful neutrality but could not entirely undo the tightness that gripped his jaw. How any mother could inflict on her own daughter the pain that Katie had suffered at this woman's hands escaped him. But he was not here today because of Katie.

Almost a full week of their two-week truce had already passed without a summons from the queen, and—finally—today he had been summoned to discuss his ransom. It was about time.

A slight smile touched the queen's red lips but did not thaw the cold satisfaction of her gaze, lingering on the torque around his throat. *A queen's magic*, she had said when she captured him. *A queen's magic to bind a king.*

Alaric bowed his head just enough to acknowledge her—for now—as his superior. "Your Majesty."

"Alaric." She drew out the word as she might a sip of fine wine, clearly savoring her ability to use his given name whether he wished it or no, when he was in no position to reciprocate. Her smile broadened, but nothing changed in her eyes. "Come closer. Come, I have no desire to shout my terms to these four walls."

He approached the throne, set on a dais so high that even seated, the queen was half a head higher than him. He was not a man to be intimidated by such theatrics. "I am pleased to hear, Your Majesty, that you have reached some idea of your terms, and I am eager to know them."

"Yes, I imagine you would like to be on your way home again, and in return for your freedom, I ask only something that is well within your power to grant."

He arched a questioning eyebrow and waited.

The queen leaned forward. Had she been a cat, he would have said she was preparing to pounce. She wore a gold coronet atop her immaculately arranged auburn hair. Gold thread and freshwater pearls adorned the gauzy cloak that floated over her dark green dress when she moved, like a mist on the lake on a chill summer's morning. She was by any measure a beautiful woman. Her voice, when she spoke, was husky. "The province of Darimbia is mine."

He took a step back before he regained control of himself. "You're asking me to capitulate in our little . . . border skirmish and cede the province to you. That's not a negotiation, that's an outright surrender."

She smiled sweetly. "And in return, I will let you live."

She was right, that surrendering the province was within his power—but it was not within his principles. He looked away from her, up into his memories. Sunlight illuminated a column capital, where a spider spun a delicate web. Darimbia had been contested between the two kingdoms for longer than either he or the queen were old, sometimes in the hands of the one, sometimes the other. Its rich veins of wild gold—the only kind suitable for fashioning into magical artifacts such as the torque that bound him—made it a prize beyond measure.

Once Darimbia had been a nation that spanned the entire continent, a nation more powerful than either of theirs, perhaps the most powerful the world had ever known. But that had been back in the era of legends. Now, the ancient cities were dust. The soil was rocky, the terrain was steep, and the people were poor, even those who mined its priceless gold.

Much of the province had fallen to Queen Claudia before Alaric was born, though his father held onto a portion of it, leading a small but fierce resistance group. Alaric had been just a lad, but word of the tragedy that unfolded in the land under the queen's control had reached even his ears. He took a breath and forced his jaw to relax. The queen had slaughtered thousands of people—everyone that might still be loyal to Alaric's father. Her army had commandeered their crops and then destroyed their fields. With famine rampant, a few copper coins were enough to encourage the desperately hungry to betray their neighbors and their families. Thousands more had died.

Alaric didn't blame the people; he blamed the ruler who created a culture of betrayal. How long could a person resist confirming an insinuating rumor against a stranger down the street, when the person's own children were starving? All the Darimbians wanted was food on the table and a chance to raise their children in peace—yet there had been so much bloodshed.

Alaric returned his gaze to the queen. "What guarantees would you give the people of Darimbia?"

She looked at him blankly. "The people? What are they to us, but labor for the mines? And perhaps a minor source of tax revenue."

The spider near the ceiling lowered itself by an invisible thread. Alaric drew in a deep breath and let it out. "I don't think you'd understand," he said softly, "but the people of Darimbia are important to me. I am not one of those monarchs who value their own lives above everyone else's. And if I were to die here, my brother would carry on the battle"—the queen blew out an audible breath of contempt at the mention of Alaric's brother—"and no doubt with more vehemence than me."

Alaric's younger half-brother Marco was probably as near as these people had to a hero. Marco's mother had been Darimbian. The province and its people spoke to Marco's heart, and he to theirs. Marco disappeared into the hills of Darimbia for months at a time, and wherever he went, Alaric's forces received excellent intelligence—and the armies of the queen met with unfortunate accidents. "But perhaps, in return for my life and an agreement to allow me to govern the province, I could agree to share the mine output with you for a period of time, say, fifty years?"

The queen's red lips narrowed into a forbidding line, and the words that crossed it were entirely too quiet. "I don't think *you* understand.

This is not a matter for bargaining, you have no leverage. I'll give you three days to think about it, and not a day more."

"Perhaps you've lost count," he said coldly. "A week remains on our truce, a week during which we agreed to negotiate."

A slow, satisfied smile spread across the queen's lips. "A week, then. You are dismissed."

"Alaric!" Katie called happily. The door to his room stood ajar; he must have been expecting her visit. She peered around the edge of the door. "The guard captain has agreed we might . . ."

She broke off. Alaric sat on the edge of his bed, head in his hands, hunched over as if he'd like to curl his entire long frame in on itself. Hearing her voice, he ran his hands through his hair and sat up straighter. "Hello, Katie. Come in."

She entered the room, quietly closing the door as much as the guards allowed, until just before the latch clicked. "What's wrong?"

He shook his head. "It's nothing you need to worry about. The negotiations with your mother . . ."

"For your release?"

"Yes, for my release."

"Oh." Katie's heart wilted. "They're not going well?"

"She is asking for the one thing I cannot—*will* not—give her."

Katie's spirits fell. She hoped so strongly for her own eventual freedom, that she'd become invested in this man's much more imminent prospects. Now that his chances seemed to have dimmed, she almost felt as if she too had been denied her freedom. "Would you like to talk about it?"

He looked at her appraisingly, an eyebrow raised, almost as if he were assessing her ability to understand difficult concepts.

"I'm not stupid."

"Oh . . . Sorry, Katie; it's not that. But the issues get into the politics between your mother's family—between *your* family—and mine. I was just wondering . . . I don't want to put you in the middle."

Did she care that he might say unpleasant things about her mother or sisters? Her heart felt as if someone had just twisted it, but in truth, she was already well aware there were unpleasant things about them. She needed Alaric's honesty more than any cover-up. "No, I want to know."

He nodded, once slowly. "It's about Darimbia."

She'd heard of Darimbia, of course. Her mother's army was fighting there, and that was where Alaric had been captured. But what did she know other than that? She looked at him blankly.

"You don't know about Darimbia?"

She shook her head. "Not much."

"Darimbia is a region located directly on the border between your country and mine. It's small but very mountainous, the eastern slope of a range high enough that clouds driven by the prevailing westerly winds can't easily pass over it. So, while the western slopes are well watered and fertile, the eastern slopes are arid, and the people are poor."

"So, neither of you wants it?"

Alaric laughed. "Unfortunately for everyone, Darimbia is the only place in the world where anyone has discovered the ore of wild gold"—he touched the invisible thing at his neck—"from which every magical artifact in existence is made. And given its geographic location, ownership of Darimbia has been contested between our two houses for generations. Right now, Darimbia is mine."

Katie frowned, thinking. "But my mother wants it."

"Of course. And I won't let it go."

"But why? It sounds like you both have a claim to it."

Alaric nodded thoughtfully. "You could say that. But the last time your mother had control of the place, a great many people were murdered. She wanted to 'cleanse' the area of sympathizers to my cause, but the way she went about it . . ." He hesitated. "She commandeered their crops and burned their fields. People starved. For enough money to buy a little food, neighbor turned against neighbor, nephew against uncle. Thousands died unnecessarily. And your mother has given me no reason to believe it will be any different if I cede the province to her again now." He shook his head. "I am responsible for those people's welfare. I cannot allow another period of such brutality. I have offered your mother half of the wild gold we mine, but I will not let her kill the people, not again."

Alaric took a deep breath and let it out. "Now you know how it stands between me and your mother. I hope you'll still be my friend, but I would understand if—"

"What?" she cried. "Do you think I'd stand for a minute in favor of killing, what did you say, thousands of people, just because it's my mother that's doing it?"

"There would be no blame in siding with your own mother."

"Then you don't know me at all." Katie was near tears. "I know what it's like to live under . . . unpleasant circumstances, and it must be much worse for those people. Much, much worse. I want to help you."

He smiled at her, that warm smile that seemed to say she was someone very special. A silly idea, of course, but it made her unreasonably happy. Through her tears, she returned the smile.

"Thank you." He pulled at the invisible thing around his neck, tilting his head to one side as if to relieve chafing. "If only I could use just a shred of my magic . . ." He clapped his hands to his knees with a sound that startled her. "But never mind all that. I could tell when you came in that you had something special planned for today. Tell me."

"Yes . . ." She lost her train of thought for a moment as a new idea crowded in. She lowered her voice almost to a whisper, so that even in the small room he had to lean forward to hear her better. "Yes, but wait, Alaric. I think I can help you—"

"No," he interrupted. "I don't want to be the cause of friction between you and your mother, and I don't want you to risk the consequences if things don't work out."

She laughed, a barely exhaled breath with no humor in it, and continued speaking very softly. "Things have already not worked out between my mother and me. As far as she is concerned, I am her greatest failure. It has nothing to do with you."

Alaric started to speak, but she held up a hand to stop him. "I want to help you. I know all kinds of ways around the castle. If we can just figure out how to get you out of this room without the guards noticing, I bet I could get you out of the castle. Then you wouldn't have to negotiate with my mother. You'd be free!"

He shook his head, and his smile turned sad. "Katie, you are a wonder of kindness, and I thank you. Truly. But as long as I'm wearing this, I am at your mother's mercy." He ran his fingers over the invisible torque. "With magic I could move quickly enough to escape her reach, but without it . . . Your country is large, the border is distant, and your mother has thousands of soldiers. She would almost certainly find me before I could make it halfway to the border, and even with weapons I wouldn't stand a chance against her soldiers."

"Oh." Katie's heart sank, and she slumped into his guest chair. Another worthless idea. No wonder her mother always said she'd never amount to anything.

Alaric took her hand. His hand was dry and warm, and his touch made her feel so tingly she could almost believe that he must still have magic. He was smiling that you're-special smile at her again, and she managed a wan smile in return.

"Tell me what you had in mind for us to do today," he said. "You were so excited when you came in."

"Oh. That. It's nothing, really. Just that I got the guard captain to let me take you to the library." She'd worked on the guard captain for two days in order to get that permission—and to get him to agree not to tell her mother. She'd raided the kitchen and brought him some of the pastries the cooks were making for the queen's dinner. And then she'd raided the wine cellar and brought the guard some wine, dusty old bottles from the back of the cellar that her mother would surely never miss. And when he'd drunk enough of the wine, he'd agreed as how he couldn't see that a library would do anyone any harm.

"The library? Really?" Alaric practically sparkled with energy. "Now?"

Her initial excitement returned, ignited by his. It felt like . . . like the way she'd always imagined magic must feel. "Yes!"

Dust motes shimmered in the sunlight that slanted through the tall windows of the library. The room was large and high enough that Alaric suspected it might once have served as the royal chapel. The windows were narrow, though, just the width of the aisles between rows and stacks of books.

Katie sneezed.

"Be healthy," Alaric murmured.

"Thank you. I think I must be allergic to dust. Perhaps I should get someone to come in and clean it."

The place smelled of dust and mold and old books long neglected. It was a pity, and also an opportunity. Alaric could imagine mildewed treasures among these forgotten volumes. "Perhaps it would be better not to. Let's keep this place to ourselves, shall we? Besides, some of these books are so old that a careless attempt to clean them might destroy them instead." Alaric ran his fingers lightly across the spines of a row of books, leaving a trail in the dust and feeling their fragility. "Military history," he mused. "Barnard's *Corlegian Campaign*. Wellbridge's *Victories at Sea*. Good books, but not for today."

Katie trailed after him as he turned into the next aisle. "What's for today, then?"

"Magic, of course." He turned his head just enough to see her reaction.

She cringed, missing a step, and reached out to one of the bookshelves for balance. She touched one of the old books, then frowned at the dust on her fingertip.

Alaric took her hand and brushed away the dust. "I meant, for me," he said. "While I'm here, I want to see which references you have. I'd love to get my hands on a copy of Dunbaster's *Incantations of the Ancients*, if you have it. For you . . ." He paused, still holding her hand, and studied her as he might a painting suspected of being a forgery.

She held her breath.

"I was thinking we might look for Stedman's *Physical Properties of the Elements*. It's about matter." He waved his free hand vaguely toward the room around them. "Physical matter. It's not magic, but it is something a sorcerer should know. You can't hope to manipulate physical objects without some understanding of them."

Katie pulled her hand from his. "Not magic, though."

"No, the book is not about magic, it's about physics—the properties of matter. I think you might find it interesting; matter is not what it appears to be. But about magic, Katie, I hope you don't take this as nagging, but I do want you to try a few experiments with me, just for fun. To satisfy my curiosity. Just small ones."

"What's the point? They won't work." She crossed her arms over her chest, her shoulders hunched. She looked like a small child. "They never do."

Maybe not yet, but there's always a first time. He kept his expression relaxed. "Never mind," he said. "Maybe later."

"Right. Later." Katie sounded relieved. "Meanwhile, do you think we might find something on Darimbian history? I'd like to know more about it."

Alaric tugged thoughtfully at his beard. "Well, Zylberblum's *Darimbia Reconstructed* is a bit dry, but it is the definitive history." Three volumes, hundreds of footnotes. "Then again, maybe it's a bit *too* dry. The history is really quite interesting. Once, a long time ago, back in the era of legends, Darimbia was a mighty nation—mightier than either yours or mine. It spanned the entire continent and may have been the greatest nation the world has ever known. Let's look for Arnold's *Tales of the Darimbian Empire*. It focuses more on the personal stories of that time." The tragic tale of Darimbia's last ruler, young Irinia Orcutt, would be much to Katie's liking, though scholars still debated whether or how much the story was grounded in truth.

He found Stedman on an upper shelf in an aisle devoted to treatises on mathematics and the sciences. But there were no books at all about Darimbia. He would ask Marco to send a copy of Arnold along with his scheduled delivery of additional clothing. "I'll see if I can get the book here soon, but meanwhile, let me tell you what I remember about ancient Darimbia," he said to Katie. "It's quite amazing, and I think you'll enjoy the story."

The next morning, the queen summoned Katie to her chambers. Though Katie would have preferred to avoid her mother's disciplinary sessions altogether, at least she had been ordered to her mother's informal sitting room, and alone. Had it been the throne room, others would have been there, and no doubt her mother would have had ready a pithy and entertaining rebuke, played for all it was worth to a laughing audience. Here, she could hope for just a quiet mother-daughter talk meant to address her deficiencies. Her many deficiencies.

Katie wished she were anywhere but here.

Her mother's eyes gleamed coldly, like faceted emeralds set in her perfect face, so sharp they could cut. Katie couldn't bear to look into them. Instead, she examined her skirts and noticing a wrinkle, tried to fold it underneath where it wouldn't show.

"Stop fidgeting," her mother said. "Sit down. Look at me."

Katie found the chair nearest the door and lowered herself onto the edge of it.

"Don't look at me that way, honey," her mother said. "You know I want only what's best for you. How many times do I have to tell you? Like it or not, you are the daughter of a queen, and you must learn to act with regal dignity and authority. Whatever is going to happen to you when I'm no longer here to look after you? Sit up straight."

Katie corrected her posture and murmured something that came out sounding almost like, "Sorry."

"Now, tell me what's going on between you and my prisoner."

Katie's face went all hot and, judging by her mother's raised eyebrow, red. She couldn't even hide her emotions properly—no wonder her mother continued to treat her like a little girl. Her throat went tight and her lip started to quiver as if she might start to cry. This made her so angry that the feeling went away. "Nothing," she said. "There's nothing going on between me and Alaric."

The eyebrow went up further. "Alaric? The two of you are on a first-name basis now?"

"*King* Alaric," she corrected herself. "We're friends, that's all. Friends are on a first-name basis, usually, aren't they? I read him stories. He teaches me . . . things."

Leaning forward in her chair, eyes piercing, the queen said, "Magic?"

"No!" Too loud. Too fast. "No, not magic. I wish you would stop pushing me about magic all the time. I'm sorry I'm such a disappointment to you, but I just can't . . ." Now she really *was* starting to cry.

Her mother raised her hand from the arm of her chair. "Stop that. Do not cry. Crying is for babies."

Katie winced, drawing away from the impending slap.

Her mother lowered the hand and heaved a long-suffering sigh, as if Katie were threatening her, rather than the other way around. "I know this is hard for you as well as for me. I keep hoping . . . maybe . . . It's not too late for some kind of a breakthrough. I thought maybe your *friend* Alaric might have some idea, something I haven't thought of yet. Perhaps you could ask him to try. Just don't let him give you any crazy ideas."

What kind of ideas would her mother consider crazy? Looking out for other people? Making sure the people who worked in your mines had enough to eat? In her most placatory voice, she said, "Don't worry, Mama. I won't." She wiped her eyes, trying to make the gesture look natural, grateful that in the fragile truce, her mother refrained from criticism.

"So what sort of *things* is he teaching you?"

Glad for the change of subject, Mouse brightened. "Oh, lots of things! History and philosophy and geography—a little. And we just started studying physics, too—Stedman's *Physical Properties of the Elements*." Mouse laughed. "What a strange book!"

But her mother was frowning, and that made Mouse's laughter fade.

"Stedman? Why would he be teaching you that? It's part of a sorcerer's training, of course, but if he's not teaching you magic, it's quite useless."

"That's what you say about my romance novels, too, Mama, that they're useless."

With a slight motion of her chin, the queen agreed. "And so they are."

"He says I should have a well-rounded education, that's all."

There was a knock at the door. The queen glanced over Mouse's shoulder and nodded at whoever stood there. "Be right with you." To Mouse, she said, "I guess a well-rounded education never hurt anyone, and it will keep the two of you out of trouble. But do see if he'll try to teach you some magic as well. I doubt he can do much, what with that torque, and"—she looked Mouse up and down—"the material he has to work with. But just on the off chance . . ." She stood, and with an exaggeratedly long sigh, finished their little mother-daughter talk.

Near tears, Katier returned to her room. She was more determined than ever to learn everything Alaric wanted to teach her—except, of course, magic. There was no point in that. Or was there? Katie decided to ask the doll. She took the tattered toy out of the box.

The doll looked around the room cautiously. "You mean your mother doesn't want you to see him so much either?"

"No." Katie arranged the doll's dress neatly over her legs. "I really should try to sew this. Or maybe even make you a new one."

"No!" said the doll emphatically.

Katie glanced at the door to her room to make sure it was shut. "Shh."

"Now you sound like me," the doll said, "always shushing. Why do I sound like your mother, then?"

"Because you're both so bossy. She says, 'Tell him to teach you magic,' and you say, 'Don't see him.' Well, I want to see him, and I like what he's teaching me."

"I'm just trying to keep you safe." The doll sounded petulant, almost unappreciated. Was Dolly on the verge of tears?

Katie couldn't remember ever seeing Dolly cry, but she didn't doubt that she could. She cradled the doll in her arms. "I know you are, sweetie, and it means a lot to me." She rocked back and forth, her whole upper body moving in the comforting rhythm.

Outside, the last orange rays of the sun broke through a cloud bank and streamed through Katie's chamber windows, throwing bright orange squares onto the east wall of the room.

"Teach me," said the doll.

"What?"

"What are you learning? Teach me."

"Oh. Okay. Today, first, we talked about Darimbia."

The doll lifted an eyebrow, and her mouth formed a neat oh. "That's interesting. What did you learn?"

Katie looked up, trying to remember. "A long time ago—maybe a thousand years—Darimbia was the most powerful country in the world. It spanned the whole continent, from one ocean to the other, thousands of miles. They had giant buildings hundreds of feet tall and great ships that sailed in the sky, and all the people were strong and beautiful."

"Wow," said the doll. "I bet your mother would have liked to be queen of that."

Katie giggled. "Probably. But they didn't have a queen or a king. All the people got together somehow, and they chose who would be their ruler. The ruler didn't have to be noble. They didn't have to have any magic at all, though Alaric says he thinks most of them did."

The doll frowned. "How can a person be a ruler without any magic? Why would anyone listen to them?"

That was a good question. "I'm not sure. I know they had soldiers and powerful weapons, so maybe people were afraid to disobey them."

"Kind of like with magic."

"Yes, but that doesn't entirely make sense. The people chose the leaders in the first place. Maybe they obeyed because they just wanted to. Anyway, it didn't go on forever. Darimbia had enemies across the oceans, and there came a ruler in Darimbia who wanted to use his most powerful weapons and smite these enemies once and for all. He killed many, many people across the oceans, but still there was no peace, and the whole thing cost so much that Darimbia became very poor. When that happened, some of the people stopped wanting to obey that leader, and others wanted to punish the disobedient ones. So, then there was a great civil war, and the government fell apart fighting against itself, and the whole country fell into ruins. The great cities were destroyed, and millions of people died. The infra—infrastructure?—broke down, so there was no way to get food and supplies from one place to another."

The doll fidgeted on Katie's lap, and then settled into a new position. "They should have had a queen," she said. "With magic."

"They did, sort of, in the end. There was a woman named Irinia Orcutt, and Alaric says he's sure she was a sorcerer because everyone loved her. The whole country chose her to be their leader. She was young, maybe only a few years older than me, and very beautiful. She was so popular that crowds gathered wherever she went, just to see her." Katie paused, trying to imagine herself as brave and beloved as Irinia Orcutt. Oh, if only it were possible! "And she went everywhere. She helped the people produce what they needed locally, and she had plans to rebuild the inf—infrastructure.'

"But she didn't do it, did she?"

"No." Katie felt her throat tighten at the thought of the dedicated, kind young woman who was so much like the person she wanted to be. "Even though her guards said she should keep a distance from the people, she was always going out among them. And one day, a man came right up to her and stabbed her to death."

Katie swallowed. She and the doll both blinked back tears.

"After that, the country just fell apart. Lots of kingdoms and other countries sprang up, like ours and Alaric's, and Darimbia became a kind of backwater province."

"That's very sad," the doll said. "I don't like history. Let's talk about something else."

"All right," Katie said. The story had left her feeling sad, too.

"What else did you learn today? But don't tell me, if it's sad."

Katie laughed. "Well, we talked about the physical properties of matter. Physics. That's not sad."

The doll wrinkled her nose. "That," she said, "does not sound at all interesting."

"Oh, but it is. Listen to this." Mouse was so excited that she propped the doll more upright, as if in a posture of great attention. "Matter is mostly empty space!"

The scratches on the doll's porcelain face arranged themselves into a frown, and her pretty red mouth pouted. "Right. Sure. Empty space. You and me. The floor. The walls."

"Yes, all of that, even the walls. Listen. All of matter is composed of atoms."

"I know that." The doll's tone suggested that she did not appreciate the insult to her intelligence.

"Well, then maybe you also know that all atoms of all kinds of matter are composed of smaller things called protons and neutrons and electrons. And some other, um, particles that I don't know much about. But the point is that *inside the atom* there are vast empty spaces. Huge, compared to the size of those particles."

"Inside of you and me and the walls," the doll said skeptically. "The stone walls."

"Yes."

"So, if we bump against a wall, why don't we just melt inside it, into all that extra space? Instead of bouncing off the wall and hurting ourselves? Tell me that."

"That's a good question." Katie chewed at her lip as she considered it. "We *should* just melt inside, shouldn't we? If Alaric's book is right—and both he and my mother think it is—then there would be lots of room in there for us."

She stood, carrying Dolly with her as she paced across her room. When she came to the wall, she knocked on it, receiving only a sharp pain in her knuckles for her trouble. "Ow!" She looked at her hand. "Maybe we don't melt into the wall because we *believe* that we won't. We believe that it's solid. But it's not magic, it's just plain physics, and now that you and I know the truth—"

There was a knock on the door, followed immediately by the sound of the door latch starting to turn.

"Oh, no," squeaked the doll. "It's the chamber maids."

"Or my mother!" They had talked for too long. There was no time to put the doll away, no time to get out of the room and avoid her mother's lectures or the servants' pitying stares. There was nothing Katie could think to do but to hide. And there was only one place she might hide.

For a moment, she hesitated.

"You said it's just plain physics," the doll said. "Hurry!"

It's not magic, it's just plain physics, Anyone who knows physics can do this if they believe they can. Clutching the doll tightly to her breast, she stepped inside the wall.

CHAPTER FOUR

Alaric proposes a union

O nce again the queen had summoned Alaric into her presence. There had been no advance notice, no polite request, just an imperious "You—come now" from a soldier at the door.

More than half of his two weeks' truce had already passed. Alaric needed to see the queen as much as she clearly wanted to see him. But he refused to be ordered about by her lackeys. He put his book down slowly. He stopped by the room's small mirror and ran his hand over his already-combed hair.

The soldier cleared his throat and shifted his weight, moving his hand to the knife at his belt, as if he would dare to use it.

Alaric called the soldier's bluff. He met the man's eye, then deliberately rummaged through the small pile of clothing Marco had sent him and selected a short cape, putting it on carefully in front of the mirror. He then exited the room decisively, leaving the soldier to fall in behind.

The queen sat on her throne in her audience hall. She waited until Alaric stood before her. "This room is stuffy," she said. "You will give me your oath that you will not attempt to harm me, and we will walk together outside."

Alaric arched an eyebrow. To attempt any harm to the queen while he was her prisoner would be futile. The only certain outcome would be his own death, either at her hands or those of her guards. No, he would defeat her, but it would have to be later. Still, he couldn't blame her for requiring his oath; magic or none, his oath was good. He would have done the same in her position. Besides, the throne room *was* stuffy this morning; whatever had been going on the previous evening had left a residue of smoke and sweat and rancid perfume. "You have my oath, Your Majesty. Indeed, you had it when you first brought me here. I shall attempt no harm to you while we walk outside this morning."

A smile flickered across her face so quickly he almost missed it. "Carefully phrased."

He tilted his head in acknowledgment.

She dismissed her guards—though he was certain they would be watching carefully from more remote locations—and led the way through a side door out onto a portico. "I understand you have seen my daughter Mouse a number of times."

"Yes, Your Majesty, she has been kind enough to visit me."

Queen Claudia glanced at him. "May I ask, what on earth do you two talk about? The child seldom puts two words together, at least, not that I've heard."

Child? Katie was the youngest daughter, to be sure, but she was also as much a woman as any of her sisters. "Indeed? I find we have enough to talk about. And . . . she reads to me."

The queen stopped walking. Below, in the courtyard, a groom led two saddled horses to a mounting block, where the two eldest princesses waited, both of them wearing jeweled and close-fitting riding clothes. They were quite lovely, those two, the red hair of the one tucked up beneath her riding cap, and the other's black hair in a long braid down her back. Saddles creaked as they mounted.

"That's very clever of you, Alaric," the queen said. "The girl likes to read. But why would you ask her to?"

He smiled, remembering Katie's pleasure at reading her book to him, a silly romance involving the summer holiday of a schoolteacher and a young ne'er-do-well who loved nothing more than surfing in the ocean waves. How she had loved that story. The idea of a holiday in an exotic location so excited her. He remembered, too, the catch in her voice as she'd read about the hero and heroine's first kiss. Katie had glanced at him then, and even now, his heart beat faster, and his body . . . No, best not to think of that now, lest the queen notice.

In return, he had shown her books on history, culture, and other subjects he thought she might like, and he had been rewarded with her growing enthusiasm. Katie was blossoming. "My eyes," he lied. "Without magic, they aren't as good as they might be. I like having someone read to me."

"And is my daughter . . . entertaining?"

Oh yes, indeed. "As well as may be."

"I can imagine." Her voice was as dry as an autumn prairie long without water, the drought of her daughter's continual lack of accomplishments. "Have you found any evidence that the girl has any spark of magical capability? Any at all?"

Evidence? There was only his instinct in the matter, but he would choose his instinct over any evidence concerning Katie; his heart had seized with the unshakable sense that she had more magical power than her family had yet seen. "If I had any magical capability my-self"—his fingers pulled at the edge of the torque—"I would be able to see such things more clearly."

The queen laughed once, an expulsion of air that might equally have been derision.

"But as it is," he continued, "I must answer no. She has performed no act of magic in my presence, no matter how small, and she has given me no other sign. In fact, she denies it vehemently."

"That's my Mouse." The queen's voice was tinged with bitter resignation. She shook her head. "She's a throwback. A mutant. The child has been a disappointment since the day she was born."

Now fully mounted, the two princesses in the courtyard below merrily challenged each other to a race, rode to a gate at the far side of the courtyard, and passed out of Alaric's sight.

"Perhaps the father—"

"The girl's father has nothing to do with her lack of ability. We will not discuss him."

The vehemence of the queen's bitterness surprised Alaric, but it also provided an interesting opening. With less than a week remaining in their truce, any idea was worth pursuing. "And yet," he mused, "this bloodline problem does suggest an idea to me of an entirely different way around this impasse we find ourselves in. Until recently, among the noble and magical families of the realm, only yours and mine have bred true."

"Until Mouse, you mean."

"Yes. Until her. That leaves my family alone. Given our historical animosities, there has never been a match between your family and mine, not in the last dozen or so generations. Perhaps now is the time that your line might profit by an infusion of new blood."

Her face darkened, a sudden gathering of thunderclouds. "If you are suggesting some kind of dalliance—"

He held up a placating hand. "Not at all. Just hear me out. I am an unmarried man. I am suggesting a true alliance between myself and one of your daughters."

"One of my *magical* daughters," she amended. "Not Mouse."

He drew in a breath, let it out, and then nodded. "Very well. One of your magical daughters. We can work out a peace agreement in Darimbia province as part of the negotiation of dowry and bride price."

"And ransom, don't forget."

A tough opponent, this woman. "And ransom. Yes. We may work out a division of the wild gold, but I must be the one to govern the province."

"Then you will do it while living here with your wife."

He stopped walking and looked at her. Though at least two decades older than him, the queen was a beautiful woman in her brocaded emerald gown, her shining red hair, her flawless skin and full, red lips. She didn't look past childbearing age, but his instinct that she was had been correct. If she could still have children, she would have preferred the alliance for herself, not one of her daughters, in order to control him more closely.

"You know I can't live here. I have a kingdom to govern. Darimbia—whether we are fighting a war there or not—is just one part of it."

The queen scowled, an angry sky that augured a storm. "You have no standing to gainsay me. Remember, Alaric, you are a prisoner whose life must be of some value to me, or I will have no reason not to simply kill you." She raised her voice. "Guards! Take this man back to his cell."

Two soldiers sprang from the shadows. One seized his arm by the elbow, and Alaric shook him off with an angry gesture and a glare so full of authority that the man did not attempt to touch him again. Alaric took three long, decisive strides. The soldiers behind him half-ran to keep up.

"Stop!"

Alaric turned to face the queen. He unclenched his fists and schooled his features. He forced himself not to attempt the magic to smite her. The magic that would smite him first.

She waited, but he refused to give her the courtesy of a nod and a 'Your Majesty.'

When the silence had drawn out long enough for the insult to be clear, she said, "You forget that you are my prisoner, Alaric." She pronounced his given name as if it were a knife she twisted in his throat.

Oh, he had not forgotten, but he had indulged himself in a pointless display of anger that did nothing to further his cause. He shoved his anger deep inside where its heat forged his spine into steel. With a minimal incline of his head he said, "My apologies, Your Majesty."

She smiled, but her eyes were hard. "That's better. If I agree that you may interview my daughters—my *magical* daughters, you must swear to me that you will do the girls no harm."

What did she think he was? It was one thing to inflict harm, sorcerer to sorcerer on the battlefield, quite another to, what, slit an innocent girls throat in her own home? "Of course. I swear that I will not harm your daughters during those interviews."

If she'd noted how he hedged the promise, she gave no sign. But neither did she smile. "Very well. I will arrange it. Should we come to terms, we will swear it on my oathstone. It will be in everyone's interest to move quickly."

Late the next morning, Alaric stood by a column in a corner of the courtyard, surveying the bustle before him with equal measures of amusement and disdain. How many people could it possibly take to prepare for a picnic luncheon for four people? Alaric stopped counting when he reached twenty. How many of them would actually be going on that picnic? Guessing from the number of horses that were saddled and ready, stamping their feet nervously, there would probably be at least a dozen, with three more horses to carry the gear.

Five men loaded the pack animals with blankets and baskets, from which wafted the scents of an elegant meal to come. But unless the royal princesses had much greater appetites than he imagined, the poor animals would be bringing much of it back home again.

He'd given his oath, of course. No harm to the three princesses, no trying to escape while outside the castle walls, all the usual precautions. Still, six well-armed and gaudily uniformed soldiers attended their mounts across the way, and judging from the distrustful glances they flicked in his direction, they meant to keep a close eye on him. Perhaps they accounted for all the extra food. They were welcome to it, as far as he was concerned. He hoped they'd keep a respectful distance, at least. He hoped that they'd stay silent and not offer too many distractions. Most of all, he hoped they'd keep their weapons sheathed and out of sight. Some courtship!

For that matter, he wondered whether he would compare unfavorably with the soldiers' youthful vigor and boyish good looks. Next to them, his twenty-six years seemed ancient. He straightened the sleeve of his surcoat.

He'd combed and braided his hair, trimmed his beard, and selected from among the clothing Marco had sent, an outfit suitable for riding into the countryside yet rich enough to avoid embarrassment. And he'd chided himself for his vanity. But there it was. A picnic for himself and three princesses, six soldiers, and who knew how many ladies-in-waiting and servants with silver platters—and he felt like a boy alone for the first time with a maid, concerned about making a good impression.

The chatter of feminine voices and a burst of laughter like the pealing of bells on a holiday broke Alaric's reverie. For a moment the bustle in the courtyard ceased and the noises stilled. From the opposite corner of the courtyard two princesses emerged, wearing bold colors and jewels that made his own gold-embroidered gray silk seem drab. But what had he expected? Alaric smiled, charmed despite himself.

Jocasta, the eldest, strode toward him. She was taller than her sisters and held herself rigidly upright. Her black hair was braided tightly; her jacket of fine, deep blue satin was buttoned to the throat. She stared at him, appraising, until he looked away, reminded who was the prisoner and who was the royalty here. "My lady," he murmured, bowing his head just enough to acknowledge her station.

"Alaric," she said, "I hope you enjoy riding."

She might have slapped him and given less offense. He might be her mother's prisoner, but he was still a king, and her superior. He looked at her sharply, one eyebrow arched. "I don't believe, Princess, that we are yet on a first-name basis."

"As you wish, my lord." Her smile was cold, her eyes blue ice. She would be a formidable challenge, that one. She reminded Alaric of her mother. Whichever princess he chose, it would not be Jocasta.

He smiled, matching her coldness with coldness. "Yes, my lady, very much."

The second princess had joined them. "My lord, I am Princess Mercuria, the queen's second daughter."

But for the age difference, she could have been the queen's twin. Alaric's smile warmed. "I would have known you for her daughter had I seen you, a stranger, in the marketplace."

Mercuria frowned. "Pray, what would I be doing in the marketplace?"

Her sister had not moved aside to make room for her, and so Alaric did so. He inclined his head slightly. "I was merely speaking hypothetically."

Her bold green and blue patterned riding outfit brought out the red of her hair and the green of her eyes. Her skin was flawless alabaster. "Hypothetically?"

"I meant only that you resemble her."

She smoothed her hair. "Yes, people say that all the time. But I am younger. And prettier."

She was indeed lovely, and Alaric wondered that she would fish for compliments. "I'm sure people say that all the time, too."

"Yes," said the princess, studying her fingernails, which were painted a bright vermilion. "They do."

Did the princess indulge in conversations on topics other than herself? But before he could compose the compliment she seemed to be looking for, the third princess arrived, standing a bit behind the others.

"Am I late?" she asked breathlessly. With her red lips slightly parted and a hand clasped to her breast, Stefania was the very image of femininity. Her blond curls were bound back loosely, and were already straying around her smooth face. Her crimson dress accentuated her fair complexion and revealed perhaps a bit too much of that heaving bosom.

"Yes," said Jocasta. "As always. You are completely hopeless."

Stefania seemed unoffended, perhaps inured to her sister's criticism. She tossed her head. "Whereas you would have ridden off without me, and taken pleasure in it."

"But *I* would not," Alaric interjected. "Besides, they're only just now finishing packing everything up." He smiled at her, and she dimpled a smile at him in return. There was something about her that seemed a little *too much* of . . . whatever it was. A glamour of some kind, perhaps. If he could only have used his magic, he would have known for sure.

They rode from the castle in a long column, two soldiers in front setting the pace at a brisk walk, then the princesses with their two matronly ladies-in-waiting. Alaric rode next, followed by an escort of two soldiers, and then a long retinue of servants and supplies. At the end of the column rode another pair of soldiers.

After about fifteen minutes of riding through rich farmland, Jocasta dropped back to ride with him. "Care to race?"

Alaric had been given a black gelding that had seen livelier days. Not a decrepit beast by any means, but certainly not one to make a daring escape on. Or to win a race, for that matter, particularly against the spirited chestnut stallion the princess rode.

But to gallop through the verdant countryside, to feel the wind in his face, the horse's muscles bunching under him! His heart beat faster at the thought of it. "I'd love to."

She spurred her horse to a sprint, and he followed at full gallop, veering across a field and away from their escort. Four soldiers scrambled to keep up with them. To his surprise, Alaric drew even with the princess and then pulled slightly ahead, laughing with the joy of the ride.

His lead didn't last long. They jumped a low wall, and then Jocasta passed him, using her riding whip on her horse's rump.

"I win!" she cried, pulling to a trot and then a walk as she circled around a large oak tree that stood alone in the center of the next field.

He joined her as they trotted back to their group. "You win," he agreed. He'd bet anything that Jocasta *always* won.

Mercuria was easier to engage in conversation. As the picnic was being set out, he stepped apart with her, the watchful soldiers keeping a discreet distance. He asked what her favorite activities were, and then simply walked beside her and listened for the next fifteen minutes. She spoke of balls and parties, of how she loved to dance and gossip, of beautiful dresses and handsome beaus. Her every sentence began with "I." All that was required of Alaric was an occasional "Mmm," "I see," or "Of course." Easy to get along with, yes, and easy to forget.

During the lunch, Alaric said little. He didn't need to. He listened to the princesses chatter, watched their interactions, and observed how they treated the servants. They were all preening in front of him, but none of them showed any actual interest in him. And he discovered he wasn't interested in any of them, either.

Stefania claimed him at the end of the picnic, when the sun brought out the smell of fresh grass and wildflowers, and the bees hummed from one flower to another. "Let's go talk together a bit, shall we?" she asked.

Alaric agreed and got to his feet, feeling pleasantly full and sun-warmed. The meal had been good—indeed, fit for a king.

When a soldier stood to go with them, Stefania ran her fingers lightly across his cheek and said, "Now, be a dear and don't follow too closely." She gave the soldier a wink, and he obediently dropped back. Then she took Alaric's hand, leading him toward the shade of a band of trees and bushes that marked the edge of the field.

Stefania's hair had become unbound during the afternoon, and it floated in lazy curls over her neck and shoulders. She squeezed Alaric's hand. "Sit with me in the shade over here." And then in a voice throaty with desire, "Behind these bushes, where that nasty soldier won't see us."

He could tell where this was headed, but the temptation the princess offered was utterly wrong.

It was the wrong place, the wrong moment, the wrong reason. Most of all, it was the wrong princess. His memory flashed to Katie—her generosity, her kindness, her utter lack of awareness of her beauty. She was a princess he could happily marry, but Stefania—

Something was not quite *right* about Stefania—not right with her, or not right for him, or both. He didn't want to be caught up in it. He smiled and kissed her hand. "An attractive offer," he said, gazing into her eyes, "but one I must respectfully decline. This is not the moment." He lowered his voice and added, "You know your sisters will miss us." With a courteous bow, he returned to the group.

On the way back to the castle, Alaric rode with the soldiers.

CHAPTER FIVE

Alaric makes his wishes known

K atie didn't visit Alaric the next day, or the day after that. She stayed in her chamber and waited for the announcement of an engagement. When none was forthcoming, she could cloister herself no longer.

She dressed very carefully in her finest, a dress of deep maroon silk woven with a jacquard of stylized lilies. She stormed the steps of Alaric's tower, to the astonishment of the guard sitting half-asleep at the door, who jumped up and barely had time to announce her.

Alaric's hair was bound loosely at the nape of his neck, and he wore clothing so simple it might have belonged to a commoner. Comfortable clothing. When she refused both his open greeting and the chair he offered, his gaze turned sad. She stood next to the window, her back against the wall. She spoke without preamble, ignoring the catch in her throat. "I heard you went out riding with my sisters."

"So I did." His head tilted a question mark, one eyebrow raised.

"Did you enjoy yourself?"

"I liked getting outside. The air was fresh and the sunlight warm."
He said nothing about her sisters, an omission so glaring it couldn't
possibly have been accidental.

"I would have taken you out, but I was not allowed." Her voice
quavered.

He took a deep breath. "I know, Katie. I would have had a most
enjoyable time with you, but I too was not allowed. I suppose you also
heard that your mother and I have agreed that I'll marry one of her
magical daughters. As part of the ransom arrangement."

She blinked back tears and swallowed a lump in her throat. She
made her voice hard and held her head defiantly high. "And have you
chosen one?"

"No, I haven't."

"Well, what are you waiting for?"

He tilted his head and looked at her, rubbing his chin. "Katie, are
you angry at me?"

She wrapped her arms tightly across her chest. "No. Why should I
be? I would do the same thing in your circumstances."

He raised an eyebrow. "Would you?"

"Yes, of course! Its your chance to get out of here. You're lucky
to have it. You should take it and marry one of them." She tried to
swallow but choked instead. Tears overflowed her eyes. She couldn't
stay, couldn't let him see her like this. She rushed to get past him and
out the door.

Alaric stepped in front of her, blocking her way. One hand, he
placed on her shoulder, and with the other hand he reached to wipe
the tears from her cheek.

Her breath caught in her throat, but she didn't push him away.

A moment passed. He moved his hands to cradle the back of her
head, leaned down slowly, and kissed her softly on the cheek.

Katie stiffened and involuntarily took a small step back. Then she wanted only to be close to him. She met his eyes and touched his face, his unshaven beard rough on her fingertips. She closed the distance between them and rested her head against his chest.

He folded his arms around her and held her so tightly she could feel the beating of his heart. They stood that way until she stopped sobbing, and for a long time after that.

"Katie, listen to me. I am not going to marry any of them, and I'm not going to leave here without you."

She pulled away from him. "No. Its kind of you to offer, but no. If you get a chance for freedom, you should take it. As for me, I won't be a handmaiden to any of my sisters. It would be better for me to stay here."

To stay and if necessary, to marry Lord Tobey. At least she'd be mistress of her own manor. Involuntarily, she shuddered.

"That bad, are they?"

She felt her cheeks flush. "I didn't say that. They're all several years older than me. We were never close."

"Many older girls like to coddle their baby sisters."

"Not those three." Katie pulled away from him and crossed her arms.

"They hurt you." He spoke gently and touched her arm. She looked up at him, surprised that he'd guessed.

"Nothing . . . major. Little scratches with a pin. A push when no one was looking. They found ways to let me know it could have been worse. Would be worse if I got in their way. Not that they were much nicer to each other, and my mother encouraged the competition. I had a doll I loved, a very special doll, and one time they took turns tearing her hair. One of them ripped the doll's arm out"—she swallowed—"out of its socket. To show me what they could do to me if they wanted. All that was *before* they came into their magic. Believe me, after that I kept out of their way as much as I could."

"Then I shall keep out of their way, too." Alaric folded her in his arms again, and a comfortable silence fell between them.

"You kissed me," she said. She could still feel his lips on her cheek, the brush of his beard on her chin.

"Is that all right?"

Did friends kiss each other? Katie wasn't sure. But this didn't feel like friends. It felt like something she wanted to do again, and often. If it led to being something more than just friends . . . She might like that, too. She looked up at him, at the concern in his gray eyes. Then she reached up and pulled his face down to hers, and she kissed him, very softly, on his lips, an act that would have been impossibly audacious, had she not done it before she had time to think.

He made a noise that might have been a groan.

Suddenly abashed, Katie felt her cheeks grow hot. How could she have been so forward? What must he think of her? She glanced up at him while trying not to meet his eyes, half afraid of what she might see in his expression.

Whatever she'd expected, it wasn't his intense gaze, pupils large and dark. He brushed back a loose strand of her hair and let out a long breath. "Well, then, we'll work something out, you and I."

She wasn't sure what he meant, but at least they were still friends, and maybe they might kiss again sometime. She liked that idea and settled contentedly back into his embrace.

"Katie, what happened to the doll?"

She stiffened. The room was suddenly uncomfortably hot, his arms too constraining. Her heart raced. She stepped away from him and breathed in, out, willing herself to appear calm. "It was just a toy, a long time ago. What does it matter?"

He shrugged nonchalantly. "Of course, just a toy. But it must have been dear to you, or your sisters wouldn't have done what they did."

Slowly, Katie relaxed again. "Yes, it was. My little friend at the time, my closest one. All my sisters were older, and I was so shy."

"I'll bet you were." He tried to suppress a smile, but it slipped out.

She saw it and laughed. "Okay, I still am. And I'll tell you a secret—I still have the doll, too, poor battered thing." She tensed, wondering if he'd think her too childish.

"Good for you," he said, his smile widening. "Good for you."

She felt a wave of relief. "So, now that I've told you about my Dolly, you must tell me a secret of yours. Which one of my sisters will you marry?"

He touched her lips with his fingertips and then took her hand. He raised it to his lips, placed a kiss in her palm, and folded her fingers over it, cupping her hand in his. "None of them, Katie. You are the only one of your mother's daughters I would marry."

Slowly, as if the air had turned to a thick liquid too viscous to push through, Katie put her other hand over his. Her hand trembled slightly. She shook her head. "No! Not me. You mustn't!"

Either she was crying, or all the moisture was condensing out of the air and settling on her cheeks. She sniffled. Definitely crying—but whether from joy or . . . maybe regret, she couldn't have said.

"Is the prospect so terrible?" His voice was raspy, like something was caught in his throat. "I know I'm a little bit older than you, and a foreigner, but I promise I would be kind and . . . gentle, and—"

"Its not that!" She clutched his hand tightly so that he wouldn't let go. "You keep saying you're older, but it's not by much. I bet my sisters are older than you are. Besides, what difference will a few years make when we're sixty, or eighty? But I don't want to be stuck in one place. I want to visit other countries, maybe see if I can find some hint about who my father was, if he's some kind of foreign prince like my mother told me when I was little. You're my friend—my dear friend, but you must marry one of my sisters, not me, so that you can be free. Isn't that what you and my mother are negotiating? One of her daughters with magic who will bear you magical sons and my mother magical granddaughters. Not someone plain like me."

"I am negotiating . . ." He spoke slowly, deliberately, as if each word had weight that must be measured separately. ". . . to marry one of your mother's magical daughters. Since you're her only daughter that I would marry, we will have to figure out how to bring out some magic in you."

Despite herself, she found herself laughing. With the back of her hand, she wiped the tears first from one cheek and then the other. "You just don't give up, do you?"

"Never. I'm hoping that's a yes."

Katie drew a deep breath and let it out. "It's not a no, but . . ." By all the stars in the heavens, she liked the man so much. He was her good friend, so why was she hesitating? She felt all around the pain in her breast, sure the answer was inside the spot where it hurt the most. "It's just that getting free is so important—for you and for me, and maybe for those poor people in Darimbia, too—that I would never forgive myself if I ruined your chance. I know what's at stake here, and it's more than just you and me. Besides, my mother would never allow us to marry, not while we're both still here. So, let's figure out how to get out of here first, and then we can talk about whatever comes next."

He kissed her on the forehead, on both damp cheeks, and gently on her lips again. He was smiling. "Good. Let's do that. Meanwhile, let's start with the magic, all right?"

Drat. Magic. How had she let herself get trapped into this?

Four days had passed since Alaric rode out with the three princesses. During this time, he and Claudia finalized their agreement. The price was steep, but Alaric had little leverage in negotiating, and time was running out. He was, as she reminded him more than once, lucky still to be alive.

Late in the afternoon, the queen finally summoned Alaric to the oathstone chamber. The stairs leading down were steep, but wide, cut from the natural rock upon which the castle had been built. The queen led the small procession, and she entered the chamber first. Two soldiers who followed at her heels paused at the doorway, then stepped to either side. Alaric, too, paused in the doorway and took a deep breath. The air smelled musty, of rocks long underground and never touched by sunlight. He prepared himself to swear an oath he might not be willing to keep—and if he did not keep it, the forsworn oath would tighten like a band on his heart until it killed him.

He entered the chamber.

The oathstone glowed with its own light, throwing dark shadows upward in the cold crypt. Magic hung in the air, heavy and pungent, urging Alaric to pull up his own inner vision, to understand the oathstone's magical knots and joinery, ancient magic far beyond any spells that could be woven today. But the stone of the walls was cast in shadows, and the torque sat heavy on his neck.

He looked from the glowing monolith in the center of the chamber to the queen who stood opposite him. Her green eyes seemed to reflect the stone's eldritch glow. Alaric shivered. The power in this room could destroy both of them.

"What we say here binds us," the queen said. Her words echoed off the walls, off the frigid stone slabs of the floor.

"What we say here binds us," Alaric repeated. The cold air seemed to wrap him like a shroud.

The queen touched the stone. A frisson of energy shook her visibly. Alaric met her eyes, and she inclined her head slightly.

This was his last chance to change his mind—but no. He would not. He touched the stone.

A thunderclap deafened him. The light from the oathstone flared out like lightning, but Alaric did not remove his hand. Energy from the very core of the world flowed through him. His knees went weak, but he refused to allow them to buckle, refused to fall. The stone gripped his hand and held it fast.

"I will set you free to live in your own land," said the queen, "and in return . . ." Her voice was strong, but shook with the energy in the room.

"In return, I will marry one of your daughters with magical powers, who shall be the one of my own choosing, but only with her consent." Alaric swallowed. "If she does not consent, this oath is void."

"My daughter will consent, you can be sure of it." The queen's mouth was a tight red line of determination; her eyes were hard.

A rumble like distant thunder echoed in the room. It vibrated through the soles of Alaric's shoes. "You may not swear for another," he said.

The queen lifted her chin. "I will do my utmost to ensure my daughter's consent."

He nodded. "Very well. I will sire my wife's children, if she is able and willing."

"She will—" The queen interrupted herself. "I agree. And as my daughter's dowry, I will cede Darimbia to you." She gave him a saccharine smile and an all-but-imperceptible nod.

"As the bride price, I and my heirs will deliver to you and yours three quarters of its wild gold production for the next fifty years." *Not much of a dowry*, Alaric thought grimly. *I do all the work, and give you three quarters of the output. But ending this conflict is worth a great deal to me. I will give the people freedom and protection, and I'll make sure they don't starve—which is more than you would have done.*

The queen broke into his reverie. "In addition, you will deliver at least ten kilograms of the refined wild gold to me this year, if not produced, then of your own stock."

"Yes, this year, for my ransom. I so agree," Alaric said. He felt old and drained. Much had been given, but much had also been gained. "Let the oathstone remember."

The queen nodded slowly. "Let the oathstone remember. And we shall not forget."

"We shall not forget."

Again, a flare of light lit the chamber. Both of them stumbled backward, a moment of imbalance as their hands were freed from the stone with a perceptible force. The oath tightened like a knot behind Alaric's heart, like a hunger that must be satisfied. He hoped he was right about Katie, because otherwise . . .

"That's done, then." The queen wiped her brow and turned toward the stairway. "Let's get out of here."

The next afternoon, Katie sat on the chair in Alaric's room, her face squeezed in concentration. Before her, a candle burned in its holder on Alaric's table. She grunted with effort.

Nothing happened, just as she expected. Just as she'd told him. Why, oh why, had she ever agreed to this?

"This is not a matter of effort, Katie," Alaric said. He moved closer, just behind her, and put a hand on her shoulder. His fingers were warm, but her muscles were as tight as a sailor's knot.

"This is a *waste* of effort, is what it is," Katie said, her voice rising even as her heart sank. "'Lighting candles is easy magic,' you said. 'Extinguishing them is even easier,' you said. But look at me. Nothing!" She balled her hands into fists, drew in a breath, and blew out the candle. "There! Its extinguished, and as usual, I've disappointed everybody, even you. I think I'll go now."

She started to rise, but he kept his hand on her shoulder, suggesting that she stay.

"Please don't go. I'm sorry; this was my fault. I pushed you too hard and without adequate instruction."

She turned toward him. His face was a map of concern, and more. Worry? Desperation? Was she doomed always to be a disappointment to everybody? The dam holding back her emotions broke, and tears overflowed her eyes.

"Oh, Katie, I'm so sorry." He crouched down to her level and reached out with a trembling hand. He brushed the tears from first one cheek, then the other. For just the tiniest instant the tenderness in his eyes almost made her think he would kiss her again, this time maybe the way the heroes did in her books, and her heart gave an out-of-rhythm jump. She'd been hoping for another kiss since that day he'd sort of almost proposed and she'd not quite turned him down.

But no, Alaric was the soul of propriety, and the look vanished so quickly she might have just imagined it. "Listen," he said. "This doesn't matter. It's you I care about, and I'll care even if you never manage to extinguish or light a single candle. I promise you will never disappoint me."

She gave a small sniffle. How could he make a promise like that? "Everyone wants me to be magical," she said.

"You, most of all."

She looked away from him, away from the awful candle. She had never noticed before how unevenly matched the wooden boards of his floor were. She wanted to say, *That's not true*, but the words seemed stuck in her throat and wouldn't come out.

"And, Katie, I believe you are," he continued. "I *know* you are. We just have to find the right way to approach it."

She bit her lip and said nothing.

"Let's try one more time, shall we?"

Katie took a deep breath and let it out. How could he possibly still believe in her after she'd so emphatically demonstrated her lack of ability? But clearly, he wasn't about to give up. And so she had to try again. For him. And yes, for herself, too, a final chance to win her mother's approval. For both of them, then. She nodded shakily.

He stood and raised a hand. Then he sighed and lowered it, shaking his head. *He has no magic*, Katie remembered.

He struck a match, and lit the candle. "This time, don't use effort. Use will. Create a fact—not an action. There's a difference, you know. Facts just *are*, but an action means you are trying. This is not about trying. *Intend* for the candle to be out. Know you are stronger than the candle. Brook no argument from it; the candle is *out*." He moved behind her and placed one hand on each shoulder. "Concentrate."

All right, she thought. She reached back and touched his hand. *I am stronger than the candle. The candle is out.*

Nothing happened.

Anger welled hot in Katie's breast and flowed out to her clenched hands. *Out, damn you, candle. You. Are. Out.*

The candle went out.

Katie turned accusingly. "*You* did that!"

Alaric shook his head as a wide smile spread over his face. His eyes were glowing so brightly they could have been silver. "No. I didn't. You did."

"Liar! *You* did it."

"Katie. I'm wearing this torque. I cannot do magic. Not even a magic this small, not even if my life depended on it."

She searched his face, his eyes, looking for the least hint that he was playing a trick on her, but finding only his surprisingly boyish grin of delight. She began to smile in return with a happiness that spread across her face and into her heart and out to the tips of her fingers and toes. "I did it," she whispered. And she laughed in wonder.

Then they were both laughing, and he picked her up and twirled her around three times.

"Hey, take it easy in there!" came the guard's gruff voice from the hallway.

"Sorry," Alaric called, the laughter still bubbling in his voice.

All at once, Katie had a clear vision of her mother demanding that she practice magic, constantly escalating both her demands and her criticisms. Katie's heart sank and her laughter faded. "Whatever you do," she said, "don't tell my mother."

"That would put a crimp in my negotiating ability." His voice was the very soul of regret, and he frowned in thought. "I've sworn on her oathstone to choose one of her magical daughters to marry, and tomorrow is the last day of our truce. I'm going to have to let her know my choice. And since I'm not marrying any of your sisters, I'm going to have to let her know I choose you."

The feeling in Katie's insides grew more pronounced, like there wasn't enough room for both her stomach and her heart. "Wait. You were serious about that yesterday?"

"Perfectly."

"But I never said—"

"Don't worry, no one has promised that the daughter I choose will accept." His gray eyes searched hers. "But I hope you will at least consider—"

"I need time. I like you very much. There's no one else I want to marry, but I've always dreamed of being free. Of traveling places. I need time to think about marriage, and we need time to talk, but not here. As soon as you tell my mother, I won't be safe. She'll be making all kinds of demands on me, and not just her. My sisters . . ." She shivered.

"What do you want to do, then?"

"Actually," Katie said, "I've been working on this for the last week or so, and I think I know how I might sneak you out. I could sneak us both out."

"But—"

His fingers went toward his neck, and she reached out to stop him. "I know, I know. The torque. That's why we'll keep working on the magic, too. But don't tell her until my plans are ready."

"I have to tell her tomorrow."

"Tomorrow? Can you wait that long, anyway?" She had a sudden realization and breathed out a bitter laugh. "Besides, she probably won't believe you even if you do tell her. You'll just make my mother angry."

CHAPTER SIX

Katie comes up with a plan

Alaric avoided meeting with the queen as long as he could the next day by feigning illness, but at noon, the queen notified him that they would meet just after lunch, illness or no. He had no power to refuse.

True to her word, two hours later she summoned him to a small audience chamber. She sat on an ornate chair that might almost have been a throne, especially since it was on a dais two steps above the floor of the room. Dressed to dazzling perfection, she wore a pale green gown lavishly embroidered in silver thread, and complemented with jewelry of diamonds and white gold. "So, tell me, Alaric"—her mouth tilted into a slight, satisfied smile as she pronounced his name—"have you chosen your bride yet?"

"Indeed, " he answered with a solemn nod.

"And—? Do not play coy with me."

"Your Majesty, I shall marry your daughter Katie."

Her jaw fell open. She clamped it shut and drew back a hand as if to slap him. Slowly and deliberately, she lowered the hand, and spoke in a voice as cold and hard as ice. "This is not a matter for jokes. Which of my *magical* daughters will you marry?"

The conversation was not going well, but there was no turning away from it. "I assure you that I am not joking. Katie has used magic to extinguish a candle, and so she qualifies under the terms of our agreement."

The queen's face paled, and her voice came out ragged. "You have deceived me!"

"Your Majesty, I—"

"I will not permit you to toy with me, Alaric." She rose from her throne and descended the two steps down from the dais, glaring at him. "I should just kill you and be done with it."

"When we made our oath, I didn't know—"

"How very convenient. And now, suddenly, you do know? Or perhaps you and that pathetic child have agreed upon a convenient lie that will allow you to slip out of your oath."

A lie would not save him from his oath. They both knew that.

The queen circled him, her arms folded over her chest. "I won't have it. You are violating the spirit of our agreement, if not the substance. Marry one of my *other* daughters, Alaric, one with proven magic. Real magic, not just a candle trick. Not her."

"I believe that we agreed I may choose among all your daughters with magical abilities. We did not specify how great. I choose Katie."

"She may not." Her voice grew louder and half an octave higher than normal. "*You* may not. I forbid it."

Alaric fingered the torque on his neck. He watched her frenetic pacing back and forth, back and forth, and he felt old and worn and inexplicably sad. "I believe I may," he said. "We have sworn this agreement on your oathstone. Let the oathstone decide." He felt sure the oathstone would decide for him..

She stopped her pacing long enough to glare at him with a heat that almost burned the magical metal at his throat. Then she resumed pacing. "You have tricked me."

His shoulders shrugged in a small unconscious movement. "No," he said, "I didn't. At the time, I hoped, but I didn't know."

"If you didn't know, as you've admitted just now, then that's not what you swore to, is it? You don't want to take this to the oathstone any more than I do. You're too clever by half, but whatever this game is, I'm not playing. I won't release you. Our truce is finished tomorrow, and you must marry another of my daughters—not Katie."

"I have already asked Katie to marry me. I will not be false to her."

"I am to let you go then, with your *wife*?" She spat out the last word as if it were something filthy. "You are a fool, Alaric. I will not remove the torque." Her face lit up, and a smile spread across her lips. "I never swore to remove it, now, did I? Let your *wife* do it with her magic, if she can. Hah."

Easy enough for the queen, or for any of her daughters with magic, but this was a problem. With no magic, he could not release any pent-up or hidden magic Katie might have. And the amount she had shown was much too small. Katie was not up to a task of this magnitude. Without sufficient magic, Katie could not release him. "Let us put our hands on the oathstone," he said. "Then we will know whether you must remove the torque or not."

"No. You have reduced your side of the bargain by choosing my daughter who had no magic when we swore, and so now I am reducing mine. I'll give the girl twenty-four hours to demonstrate her magic by taking off the torque. By then, we'll no longer have a truce, and I'll have you both killed and be done with you. Now get out."

The queen wouldn't kill her own daughter, of course. At least, Alaric hoped not. Nor would she kill him without an appeal to the oathstone. The oath had been sealed, and to forfeit the oath would cost her own life. But she could make his imprisonment much more painful for him. She could make things even worse for Katie.

He had no power. He could force the queen's hand only so far. He turned and left her throne chamber, two somber-faced guards dogging his heels.

Katie nibbled at a fingernail as she waited for Alaric to return from his audience with her mother. It wasn't going to go well, she could feel it in her bones and in the chill that, despite the warm weather, seemed to envelop her hands and feet with a life of its own.

"How long you plan to wait here?" the room's guard asked. "Maybe he ain't coming back. Maybe Her Majesty throw him in the dungeon instead of here."

Katie shivered. From where she sat, she could see the guard clearly. "He's coming back," she said. "He has to."

The guard shook his head. "Boring job, watching him."

She'd never thought about what it must be like for the guard. "Really? Would it be better for you if you had to watch him in the dungeon?"

"What would be better for me," he said, "would be to have some booze to give me something to do while I was watching him." He covered his mouth with his hand. "Sorry, Princess, I spoke out of turn. I didn't mean that."

Sure you did. And this gave Katie the beginning of a plan.

Alaric agreed to Katie's plan. There was no other choice, not really. The queen had given them twenty-four hours, and they had to make the most of the time. Even with the best intentions, Katie wouldn't be able to remove the torque while they remained in the castle. Fear of her mother and sisters hung over her like a dark cloud. They needed to get away if she was to have any chance of success. And so they waited until dark, when they might leave undetected.

If he'd had a clock, Alaric would have checked it again—probably for the hundredth time. Seven hours had passed since his meeting with the queen—seven of the twenty-four she'd given him. He paced the length of his small cell, pulling at the stiff-edged torque around his neck. Up two strides. Turn and back two strides. He didn't suffer powerlessness easily. Turn. Repeat.

A scratching at the door interrupted his brown study, so tiny he wasn't entirely certain he'd heard it. But an instant later a key fumbled in the lock.

One step, and he was at the door, opening it as soon as he heard the tumblers click into place.

And there was Katie, booted and cloaked and radiant. She wore a satchel over her shoulder, smiling like a child with candy.

"Shh." She gestured with her chin toward where Alaric could dimly make out a guard sprawled in his chair, apparently sleeping. "Are you ready?" she whispered.

"Yes." He threw on his own cloak and picked up his satchel—a sad thing with only three books in it—though the books were valuable enough. There would be no need to take any of the clothing Marco had sent to him. If Katie could develop her magic quickly enough, they would be across the border before he needed the change. If she didn't . . .

He shook his head to clear thoughts of negative consequences. And to look at Katie. She positively sparkled. The way she looked now, energy glowing in her, she might be the most powerful sorcerer in the world. He could believe she was—or would be. She was transformed—beautiful. His heart swelled and pressed against his chest with an aching desire to kiss her. And more.

But not now. With any luck, that would happen later, when the torque was off and they were free. When they were married.

They slipped out the door. Katie closed and carefully locked it, and she placed the key on the floor near the unconscious guard's hand.

Alaric examined the guard. Not unconscious, but asleep. Dead drunk asleep. He sprawled in his chair, snoring. His shirt was pulled loose from his trousers and unbuttoned at the top, where the open V revealed a mat of dark hair. The man's hands hung by his side, an empty wine bottle still held in his loosely curled fingers. Two more empty bottles lay on the floor nearby, and three full ones stood along the wall at his side.

The bottles were dusty, and there were smudges on the man's hands and face. Even over the man's sour sweat, the wine smelled aged, a hint of raspberries and herbs on the nose. Alaric picked up one of the full bottles. It was a rare vintage, worth a small fortune in the country where it was grown and a considerably larger one here, one of the best vintages ever produced anywhere. He let out an appreciative sigh.

Katie's eyes flicked from him to the bottle he held and back again. "They're just dusty old bottles from way in the back of my mother's cellar. Don't worry, she'll never miss them. She probably forgot about them years ago."

Not a chance of that, but whatever upset would occur when Queen Claudia discovered that the bottles were missing wouldn't concern him and Katie. With any luck, they'd be long gone. Alaric placed the bottle back near the wall and followed Katie down the stairs.

The sound of raucous voices from the guard station on the ground floor grew louder as they descended. Katie stopped on the landing of the floor above. "I could slip by unnoticed," she said after a moment's consideration, "but you . . ." She scanned Alaric up and down with a critical eye, seeming to take in his tall frame and upright bearing. Her head moved almost imperceptibly from side to side, a negative judgment that he could see forming.

But the matter was taken out of their hands.

"Quiet!" A booming voice from within silenced the others. "Jamaal may like his wine, but he would never drink on duty. I'd stake a week's pay on it."

Several voices clamored to accept the bet.

Katie and Alaric looked at each other. Concern twisted in the pit of his stomach, but Katie's face grew brighter. She pushed at the door exiting the stairway at this level, but it refused to give. Alaric added his shoulder to it. The door didn't budge.

"Locked from the other side," Katie whispered. Her eyes were wide, and she looked rapidly to both sides. "I'm so sorry. I should have thought of that and undone it."

"So, now what? Upstairs and try the next level?" Alaric's heart was pounding, but he trusted Katie's judgment—Katie, the Mouse.

"All right, let's go see if he has or hasn't been drinking." Jamaal's supporter spoke loudly. "Max, you and Udi come with me."

Katie gasped and grabbed Alaric's hand. Before he could ask, "Which way?" she pulled him into the wall.

Tons of crushing rock pressed all around, squeezing his lungs, his heart. He gasped for breath, but in vain. There was no air inside the stone wall. He gripped Katie's hand tightly.

Then they stepped out the other side.

Katie glowed as if magic were crackling in the air around her, sparkling in her hair, cascading down through her fingertips and toes. Her eyes were alight with the pure joy of it.

He felt himself grinning, but he had to be careful. "That's a good trick," he said. "Have you always been able to do that?"

"No . . . I just figured it out when we were studying physics." She must have seen the question still lingering on his face. "With all the space between subatomic particles, it had to be possible to push right through them somehow, and it was."

Indeed it was possible theoretically, but not without considerable use of magic. Could it be she didn't realize this? He himself had tried when he first studied Stedman. What young sorcerer hadn't? But he knew of no one who had succeeded. Until now. He wanted to know more about how she managed this trick, but it would have to wait. He nodded sagely. "Good thinking."

He looked around. They were in a hallway of some kind, its stone walls smoothly cut and polished, with narrow mortar joints. A brightly patterned but worn carpet lay on the stone floor. "So, where are we now?"

"In the corridor between the ballroom and the banquet room—where we first met, remember?" A slight reddening of her cheeks made her perhaps even prettier. "There's a kitchen staging area beyond the banquet room, and beyond that the back stairway leads down to the kitchen and out to the delivery courtyard. No one's here this time of night."

Their footsteps echoed down the corridor. The banquet room was dark, and it had a stale smell—food gone bad, drinks spilled and soaked into the carpets and the mortar of the flooring stones, a lingering odor of sweat and perfume.

From the foot of the stairway they could see into the kitchen, which was brightly lit. A baker measured ingredients amid a slight haze where the flour hadn't settled from pouring, and her assistant grunted with the effort of kneading the loaves.

They crept past the bright kitchen and through the open doorway to the courtyard. It took a moment for their eyes to adjust. No lamps lit the area, but the half-moon hung nearly overhead. The courtyard was deserted, no sentries in evidence. Silently, they crossed to the stables.

A small door led to the tack room. It was dark but for a small lamp in a bracket. The room smelled of horses and old leather and fresh-cut hay, a good, warm smell. Katie put a finger to her mouth and shook her head. She pointed to the ceiling and held up three fingers to indicate the three stable-boys who slept above. Saddles sat on shelves, bridles hung from hooks, and folded blankets were piled in a neat heap on a table. From a shelf, below which a small brass plaque read "Arrow," she took a saddle. She gestured to the next saddle, whose plaque read "Grumpy," and Alaric took it, along with two bridles and saddle blankets. He followed her through a small wooden door into the main stable.

Katie and Alaric saddled up quickly and led the horses to the castle's inner gate. Claudia's castle had a strong defensive perimeter, a relic of an earlier age when, perhaps, her domain had been less secure and invasion not outside the realm of possibility. But the inner gate was now open. A lone sentry was on duty in the gatehouse. He sat by a flickering fire, head slumped on his chest, snoring. "Asleep," Alaric whispered. "Good thing he's not in my army."

They passed through the gate and into the outer court. This, too, was gated, a heavy gate that took four soldiers to close and twice that many to open. It was open and unused, the heavy chain coated in rust.

They mounted and rode through the night, into the early morning. It was less than two weeks from the summer solstice, but the sky was as dark as dusk. Wind whipped the few trees into a lashing frenzy, tearing early summer leaves from their branches and branches from their trunks. Lightning traced jagged fracture lines across the clouds. Threatening thunder growled constantly, sometimes booming so close that the horses startled and struggled against the bit.

"This is no ordinary storm." Alaric had to shout to be heard. "The queen knows we're gone." He'd studied the geography of Victoria, as he had all the neighboring countries, and he knew approximately where they were. There was a small town ahead. Maybe they could find an inn where they could rest for an hour or two and give the horses a needed rest as well. Perhaps the storm would lessen a bit if the queen grew tired, or was distracted.

A soldier appeared in the road ahead, then more. An entire platoon approached, some twenty men, heads down, marching stiffly into the biting wind. Their lieutenant and an adjutant rode alongside on nervously prancing horses.

Alaric bit his lip. There was a small army base in the area. His spies had earmarked it as a training facility, so patrols were unlikely—unless, of course, they were training the recruits how to conduct a patrol.

"We have to hide!" Katie cried. "They'll bring us back to my mother."

She started to turn her horse around, but Alaric grabbed the reins. "Only if she's sent out an alert," he said. "And she might not have, not yet. She did give us twenty-four hours."

Katie breathed out a mirthless laugh. "I wouldn't count on that."

"Anyway, they'd have to recognize us."

"Or question any man and woman riding this way."

It was a good point. Alaric considered their options, trying to think fast enough to preserve whatever few options there were. If they pretended the soldiers were no concern of theirs and rode right by them, perhaps the soldiers would see them simply as harmless and uninteresting civilians just... Just returning to town after a night in the stormy woods? That seemed highly unlikely. No, the lieutenant would want to question them even if he had no idea who they actually were.

Alternatively, they could flee. The foot soldiers wouldn't be able to follow, but the two mounted officers, on the other hand, would be very likely to view that act with suspicion. Would they leave their squad behind and give chase?

Neither of the horses Alaric and Katie rode was worth much, quite possibly the most useless animals in the queen's stables. They had thought there was no need for better animals; the queen's soldiers could catch them before they reached the border even if they rode racehorses. The torque would be a beacon to the queen if they could not remove it, and if they could, horses would be unnecessary. No, there was no sense in making the queen any angrier than she already was, by stealing her best steeds. But now, the odds were high they'd be caught if they ran. Whether they were caught now or later — did it make a difference?

Yes. It did. If they could buy some time, maybe, just maybe, Katie might be able to remove the torque. At least, she'd have time to try.

Alaric let go the reins of Katie's horse. "Go."

"You too?"

He gave her a nod. "Yes, of course. You lead. I'll be right behind you." Alaric wasn't accustomed to letting someone else take charge. But he recognized ability when he saw it, and Katie had an uncanny ability to avoid being noticed. She would lead, and he must hope her talent would shield him, too.

They turned from the road and entered the woods. They rode as fast as they could, but the narrow deer path they followed slowed them as they dodged around low-hanging tree branches and clawing bushes. Katie guided her horse through turns Alaric didn't see until she unexpectedly disappeared for a moment, only to come into view again at the last minute before he had to make the turn. She took a path so crooked he needed all his concentration to follow.

Behind them, hoofbeats thudded along the dirt path, and a strained male voice shouted, "Halt!" The two mounted soldiers had decided to follow them, and they were drawing closer.

Katie turned yet again, almost doubling back where a narrow path joined their own from the left. Alaric's horse slipped in a puddle he hadn't noticed, barely keeping upright. Foam flecked from its mouth, and the whites of its eyes were visible as it resisted the pull of his reins. They wouldn't be able to keep this up for long, not while the soldiers continued to close in.

Why, oh why, had he not thought to steal a weapon, even just a simple kitchen knife, as they passed by?

Katie made another turn and disappeared behind a large boulder. She reined her horse in, and Alaric drew in alongside her.

There was a slipping sound, a shouted curse word, and a sickening thud.

A female voice shouted, "Whoa!" More slipping sounds, and the hoofbeats drew to a halt. "You okay, sir?" asked the female soldier.

Their voices were so close they could have been just on the other side of the boulder where Katie and Alaric hid.

"Fine," grumbled the man. "Give me a hand, would you?" The jingling of harness fasteners accompanied the man's cursing. "Damned horse is limping. My luck, he'll have to be put down."

"Maybe not, sir," said the woman. "He's putting his weight on the leg."

"So he is. Lucky, that. It's probably just a bit of a sprain, but let me ride behind you back to the platoon. No use adding to the creature's injuries. I'll get him looked at back at the base."

Alaric and Katie listened as the two soldiers mounted, and stayed silent until they rode out of their hearing.

Katie brushed a stray sweat-soaked lock of hair away from her face. She looked exhausted. "That was lucky for us," she said.

Alaric didn't think it was luck. Katie was too good at hiding for it to have been mere luck. But this wasn't the time to compliment Katie on her magical abilities. "I don't think we ought to go into the town after this," he said. "Let's get out of this area and then look for shelter somewhere."

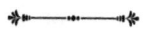

Two hours later, they worked their way up the side of the mountain that overlooked the town and the military base. Their poor horses moved so unsurely on the steep path that Alaric thought time and again of dismounting and leading them. But when he looked at Katie, her eyes dark-circled and her face drawn, he couldn't ask her to walk. And so they made perilously slow headway in the storm.

When Alaric spotted what looked like a cave mouth, or at least an indentation in the face of the rise they'd been climbing, he took hold of the rein of Katie's mare and guided them toward the shelter. A sudden torrent of hail pelted them across the last several yards.

Though shallow, the cave sheltered humans and horses alike.

"Maybe it will let up soon," Katie said, her voice shaking between chattering teeth.

"No, not soon." Alaric stared out into blackness. A flare of lightning lit the distant silhouette of the castle against the horizon. An instant later, thunder shook the cave's stone walls. "Your mother is making this storm, and it won't let up until she is exhausted. Maybe later, when she sleeps."

But by then, of course, her soldiers would be closing in. This was not something Alaric wanted to tell Katie, not yet. What, after all, could she do about soldiers, except worry? And worrying never accomplished anything.

Katie shivered, and Alaric put his arm around her. She was soaked. He took off his cloak and put it over hers to warm her, not that his own cloak was any dryer than hers. A gust of wind-driven rain pasted his shirt to his skin.

He decided to dare a fire, a tricky business without magic to dry the tinder and light the spark. "She'll know where we are as long as I wear this torque," he said after he got the fire going, "so we might as well be warm and dry. We're safe until this afternoon, when my twenty-four-hour deadline is past. Quite possibly, she won't try to injure us even after that, as long as we keep heading out. She won't want to risk forswearing her oath." He could still feel the knot of his own oath near his heart, how easily it could expand and leave his heart no room to beat. He wondered if it would end that way for one or both of them. "It could kill her." Of course, this left open the likelihood of their recapture, a probability Alaric decided not to mention. "But once we leave her domain . . ."

"She knows where we're heading." Katie spoke through lips numbed with cold and fatigue. "All she has to do is have her soldiers lie in wait for us."

What kind mother is Claudia, to put Katie through this? Alaric wanted to protect Katie and keep her well. At the least, he wanted to get her warm again. It would be easy enough, if only he had access to his magic, but under the circumstances, the normal methods would have to do.

"She knows our destination, yes, but my borders are well protected by my magical wards. We'll be fine once we're there, and her own oath will protect us here. What I worry about is where and when we cross the border. It would be good if we could prevent her knowing that."

"How?"

"By magic, of course."

She drew in a breath, eyes wide. "But we don't—"

"Not yet, we don't, no. But we're going to try."

She looked at him, sunken-eyed, exhausted. Wordless.

"Later," he said. "Not now. Now, you must warm yourself and rest."

CHAPTER SEVEN

Katie performs a serious magic

Katie didn't know how long she had slept. Alaric held both her hands in his. "Wake up, Katie," he said. "Its time. We can't wait any longer."

She stirred. She felt heavy and sluggish, wrapped in warm, damp cloaks. She had been dreaming of . . . what? The memory vanished as she opened her eyes.

The cave was dimly lit by the banked fire he had made. A pile of reasonably dry wood lay nearby. She blinked, remembering their wild ride in the storm. Where had he found so much wood? In the back of the cave somewhere? It was too dark back there to see.

"Do you think you might be up to trying some magic?" he said.

Her heart fluttered like a swarm of butterflies trying to escape her chest. She was fully awake. "Try?"

He took her hands and looked searchingly into her eyes. "Only if you think you can."

"Oh." Her voice sounded faint in her own ears. Katie didn't know whether she was more afraid that for the final time she would know with certainty she had no more than a smidgeon of magic—or that she might prove to have quite a bit of it. But if she couldn't face those fears now, when would she? She steeled herself, drew in a breath, and held her chin high. "Yes. I can."

His eyes glowed with warmth. "Good for you. Then you must follow my instructions exactly."

She nodded.

"You brought the doll?"

How strange a question! But she nodded again.

"Let me see it."

Katie reached into her saddle pack and retrieved the doll, a poor, sorry, dirty thing worn almost threadbare through years of constant childhood loving. Its clothing was as nondescript as her own, but tattered and patched. She held the doll for a moment, tight against her chest. "Silly that I even kept this doll all these years."

He watched her without any sign of judgment or impatience, and to her relief he didn't say, "Yes." He just waited.

When Katie held the doll out for him, her arm wouldn't straighten, reluctant to let it go. Her hands trembled.

Alaric cradled the doll gently, as if it were a small wounded creature that needed comforting. He stroked its matted hair and studied with great tenderness the scratches on its porcelain face, the places where fabric had worn threadbare and seams had opened. At last he turned to Katie. "What's her name?"

She knew the doll's name like she knew her own, but it refused to come to her. Blood rushed to her face. "Its . . . Its M—Mattie? No, that's not it. I don't remember." Her blush deepened.

A wet branch in the fire released steam in a hiss and then flared into flame.

A furrow of concern etched the space between Alaric's eyebrows. "Then you must ask her what her name is, and when she tells you, you must use the name to get your magic back. For as I live and breathe, this doll is where you have put it. I can feel it in every stitch of her fabric. And the name is the key."

She took the doll and looked up at Alaric. "What should I say?"

"Ask her name."

"I'm embarrassed."

"Perhaps she doesn't want to speak it out loud. Whisper to her. I won't listen." He walked to the cave entrance, ignoring the rain that gusted in as the wind blew.

Katie began the strangest conversation she'd ever had. She spoke both sides of it in a whisper, her voice altering and becoming higher and more childlike as she spoke for the doll.

"I can't remember your name," she said.

"Well, if you can't remember, I'm certainly not going to tell you."

"No, please."

"You'll just tell *him*," the doll said, frowning.

"No, I won't. Not if you don't want me to."

"You promise?"

"Yes, I promise," Katie said as gently as she could.

"I don't want you to. If you ever tell anyone, they'll hurt us both." Katie's eyes filled with tears as she looked into the dead crystal eyes of the doll.

"Yes, I know they've hurt you," she said. "Hurt us. But he won't. He'll keep us safe."

"*I* will keep us safe," said the doll. "We don't need him."

Katie blinked the tears away. "*You* will? But how?"

"Haven't we been safe for all these years? I've hidden your magic, and I've kept your secret name that is the key to it, and you've hidden me. Everything was fine. Now you're messing it all up by going away with him. He's trouble for both of us."

Katie studied the doll and thought about all the years she'd buried it in the bottom of the chest underneath all the extra blankets and wraps, a place her sisters wouldn't go to the trouble of looking. She'd taken it out at night when she was alone in her room, on those nights when she had trouble sleeping—often enough when she was young, less often as she got older. "You call this fine?" she said. She forgot to whisper. "What kind of life did we have? Both of us hiding, hiding all the time. I gave you the name, and you kept it safe. I gave you the magic, and you hid it, even from me, but now it's time for you to give it back."

She glanced at Alaric, but he remained motionless in the cave mouth, his back to her, silhouetted briefly in a flash of lightning.

She whispered again. "You took good care of my magic and of us, but now I'm grown up and it's my turn."

The doll said nothing for the longest time. A branch in the fire fell, and the firelight flared up.

"Margreta."

"Oh, Meggie!" Alicia Aurelia *Margreta* Katrina Emilia. How could she have so thoroughly forgotten? She held the doll to her chest and rocked it and crooned to it, to the doll and to the frightened girl of years ago who had to hide her magic away.

She remembered that Alaric still stood in the gusting rain, and she called to him.

He came at once. "Did you . . . ?"

"Yes."

"Can you tell me?"

She shook her head, her eyes wide and apologetic.

"That's all right. Never mind. But can you . . . ?"

Katie stared at his neck, where his fingers unconsciously lingered. She wasn't sure if she could see the torque or not. It seemed a half-existing thing, as if it blinked in and out of existence too rapidly for the eye to follow. She made out twisted strands of white and yellow gold inscribed with runes she could not decipher, its essence composed of a kind of fog or a dream. She reached toward it, wondering if she would feel something solid or if her hand would go right through it.

Alaric watched her move, barely breathing.

Her fingers touched the torque, then slid into and through it as if it were made of a substance barely thicker than air. She backed to the surface, feeling the slight shift in texture. Just far enough to touch, not so far as to penetrate. She eased her hand around the torque. "Its . . . beautiful. I never imagined." Her fingers reached a slight protrusion. "Is this the clasp?"

He reached around to touch her, fingers fumbling over fingers. "Yes."

"How does it work?"

He moved her hand to show her. His eyes met hers, and the desire she saw there made her lose her place. *Not now, not now.* She worked back to the clasp and found the pin that held it. She tried to pull the pin, but her fingers slipped through it. She brought her other hand around his neck and—gently, gently!—pushed with one hand and pulled coaxingly with the other. Nothing happened.

He moved his hands under her cloak, around her waist. "Feel it." His voice was rough-edged.

"I can't keep hold of it."

"Never mind that. You will. For now, just feel the magic in you. How it vibrates."

Yes, she could feel it. Her skin was tingling. Her bones sang. Was this magic, or was it desire?

He brushed back her hair, ran his fingers across her cheeks, touched her lips. His pupils were so large his eyes were no longer gray but black. "Try again."

She breathed rapidly, and the cloak she wore felt like liquid pouring over the skin of her chest as it moved. The torque seemed more solid now, and she reached around his neck for the clasp. She found the pin and pushed it out. She removed the open torque from his neck.

He drew her close and kissed her, and the torque fell from her fingers.

Later, the storm calmed. The wind growled around the mouth of the cave, but it no longer roared.

Alaric stroked Katie's hair as they sat together by the fire. "I wish we could stay like this, just the two of us, but we have to leave. The queen is getting tired. She can't keep the storm up any longer. Now that our deadline has passed, she'll send soldiers. We must be gone before they arrive."

"But the horses . . . You said . . ."

"We won't need the horses. Now that I have my magic back, I can open a portal."

Of course, a portal. That was what her mother used to move soldiers and supplies to Darimbia. Probably Alaric did the same. Katie knew the concept, but she'd never seen one in person.

Alaric stood and gave Katie a hand up. Then he gathered their things together, leaving their cloaks bunched where they'd been lying in the back of the cave. He fingered the torque, and Katie wondered whether he found it as beautiful as she did. But then he set it down on top of the discarded cloaks.

"Why don't you keep it?" she asked.

"I'd like to. I'm sure I could learn something from it. But it would be a mistake to bring your mother's magic into my household. Depending on how she wove it, it might do great harm."

He didn't re-saddle the exhausted horses. "That torque is a beacon. Your mother's soldiers will be here soon. They'll find the horses and take them home again."

Alaric began moving his hands in intricate patterns in the air. He focused completely on what he was doing, which looked to Katie something like knitting the air into a complex garment, or unraveling one without breaking the threads. His lips moved as if talking, but he made no sound, perhaps subvocalizing words in an unspeakable vocabulary.

Alaric grunted in satisfaction, reached out, and—

Katie blinked, then blinked again. Alaric had pulled open a gap in the air. When she squinted, she could see the edges of the opening, an irregular oval of haziness against the sharp cave wall beyond. Alaric proceeded to widen the gap, stretching its edges as one might stretch the dough for a pie crust. Nothing was different inside the hole than outside; it was just air through and through. And yet, everything was different. The cave smelled musty and damp, but the breeze that blew from Alaric's new portal smelled of roses in sunlight. Warmth and light radiated from the opening.

Holding a side of the portal with one hand, Alaric shifted their bundles into the space beyond and out of Katie's sight. Then he turned to her and held out his hand. "Come."

Katie drew back, afraid. If she stepped through the opening, her life would change forever. There would be no going back to the safety she'd always known. Her heart pounded, and she wrapped her arms around herself against the cold. She shook her head.

"We have to leave now," he said. "Please."

"I . . . can't."

"Oh, Katie, you have a whole new life ahead of you. You can do magic—remember how it felt. The whole world is open to you now."

"I'm just not ready."

"We'll work together, you and I. We can save Darimbia. But you have to come with me." His voice was strained, his eyes pleading.

She wanted to go with him, but after this there would be no going back. What if it was all a terrible mistake? "I . . . don't know. I don't know if I can."

His face was pale. He strained to keep the passage open, his right arm tensed against it, his features drawn in pain. "What do you want, then? Shall I let the portal close? There might be time for me to teach you a few defensive charms. We might hold out here for a while, but I don't think I have the strength to open the portal again, not while also keeping the soldiers at bay. You have to decide."

She took a deep breath of air that blended roses and must, sunlight and darkness. In her mind, she balanced the oppressiveness of her home against how well she knew her way around it, and the allure of the new place against how little she knew of what she might be getting into. Her desire for the unknown against her fear of it. "I think my life has perhaps already changed, now that I know I can do magic, at least a little sometimes. I want to go with you, Alaric, but whatever this game is you're playing against my mother, this war—it's not over, is it?"

"That's up to her, but—no, probably not."

"I won't have you use me as a pawn."

He bowed his head in acknowledgment. "If this is a game, you are no pawn, and I'll not use you as one."

Still, she held back.

"But now there may be two queens on the board, and you are one of them," Alaric said. "If you come with me, then you will be taking on that role, and you'll have to play it. I won't lie to you. If your mother forces our hands, it could become unpleasant, but I won't use you. That's all I can promise."

She took a tentative step toward him. "I'm afraid."

"I can't keep this portal open much longer. Come."

Katie took another deep breath and reached for the hand of the man who had chosen her, and she stepped into the sunshine.

CHAPTER EIGHT

A new beginning

The sunlight streaming in her window was so bright that Katie pulled the covers over her head. She hadn't slept well, and she wasn't ready for morning. An instant later, she remembered where she was. She pulled the covers back down and blinked, adjusting to the light. The window was large—much larger than the small square windows punched into the thick stone walls of her home. This window was taller than she was, and broader than her arms could span. A sheer curtain of pale yellow billowed in front of it, letting in warm, fresh air filled with the scents of exotic flowers with names she'd only ever seen in books—frangipani, oleander, jessamine. She breathed in deeply and let out a sigh of pleasure.

She had done it. She had escaped.

Her heart pounding, Katie threw off her covers and went to the window. Below was a garden bright with flowers, and beyond its wall lay a city with red-tiled roofs. To her right, she could see the blue of the sea. The shore was barely visible, and white boats, large and small, plied the waters. She could hardly wait to explore. A whole new life lay ahead of her, and she wanted to know all its possibilities, wanted to set worthwhile goals and accomplish them. Yes, maybe like brave Irinia

Orcutt from the history book Alaric had given her, she too would find a way to help the poor people of Darimbia.

But first, she wanted to find Alaric and make sure he was all right. He'd been so exhausted yesterday, it was a miracle they'd gotten away. She hoped he was well, and as happy to be here as she was.

Someone knocked on the door.

Katie's first impulse was to hide. Then she breathed out a small, relieved laugh. She was no longer the Mouse. That part of her life was finished. Now, she would be . . . Queen Katrina? No, she wasn't sure Alaric's proposal had been heartfelt or simply expedient. And she wasn't sure she was ready to be tied down into that role. No, she would be just Katie, and all the better for that. But she wasn't dressed. Who . . .?

"My lady?" said a voice from the other side of the door—a timid, female voice. "If you are awake, shall I help you dress? His Majesty has already provided some clothing for you, since those you came in were wet and torn. And there's more on the way."

"Please," Katie said. "Come in."

The door opened a crack, then a little more, and a girl barely into her teens took a hesitant step into the room. "My name is Sally, my lady, and if you so wish, I am to be your maid."

Her own maid? Her mother had two maids, of course, but Katie hadn't had even one at home.

But then, Katie hadn't had a lot of things at home. This was a new home, and naturally there would be new experiences. That was what she had wanted, wasn't it?

The poor girl was looking at her fearfully, reminding Katie of her old self.

Katie gave her a smile that she hoped was inviting. "Of course. I could use your help. Come on in, there's no need to be shy."

No, there wasn't. Not anymore.

It began easily enough as a simple briefing. Alaric had set up a meeting with his half-brother Marco to get an update on the activities in Darimbia since he'd been gone. Marco awaited in his private conference room, hunched over maps that were spread out on the table. He'd opened all the windows to let in light and fresh air.

"Marco!" Alaric stepped into the room, closing the door behind him.

"Welcome back, Alaric." Marco looked up from the map, grinning as widely as a boy who'd just gotten his first pony. He walked over to Alaric, and the two men hugged warmly. Then Marco turned back to the maps. "We've been struggling to raise a ransom, of course, but here you are without one. How did you manage it?"

Alaric thought of Katie, and he smiled. "That's a rather long story, actually, but the short version is that Claudia's youngest daughter helped me. I couldn't have escaped without her, and I've brought her back with me."

Marco scowled and leaned forward, resting his hands upon the table where the maps were spread out. "Here? Now?"

Alaric ignored the aggressive tone in Marco's voice. "That's right."

"Has the queen's magic caused you to lose your senses altogether? You've brought a spy into our midst."

Alaric studied his younger brother. Not many people would risk the king's anger with such an outburst. Not so long ago, neither would Marco. But in just the few weeks he, Alaric, had been gone, Marco seemed to have matured. Indeed, he was letting his beard grow in; it was still a bit thin, but a fine contrast to that enviably thick mane of brown hair. And the laugh lines at the corners of Marco's eyes were now offset by the beginning of lines marking a worried frown. It was good he was starting to worry some; Marco's happy-go-lucky lifestyle sometimes verged on recklessness.

Arguably, it was Marco's fault Alaric had been captured in the first place. But Alaric had no regrets about that, not since he'd met Katie. Besides, he had high hopes for Marco. The lad would make a fine governor in Darimbia one day, perhaps soon, and eventually, if Alaric had no children, a fine king for Westland.

But Katie was one thing Marco didn't need to worry about. "I have asked her to marry me," Alaric said calmly, "and I hope youll give her a good report of me, should she ask."

Marco gaped.

"Also, she wants to help us in Darimbia. I think we should give her a tour there, let her meet some of the people."

Marco shook his head with increasing vigor. "She has you bewitched, big brother. She's Queen Claudia's offspring."

"And my proposal was very much against the queen's wishes. I couldn't have escaped without Katie's help."

Marco grimaced. "Nevertheless, what makes you think you can trust her now?"

"Because I know her. And I want you to get to know her, too." He smiled. "You'll like her. Just keep an open mind."

As if on cue, there came a rap on the door, and one of the sentries stationed outside took a step in. "Your Majesty," he said, "Princess Katrina awaits. Should I send her in?"

Alaric and Marco exchanged a glance, then Marco looked away.

"Yes, of course," Alaric said.

The sentry opened the door wider, and in walked Katie, wearing a dress of pale green that accented the green in her hazel eyes, and a tunic that was embroidered with peonies in shades of pink—clothing for a princess, not for a Mouse. Alaric's heart leapt. She was, he thought, the most beautiful woman he'd ever seen.

Katie took a tentative step into the room. Shelves of books lined the walls, and a large table in the middle was covered with maps. Unlike her mother's library, this room was bright with sunshine, a room she could imagine spending lots of time in. She wondered what books she might find on all those shelves.

Alaric smiled at her, and the room lit up. Or her heart did. She returned the smile before she could think about whether she should. Alaric looked quite kingly in a jerkin of deep blue brocaded with stars and moons and planets in metallic threads. Would this man, this mage, this *king*, behave at all like the powerless prisoner who had befriended her?

And who was that other man, the stranger standing at the table next to Alaric? He was nicely featured, with thick brown hair pulled back into a braid, and a contrastingly thin beard. He was young, maybe only fifteen or sixteen, barely more than a boy. Possibly, this was the first beard he'd ever grown. His eyes were gray like Alaric's, but his face was rounder, and he wore simpler clothing—finely woven enough, but without the brocade. By any measure, he was a good-looking man, but why was he scowling? Had she interrupted some unpleasant conversation? "I—I'm sorry. If this is not a good time—" She turned to go.

"It's a fine time, Katie. Come in." Alaric held a hand out to her. "Come." His fingers moved in a welcoming gesture. "I trust you slept well?"

After yesterday's events—the doll's revelation, her own magic, the portal—she'd thought she'd never get to sleep. And indeed she'd slept fitfully, haunted by dreams of unknown menace. She stepped nearer to Alaric, giving the other man a wary nod. "Yes, well enough, thank you."

Alaric put an arm around her shoulder, almost as if to protect her from the scowling stranger. "Katie, I'd like you to meet my brother, Marco. Marco, please meet Princess Alicia Aurelia . . . Katrina Emilia."

Katie thought she detected a slight pause in the place where her middle name should go, the name she'd kept secret all these years. Had he overheard her, back there in the cave? Or had she just imagined the hesitation?

Alaric gave her shoulder a small squeeze. "I would be very pleased if the two of you would consent to be on a given-name basis."

She nodded to the young man—to Marco, and said to Alaric, "I didn't know you had a brother." And what else didn't she know about him?

"Half-brother, actually," Marco said. His displeased expression lessened, replaced by something like curious appraisal.

"My father—*our* father—met Marco's mother after my mother passed away," Alaric said. "She was a leader among the Darimbians."

"It was a love match, but they didn't marry." Marco added. "That was my mother's choice. She was a commoner, and she felt she belonged in Darimbia, not here. I grew up there."

"Marco is my secret weapon in Darimbia," Alaric said. "The people adore him. And sometimes I think he'd rather be there than here at the castle with me."

"Be sure of it," Marco said with a laugh, but when he turned back to Katie, his eyes were still hard. Still assessing. "But what of you . . . um, Katie, is it?"

"Yes," Katie said, realizing with a start that here was the first person who had never heard her called "Mouse." It seemed she'd truly left that behind, along with her old life. She moved a step closer to Alaric and gave a small, self-conscious laugh. "I'm from Victoria." Since Marco showed no surprise, she added, "I guess you know that."

"But she's going to be living here with us now," Alaric added.

Katie frowned. She liked Alaric's place and wanted to stay for a while, but she hadn't decided yet what she was going to do in the longer term, now that she was free of her mother's castle. She ached to see more of the world.

Marco raised a questioning eyebrow. "Really? Why not stay in Victoria?"

Katie looked at Alaric, hoping he might answer for her. *No, I have to learn to stand on my own, and that means giving my own answers.* "There's no place for me there. I'm the youngest of Queen Claudia's daughters, and I never had any magic."

"But that's not true," Alaric protested, smiling at her. "I wouldn't have escaped, were it not for Katie. She removed the torque I was bound with."

Marco frowned again, as if removing the torque were proof of some kind of an evil plot. Katie could make no sense of that, so she ignored it. "Well," she said, blushing, "I'm the one who never used to have any magic before Alaric came along."

"I wouldn't be surprised," Alaric said, "if she's going to have more magic than both of us put together."

Now, *that* was a frightening thought. "Don't say that. I'm not sure what I did back there was actually magic, or if you're just calling it magic to be kind." Katie made to pull away, but Alaric's hand lay firmly on her shoulder. "Just because . . . one time . . . I . . ."

"I don't have much magic, myself," Marco said. "Just a little. Never much interested in it."

"Not interested?" Katie couldn't imagine that.

"Oh, I'd rather be organizing things on the ground." Marco stabbed a finger at one of the maps. "Where to trap enemy patrols, how to organize a fighting force, who would make a good scout, when to feed false information." He looked at where his finger had landed, frowned, and then broke into a grin. "That's not a bad position, actually. A little bit of magic never hurts."

"But Katie has more than a little," Alaric said, "and she wants to help us in Darimbia. So, I want you to be kind to her."

"You want to help us?" Marco asked, one eye squinting a little more than the other in disbelief.

She met his gaze and held it. "Yes. Yes, I do. Any way I can. But I wouldn't count on me for magic, if I were you."

"But you are not me," Alaric said, "and our success might somehow depend on you and your magic, so we have a lot of work to do between now and then to get you ready. How about starting this afternoon?"

Oh, great. Me and my magic. How did I ever manage to get myself into this?

That afternoon, Alaric took Katie to a terrace overlooking the ocean. She stood at the low wall that bordered the terrace and stared in amazement. The sun was brighter and hotter than she remembered sunlight ever being, and its heat reflected from the paving stones. A cool breeze kept her comfortable, though, carrying the sharp tang of seaweed and salt. Small birds dodged the waves that murmured along the beach; larger ones rode the air currents overhead screaming raucously at one another. Katie had read about the seaside, of course, but her imagination had fallen far short of the full sensory experience of the real place.

"So, what do you think?" Alaric asked.

"It's . . . beautiful. You're so lucky to live here."

"You live here too, now."

Katie had given more thought to her current situation since waking up. All her life, she'd dreamed of getting away, of seeing the world, of searching for her father. Was that all just her childish desire for escape? How could she even begin to answer that question if she never actually traveled? As beautiful as this place was, and as much as she liked Alaric, she wanted—*needed*—to see more, to experience more in order to truly understand herself. If she stayed here now, Alaric's castle would become as much a prison to her as her mother's had. She turned away. "I'm . . . not ready quite yet to think about where I want to live. There's so much of the world that I don't know."

Alaric gave her a little smile that didn't quite hide the concern in his eyes. "I didn't mean to pressure you."

"No, it's . . . I'm . . . I didn't mean to sound ungrateful, and I'd like to stay for a while."

"'A while'?" His expression was decidedly bleak.

She reached out toward him, then paused uncertainly. "That's not so bad, is it? I still want to help you in Darimbia."

He let out a sigh. "Thank you, Katie. Let's just say that for now, you live here temporarily. You can decide later what you want to do."

Relief flooded through her, and she smiled. "All right, I'll stay at least for as long as I can stand your magic lessons." She made the smile wider, hoping he would realize she was joking.

But he didn't. He touched her shoulder. "You don't have to do this, you know."

"Yes. I do have to do it." She stared at him, defying him to say otherwise.

Alaric drew a deep breath. "Well, then. Shall we begin?"

Katie glanced behind her to where Marco sat, farther along the wall. He was ostentatiously examining his fingernails, as if he had no idea anyone else was anywhere nearby.

"Do you want him to leave?" Alaric asked.

"No. It's all right. If I'm going to become reliably good at magic, I'll have to get used to other people being around sometimes, and Marco . . . seems very nice."

Marco glanced up at her, then quickly dropped his gaze.

"Good!" Alaric said. "Then I'm going to drop this ball over the wall, and your job will be to bring it back up again."

She squinted one eye at the ball and held out her hand. "Let me see that."

He handed the ball to her. It seemed a very ordinary rubber ball, bright yellow and slightly fuzzy, about the size of her fist. It was firm to the touch and not very heavy. "How? How am I to do that?"

"The same way you do all magic. With a strong will and with confidence."

"No, I mean . . ." Katie looked back over the wall at the grassy dunes some twenty feet below, and the sand beach beyond. "What if I can't do it? The ball will roll out to sea, and then where will we be?"

"Oh, if you can't bring it back, you'll just have to swim out and get it."

Katie gasped. "But I can't—" She looked back at him. He was grinning broadly, and his eyes were kind. A wave of relief swept over her. "Oh . . . You're joking. But still, how . . .?"

"If you don't bring it back—and I expect you won't, the first several times you try, till you get the hang of it—then I will bring it back for you. And as for how . . ." Alaric rubbed his beard thoughtfully. "Look at it this way. You're not doing anything difficult, like defying the laws of physics; you're just—"

"Gravity!"

"Oh, yes. That. Well, but you read about Brownian motion, right?"

"Of course. All the little atoms move randomly around in all the vast space that surrounds them. None of them, not even solid rock, is ever still."

"Very good. So then, suppose all the atoms of the ball just happened by random chance to move from the beach up to the terrace together?"

Katie gasped. "Oh . . . I never thought . . . I suppose that could happen. So, we're really talking about physics, right? I can do physics, but the odds would be very much against the ball moving upwards by Brownian motion, wouldn't they?"

He nodded. "Somewhat. Yes. That's where the magic part comes in, to make the possible real."

"Show me." She put her hands on her hips.

"Marco!" Alaric called.

Marco looked up.

"Would you like to play a little game of fetch?"

"What, with that ball? You want me to run after it like a dog?"

Alaric let out a hearty laugh. "No. I want you to magic it back here after I throw it."

"I'm not very good," Marco said, "but that's pretty elementary. I think I can do that much." He gave Katie a smile and a wink. "Okay, I'm ready."

Alaric threw the ball out toward the sea. About two seconds later, the ball stopped moving and hovered in the air, a miniature yellow sun in the blue sky. Katie gasped, then looked at Alaric, who watched her expectantly. She returned her gaze to Marco.

Marco had his eyes half closed, squinting with what might have been effort, or extreme concentration. He stretched his hand out, fingers opened wide.

The ball began slowly moving toward him, then gathered speed. It landed, finally, in his outstretched hand.

"There!" Marco said, sounding satisfied. "I'm not entirely clueless. But you're much better." Before Alaric could respond, Marco threw the ball out to sea.

Alaric held up his hand, and the ball stopped moving. "Marco makes it look more difficult than it is. All that effort is just like icing on an apple pie. Looks good, tastes good, but if the pie is good, it's really not necessary."

The ball was in his hand.

Katie had been watching, and as nearly as she could tell, it had not moved through the intervening distance. "How . . . How did you do that?"

"The same way you're going to. Are you ready?"

Katie drew a deep breath and held it for as long as she could. She let it out, and then she drew another. Her heart was pounding. She stretched out her hand and turned it over to examine her fingers. *The ball*, she thought. *Right here.* "Yes."

Of course, the ball did not end up in her hand, but just before it splashed into the water, it was in Alaric's hand again.

"Are you okay?" he asked. "Any worries?"

Katie drew herself up straight. "You said it would take several tries, right?"

He nodded slowly. "It's actually easier than the torque, once you get the hang of it."

"Well, then, what are you waiting for?" She tried to look serious, but a little smile escaped her.

Alaric returned the smile, nodded appreciatively, and threw the ball out to sea once more.

After Katie's sixth failed attempt, Marco heaved a theatrical sigh, followed by an ostentatious yawn. He rose from his seat.

"Now, that is rude! I believe you should apologize." Alaric spoke sternly, but there was a glint of humor in his eyes. Brotherly banter, Katie decided, and wondered what it would have been like to have a brother. Would he have protected her from her teasing sisters?

"It's all right," she said. "My performance *was* rather boring."

Marco acknowledged her comment with a flourish of an imaginary hat and a deep bow.

Alaric threw the ball at him, hard and fast.

Marco threw up his hands—to protect his face, or to catch the ball? Or to attempt, much too slowly, the magic necessary to stop it?

Katie's heart leapt with fear. Would Marco be injured?

Suddenly, she held something hard in her hand.

Both men looked around, as if to find out where the ball had gone.

Katie looked at the object in her hand, wondering at first what it was, and then, recognizing the ball, wondering how on earth it had gotten there.

Alaric went wide-eyed, then he laughed with delight. He put his arms around her waist, picked her up, and twirled her around. "You did it!"

But Katie didn't laugh. She was, in fact, near tears. "Alaric, am I always going to have to be in fear that someone will be injured, or worse, in order to work magic?"

He hugged her and said nothing.

CHAPTER NINE

Too much, too fast

"It's about time you took me out to say hello," the doll said, sulking. "You probably didn't even think about me once since you've been here."

"But it's only been a day," Katie protested. She sat on the bed in her room, with Dolly propped on her lap. Lamps had been lit, casting a warm glow. Katie had intended to read for a while before retiring, but, still worried about the morning's events, she had taken out the doll.

"I liked it better in the other place. You wanted me more."

"Well, *I* like it better here. And see, I still want you."

The doll's lower lip quivered. "No, you're going to forget about me."

Katie thought she detected the glisten of an unshed tear in the doll's eyes. Now that she undeniably had some magical ability, and had reclaimed her middle name, could it be that the doll was right? She hugged the old toy close against her chest. "Oh, Dolly, maybe I won't always be able to take you with me, but I promise I'll never forget you. Never!"

For a few moments, neither of them spoke. Then Katie said, "This is a good place to learn magic. I feel safe here. And afterwards . . ." She shrugged. "I'd like to travel a bit, see the world."

"I would like to see the world," the doll said. "You wouldn't go without me, would you? Maybe you'd rather go with *him* instead."

Him. Alaric. Katie had to admit that she would like to go with him. There was so much he could show her, so much to learn from him, and besides . . . She could feel herself blushing. But of course that was impossible. He was a king. He had responsibilities. He'd have to stay here.

"No," she lied to the doll. "I'd rather go with you."

"Anyway, he doesn't love you," the doll said.

"What?"

"Never did. He only asked you to marry him because he had to marry someone."

"Wait. I never told you—"

"Yes, you did. You tell me everything. Maybe you just don't remember. Anyhow, you know it's true."

Katie considered. Alaric had said they were friends, and he'd asked her to marry him. He'd even kissed her. Remembering that kiss, she felt warm inside and wanted to do it again. But had he ever said he loved her? She didn't think so. The doll was right. All Alaric had said was that she was the only one of her mother's daughters he would marry. Who knew what that might mean?

"It doesn't matter," Katie said. "I'm not about to get married anyway."

The next day, Katie stayed close to Alaric's side as they walked along a square not far from his castle. It was market day, and vendors with carts sold tomatoes, beans, lettuce, chickens, pots and pans, clothing, toys, and more. The smells of living animals blended with those of roasting meat and pungent herbs. She looked right and left, dazzled by the array of food and household goods for sale.

"Does my mother have . . ." She hesitated. "Is there a market like this in Victoria?"

"I would think so," Alaric said. "You've never been?"

"My mother always wanted us to have guards when we went out. She said it was too dangerous otherwise, and the guards made me uncomfortable. So I went out a little, but not much. Never to a market. But you go out all by yourself. I think I might have done it, if I could have been alone."

He smiled at her. "Well, here you can go out alone whenever you wish, certainly during the daytime. Even at night, it's fairly safe. No one with half a grain of sense would molest a magic user."

"Except, perhaps, another magic user?"

Alaric stopped walking and looked at her. "What are you thinking?"

"No, nothing. I meant just in theory. I think my sisters could have . . ."

"And you're worried about Marco?"

"No!" That was a little too quick, a little too easy. "I mean, I think he doesn't entirely trust me, but that would be normal, wouldn't it? It doesn't mean he would try to ambush me on a dark street." She laughed a little, nervously, suddenly unsure. "Or would he?"

"He most certainly would not."

"Flower for the lady?" A street vendor approached them, cradling a large bouquet of roses in one arm, and holding out a single red rose in his other hand. "Smell! They're sweet as well as beautiful. Just picked today."

Alaric accepted the flower and handed the man a coin in payment.

"Maybe Marco is a nice person," Katie said softly, "but I don't think he likes me."

"He just doesn't know you yet, like I do."

"He's suspicious of me because of my mother. I understand that."

"But I am not." Alaric gave her the flower and took hold of her hand. "I was serious when I asked you before. I would like you to marry me and be my queen."

"Oh, Alaric!" It was all about that agreement he'd made with her mother, of course, to marry one of the queen's magical daughters. Katie admired how honorable Alaric was, but she didn't want to be used that way. And it wasn't fair to him, either. He needed the freedom to marry someone he truly loved, and as for her . . . She too needed freedom. Freedom to see new places, to discover herself. Tears filled Katie's eyes. "You are my dear friend and companion, and I . . ." It wasn't really love, was it, like in the romance novels she'd read? "I am very fond of you, of course, and I don't want to get you in trouble by not marrying you, but—"

He gave her a quizzical look. "Get me in trouble? How?"

"The oath you swore with my mother."

He shook his head. "I'm bound to ask you, and I have. This is the third time now, by my count, and the offer stands. Please, Katie."

Katie sighed. She wasn't happy about this. "If you must marry, I'll do it, of course. Do you need that, to fulfill the oath?"

"No, Katie. An oath can't obligate a person who is not a party to it."

This was probably crazy. She'd probably regret it. But how could she move from one palace to another, and never see anything else? No, she'd never forgive herself. "Then I think I'd rather wait. All my life, I've dreamed of going to faraway places, experiencing new things, and meeting different people." *Meeting her father, unlikely as that might be.* "I'm not ready to settle down yet. Maybe we can just stay . . . friends?" She searched his face, hoping, fearing what she might see there.

His expression was strange, hard for her to read. It seemed at once sad and yet relieved, and above all, intense. At least, thank heavens, he wasn't angry. "Of course we will," he said in a voice that sounded so formal he might have been reading a court verdict.

He'd certainly answered quickly enough. The doll was probably right. Kind as Alaric was, he didn't love her. "You're not offended?"

"Not at all. You are young and smart and curious, and you should have a chance to be out on your own." He gave her a wan smile. "And I would be very pleased if, when you are ready, you would decide to return here." He reached out a hand as if to touch her cheek, but Katie turned away. Alaric dropped his hand to his side.

"I . . . don't have to leave right away." She was surprised at the hesitation in her own voice, surprised how much she truly didn't want to leave him. "I promised to help you in Darimbia, and I meant it."

"Thank you," he said. "It would please me greatly." He touched her shoulder, so that she turned back toward him. "Don't feel bad. You'll always be welcome in my house."

❖▬━▬━╫❖

The next day, Alaric invited Katie to join him for a brief trip to Darimbia. "You want to go places, right? Let's start with a first-hand look at the place where this conflict is all about."

Katie drew in a breath. "Won't that be dangerous?"

Alaric laughed. "Not at all. We won't be going in person. We'll visit via my scrying pool. It'll look real enough, but I assure you, we'll never leave the palace."

She relaxed and returned his lingering smile. "That sounds wonderful."

Less than an hour later, Katie and Alaric were back at the palace. The two of them and Marco stood in a room with no windows, roughly five or six meters on a side. Tiles ran around the edges of the room's floor, and set into the center of the floor lay the still water of Alaric's scrying pool. The three of them stood barefoot in the pool, with water up to their ankles. Under their feet, the floor of the pool held the forest of Darimbia. Treetops brushed the soles of their feet, and they floated over a forest of tall pines that marched up and over steep mountains with jagged, rocky peaks.

"A little farther east," Marco said.

Alaric made a slight gesture with his fingers, and the trio were flying over the forest. The effect made Katie dizzy, and her stomach lurched. She looked away from the land rushing past below and upward at the constant blue sky.

But it wasn't sky, of course. It was the room's domed ceiling, painted sky blue. Katie swallowed, took a deep breath, and made herself look back down.

"Katie?" Alaric said, "Are you all right?"

"Yes. Sorry. I just felt a little faint."

"You don't have to stay."

"There," Marco said excitedly, pointing to his left. "Can you zoom in over there?"

Katie nodded. "I'm fine. Please, go ahead."

Alaric gave her a small smile. He looked where Marco was pointing and then made another gesture with his fingers, as if he was closing something up. Katie could now see a few bright colors. As Alaric continued to—what did Marco say?—zoom in, the colors resolved themselves into a group of people. A few were dressed in bright clothing, but most wore clothing of greens and browns that blended into the forest. An instant later, the three of them stood on the ground amid the trees, and the strangers stood all around them.

One of the people looked up, a young man with curly, reddish hair, pale blue eyes, and a bright yellow scarf tied rakishly around his neck. "Marco!" The man broke into a grin. "I'd give you a hug, but since you're here with His Majesty"—the man acknowledged Alaric with a perfunctory bow—"I know you're not as solid as you look. I'd probably walk right through you. When are you coming back? Did you get the weap—uh, supplies?" His eyes narrowed, looking at Katie. "Who's the lady?"

"This is Katie," Alaric said. "She's my . . . apprentice. She's going to help us."

"Lem," the man said, pointing to his chest with his thumb. "Pleased to meet you. And these folks are Joe, Tessa, Mandy, and Brusio." He gestured toward the nearest people. "Will you be coming out with Marco, or staying behind with His Majesty?"

Katie looked to Alaric for guidance.

Their eyes met, and he raised a brow slightly in a question. Katie shrugged, then gave a small nod.

"I think I'll bring her out for a visit," Alaric said. "It's always good to see a place first-hand, but mostly she'll be back with me."

"I have the *supplies* you wanted," Marco said. He put a strange emphasis on the word supplies. *Weapons.* "I'll start bringing everything over tonight, if you think it's safe."

Lem made a face. "Safe? When is it ever safe here?"

"I know, but—"

"It's as safe as ever, so come on over. I think we've located the other side's supply depot, and I'd sure like to blow it up. You game?"

Marco broke into a grin. "Absolutely! I can have everything over there in, say, two days. You want them in the same place as before?"

"Yes, of course." Lem turned to Alaric. "We've had some pretty good skirmishes, but when are we going to get some real action?"

"Soon," Alaric said. He gave Katie a significant look. "There are just a few things we need to take care of first."

Katie shivered.

"Scrying is easy," Alaric said to Katie the next morning while Marco was in the process of staging supplies to move to Darimbia. Katie and Alaric stood once again in the shallow water of Alaric's scrying pool. It was clear and perfectly still, no more than twenty centimeters deep. The bottom of the pool was coated in a reflective surface, creating an illusion of sky above and sky below.

"I can bring up a vision of anyplace, anywhere?"

"Yes, pretty much. But there is a catch. You need to previously have been—or at least to have scried—the place you are trying to bring up. You need to *know* it in that intimate way."

Katie's shoulders slumped. "I haven't been very many places."

He smiled at her in a kindly, almost avuncular way. "But the places you have been, I'll bet you know very well. So, recalling them should be no problem for you."

"Well." She made an exaggerated shiver. "My mother's castle. I wouldn't want to run into her by accident. Or anyone, for that matter."

"Then go someplace where people are not likely to go. The dusty old back of that wine cellar, for example."

She thought about that for a moment. "Too crowded. The ceiling's low, and all those bottles of wine are so close together there's hardly room to stand. I'll try the library. No one ever goes there."

His eyebrows went up. "I can't imagine it."

She laughed. "I'll bet there isn't any dust on the shelves of *your* library!"

"Indeed not! And the map room you've seen isn't the main place I have books, either."

"You'll show it to me, won't you?"

"Of course, with pleasure. Now, let's begin, shall we? You'll need to look into the water and imagine that you're looking down at the library from someplace near its ceiling."

Katie pretended to look at the rows of shelves in the library from above, but she had trouble picturing it. Some of the shelves were low, but most of them were so tall that even on tiptoe she could barely reach the top shelf, much less see the top of it. What might be up there? Plain wood? Or perhaps someone had piled a few books up there, invisible from where she'd stood. Would it be dusty? No doubt—even the shelves and the books were dusty. The top must be much worse. Piles of dust. And cobwebs. Whole spider cities! Katie giggled.

Alaric looked at her sharply. "What?"

"Oh, Alaric, I can't do this. I have *no idea* what the library looks like from above. Can't I just picture it from somewhere, some perspective, where I've actually seen it?"

His mouth tightened as he looked away, considering. "That could be tricky, since you are looking *down* into the scrying bowl. So you would need to perform a mental rotation of perspective. It's not easy—but if you want, give it a try."

Katie did want. She gazed into the scrying bowl and thought of the library in her mother's castle. Of her favorite chair there, upholstered in a pattern of flowers, its original vibrant reds and pinks still barely visible in the folds of fabric where the seat pillow met the chair back, but now peacefully faded into pale rose, brown, and tan. Then she could almost see the chair, from slightly above, as if she were standing over it, about to sit down. And then she did sit down, settling into the soft cushions with a heartfelt sigh. The library air smelled stale, as if no door or window had been opened for a long time, and the air itself hung heavily upon the books, the shelves, the floor.

Katie gasped. It was *too* real. Was she really here? How would she ever get out again? Her heart tripped a panicked beat. She gripped the arms of the chair, lifting herself out of it, too frightened to breathe. Then the world twisted, just ever so slightly, and she was standing next to Alaric, looking into a pool of clear water. She choked back a sob of relief, and turned her face into his chest.

He wrapped his arms around her, and she wept.

Alaric held Katie until her sobs quieted and her jagged breathing returned to normal. "I'm so sorry," he murmured into her soft hair, wondering what had upset her so much. He'd been able to see where she was, had, in fact, followed her scrying discreetly, hovering near the ceiling of the library. And as far as he could tell, the library was deserted and nothing whatsoever had happened.

He held her hand as they stepped out of the shallow water of the scrying pool into the adjoining room. They each took a towel from a pile on a nearby low table. The two of them sat in chairs next to the table, dried their feet in silence, and put on their shoes. Then he asked, "What was it? Can you talk about it?"

"I just didn't expect it to be so real," Katie said. "I guess I panicked a little. What if . . . What if someone had found me there? My mother , , ."

"She would have seen you, of course, but you weren't there in person. You could have whisked yourself out instantly—just like you did." He decided against mentioning that a fully trained and powerful wizard like her mother might have followed her out—not in person, of course, but even as an insubstantial wraith, such a powerful wizard might have been able to harm her. Not here, of course; the room was well warded. But when Katie got the hang of scrying, she might go anywhere. Sometime—tomorrow, when she was less upset—Alaric would have to warn her.

Katie nodded and swallowed hard. "Well, I don't think I need to go *there* again." She pulled away from his embrace and glanced warily at the scrying pool. "I'm okay now. Thanks."

"But what you did was quite remarkable," Alaric said with what he hoped was an encouraging smile.

She returned a faint echo of the smile. "Oh, stop. It was just . . . I don't know . . ."

"No, I'm serious. Most new young wizards can't materialize standing on the ground or sitting, as you did, not at first. It's generally a lot easier, looking down into the water, to look down at the place where you're going."

"Like we did yesterday in Darimbia?"

"Yes, exactly. But you came in at eye level, and you did it on your first try."

"So this is the part where you tell me what a powerful wizard I'm going to be, right?"

"No. This is the part where I tell you what a powerful wizard you already are."

She shivered, as if something in his gaze might by its own magic bring about this dreaded fate. "Don't say that," she said. "Just . . . don't." She turned and left the room without a goodbye.

It was too much for Katie, too fast. She retreated to her room. She paced up and down the space in front of the fireplace, while Sally wrung her hands nervously, uttering the occasional "My lady . . ." and "Please . . ."

After a while, Katie realized she hadn't eaten anything in hours, and she allowed Sally to bring her a light meal of smoked turkey, a green salad with a lemony dressing, and hot buttered corn. After eating, Katie felt better, but she still didn't want to go out. She didn't want to run into Alaric for fear he would offer her yet another lesson in magic, which she would have to decline. And then she would see an instant of pain and worry in his eyes before he hid it from her. She'd been a disappointment to her mother, to everyone, all her life, and now . . . She didn't want to become a disappointment to Alaric, too.

And what if she ran into Marco? He never said much, but Katie had the feeling that Marco was judging her. Judging her and finding her deficient? She didn't know what he was really thinking—or what he might be saying to Alaric when she wasn't there.

It was so much easier just to stay invisible. Why, oh why, had she ever come here at all?

CHAPTER TEN

A worthwhile mystery

That evening, Alaric had dinner with Marco, not in the formal dining room, but at a small table on the terrace, watching the sun, a dull red disk in the hazy sky, descend slowly toward the darkening ocean. They ate a layered pasta native to Darimbia, a spicy dish with lamb, cinnamon, onions, garlic, sorrel, and just enough hot peppers to complement the ruby wine.

"Katie's not joining us?" Marco asked.

Alaric looked away, remembering Katie's tears. "She's had a rough day."

Marco made a disapproving noise. "What, you're teaching her portals already?"

Portals, of course, were out of the question; they were among the most difficult of magical accomplishments. Marco was being sarcastic. Not that Katie wouldn't have the power someday, but Alaric saw now that he had to take it more slowly, and to give Katie a lot of support along the way. "Scrying."

Marco nodded thoughtfully. "Where?"

"Her mother's library."

Marco lifted his eyebrows. "You got in?"

"It's warded against me, but apparently not against her. Why would it be? I slipped in with her. She sat down in her favorite chair."

"Sat down! On her first attempt?"

"Yes. I made the mistake of telling her how strong her magic is. She's taking it hard."

Marco took a bite of his pasta. He looked away, frowning. Then he said, "Strange girl, but I think you're right, there's nothing the least bit deceitful or unkind about her. Do you love her?"

Alaric took a bite of his own dinner. "This is good," he said. "If Darimbia weren't so important for its wild gold, it would be world famous for its cuisine."

Marco laughed. "Don't think I haven't noticed that you're avoiding the question."

"I've asked her to marry me."

"Yes, so you've said. As part of your negotiated release, and a win for you, as far as I can see. But I asked whether you love her."

It was a question Alaric didn't want to face. No, he had to be honest with himself. The question was unsurprising. What he didn't want to face was the feeling that welled up inside when the question was asked, and his inability to control it. "I . . . I'm very fond of her."

Marco took another bite of his pasta, chewing contemplatively; then he washed it down with a sip of the strong Darimbian wine. "But do you love her?"

Alaric swirled the wine in his glass, pretending to study the color, buying time. "I like her very much . . . but I would rather not fall in love."

Marco's eyes widened. "Why on Earth not? It's something most of us do, and we seem to survive the experience okay."

"Ah . . . You and that Darimbian girl, what was her name?"

"Maria."

"Maria, yes. She jilted you for some farm boy, as I recall."

"And we're still good friends," Marco said hotly. "Anyway, I'm seeing Angela now, and I'm very happy, and you're avoiding my question again."

"Angela? Who's she? When did that happen?"

Marco blushed and looked away. "Well . . . last week. I don't know if it will last. Now, about you . . ."

Alaric took another bite of his dinner, then pushed the plate away with a grimace. "This has gotten cold. I think there could be such a thing as loving too much." He glanced at Marco, the one person he probably already loved too much, not that he would change it. What would it be like if he loved Katie that much? He didn't know if he could survive if anything happened to her. Would it be like what his father went through when his mother died? That was twenty years ago, but the memory still made his stomach churn. "You know that my mother died in childbirth."

Marco stroked the thin hairs of his beard, thinking. "That was before I was born."

"Yes, I know. But our father must have told you, right?"

Marco continued to stroke his chin, frowning.

"Well, no matter whether he told you. The thing is, she did. She and the baby, both. With all her medicine, the midwife couldn't save them. And with all his magic, neither could our father. He loved her very much." Now that the words were out, Alaric wondered whether he should have said them so bluntly to the child of his father's mistress.

"But that was a long time ago," Marco said, "and your father is not you."

"But I was there, and I remember how it tore his heart out." Alaric's mouth had gone dry, his throat tight. "I'm not interested in experiencing that for myself." He stood abruptly, pushing his chair back with a loud scrape on the stone floor. He had lost his appetite.

It was clear that Katie had been badly shaken, though whether by the experience of her strong magic, or by his own wholehearted praise of it, Alaric didn't know. Regardless, for the next two days he made no mention of magic.

But the supplies and weaponry needed in Darimbia had been assembled, and Alaric could wait no longer to deliver them. With or without Katie, this would involve magic. He hoped Katie would be willing to join him. "Shall we try scrying once again?" he asked as gently as he could.

They stood on the terrace overlooking the sea. A chill wind blew, and Katie had a warm shawl wrapped around her—soft vicuna woven with a thread of gold. She had both hands wrapped around a mug of hot tea, but she shivered. "I wish I could be the wizard you want me to be. I wish I had so much magic I could help you win the war in Darimbia. More. I wish—"

"That's not why, though it would be helpful." Very helpful. It might well make all the difference. But he'd promised Katie he wouldn't use her, and he intended to keep that promise. "You need to do magic, and to do it as well as you can, because it's part of who you are. You won't be fully yourself until you conquer this fear."

"I—I'm not sure I'm ready." She looked out at the sea, and not at him.

Alaric resisted the disappointment he felt tightening in his chest. "There's no rush."

The ocean filled the silence between them, as waves rushed to the shore below and sucked pebbles out again.

"I have to start moving supplies from here to Darimbia today," Alaric said. "I'm going to go over there with Marco to ensure that they are ready to receive them. Why don't you come, too?"

She looked up at him, eyes wide. "I—"

"You won't have to use any magic. I promise. Just come along."

"To Darimbia."

He nodded.

"Today."

He nodded again.

Katie hesitated for so long that Alaric thought she might say no, but a smile slowly spread over her face, so wide that it overflowed into laughter. "Darimbia today! Why not?" Then the laughter disappeared, replaced by a frown. "Oh, Alaric, what should I wear?"

"We usually dress in camo," he said. "I can't protect the entire region from scrying, so it's best not to be too visible. I'll see about getting you some."

Katie watched, fascinated, as Alaric opened the portal. She and Alaric and Marco stood in a simple room in his palace. It was a lower-level room with thick stone walls and a flagstone floor. Two high windows let in daylight, and from the corners of the room rose columns supporting an arched ceiling. Bags of goods of some kind were piled against the walls. Without a word, Alaric walked to the room's center and began his magic.

It was somehow different from last time. Before, in that cave, they'd both been tired and wet. She'd seen him moving his hands in the air in a pattern that suggested weaving, but now if she let her vision blur just ever so slightly, if she looked out of the corner of her eye and not straight ahead, she could almost see the strands of air. He seemed to pluck those strands out of, well, out of thin air, and then they were somehow thick and pliable. He made seven strands of the not-quite-visible air and began weaving them in a complex pattern. It was a pattern that made Katie dizzy as she watched it forming, but it seemed to draw her in. She couldn't—no, didn't want to—turn away.

Marco, who had no doubt seen Alaric's magic many times before, gave her a nod and a smile. He leaned close to Katie and spoke quietly. "Beautiful, isn't it?"

"Yes." Her voice came out in a whisper.

"I forgot to bring in medical supplies for the clinic. I'm going to get them now. If he's looking for me, tell him I'll be right back."

Katie nodded, never taking her eyes from the pattern Alaric was forming in the air. She barely saw Marco leave.

When the seven-strand braid was closed back on itself, Katie gasped for air, and only then did she realize she'd been holding her breath.

Alaric too took in a deep breath, and then, still holding the woven circle of air with one hand, took a step back to examine his handiwork, frowning. "Not bad," he said, half under his breath. "Only . . ." He reached for something in the air and pulled at it with his free hand.

It seemed to resist him.

"Portals are difficult," he said. "Each one is unique to its creator, but what they all have in common is that they always feel like they don't want to be formed. The air resists being bent in this way." He continued to tug at the strand of air, but apparently without effect. "I'm going to need both hands. Would you mind just putting a hand on the circle here, just for a moment?"

Katie drew her hands toward herself and folded her arms across her chest. "Where?"

"Anywhere on the circle; it doesn't matter." He glanced over his shoulder at her. He must have seen her fear in her expression, and he added, "Don't worry; there's nothing magic about it. The magic is all mine, and the portal will respond only to me. I just need to keep something in the circle to prevent it from closing in on itself."

Not magic. "Okay." She put her hand on the woven-air braid and was surprised at how firm it felt under her fingers.

Alaric braced himself and pulled hard with both hands at the—whatever it was—a strand of air? He grunted in satisfaction and brought it in contact with the braided air.

In her fingertips, Katie felt a jolt of something uncomfortably tingly and sharp, like a stab with a needle. She jumped involuntarily, but she held on tight.

The view through the circle of air changed. It was no longer the far side of the room. Instead, she was looking into a grove of conifer trees with thick trunks, the ground beneath them carpeted so thickly with needles that the understory was clear of plants.

Outside the magical circle, the room was unchanged, with its stone walls and flagstone floor, bags of supplies piled high all around.

A fresh breeze, tangy with the scent of pine needles and verdant earth, wafted in through the portal.

A young woman knelt at the base of one of the trees, next to a pile of packs. She was taking something out of one of the packs, but as Katie watched, she looked up. She frowned when she caught sight of the portal and reached for something at her waist. A knife. But then her gaze fell on Alaric, and her expression relaxed into a smile. "Your Majesty," she said, with a deferential bow of her head. "Welcome back."

The first thing Alaric did was to order a thorough briefing. The reports were not good. Queen Claudia had been reinforcing her troops and bringing in supplies. Alaric met with the leaders of the resistance as well as the commanders of the troops he had sent to the province to support them. The command tent, which was little more than canvas shielding a table full of maps from the elements, was barely large enough for the six people present.

Alaric turned to the maps, shuffling aside a couple of detailed ones to expose a large map of the entire province. "Show me where they're camped now."

General Eneko, the commander of his troops and a seasoned veteran who had served under Alaric's father for years, placed a large stone in one spot. "Here, but we don't expect them to stay."

One of the resistance leaders added, "We've been able to get close enough to see something of what's going on. They're staging supplies for a move. But we don't know where, or when. Or, for that matter, why."

There were murmurs of agreement.

Alaric grimaced. "Claudia won't be thinking about peace. She wants blood—mine if possible, but all of yours will do, too. She won't wait for us to choose the location for a battle. That's not her style. She'll want to choose the location herself. She probably already has something in mind. What we need to do is to figure out where she wants to lead us. Then we can decide how best to prevent her from succeeding."

After the meeting broke up, Marco and Alaric had a moment alone. "I thought you had this under control," Marco said. He looked petulant, brows frowning, lower lip slightly forward, like a toddler about to cry. "You said that you had reached an agreement with Queen Claudia."

"Yes." Alaric studied his younger brother. Their father had lavished love and attention on Marco, leaving Alaric to manage on his own. Was that why Marco still, at times, seemed to expect other people to continue taking care of him even though he was now an adult? Alaric supposed he ought to feel grateful that his father had given him so much responsibility so young, but at moments like this . . . it seemed he had *become* his father, continuing to take care of Marco, the other Darimbians, and his entire kingdom. He had never had a normal childhood.

"We do have an agreement, she and I, but right now we're having a . . . a difference of opinion over its interpretation."

"She was going to cede Darimbia to us," Marco said. "That should be clear enough."

"Yes, and I was going to marry one of her daughters with magical ability."

"You asked Katie. She has magical ability."

"Katie is not one of the daughters Claudia had in mind. And more important, she has not agreed to marry me."

Marco drew in a breath as if preparing to speak.

Alaric crossed his arms over his chest, frowning. *You'd better not be about to tell me to force or shame her into it.*

Whatever Marco had been about to say, he apparently thought better of it, and he let out the breath. "Well, then," he said. "Let's get on with our pretty little war, shall we?"

The war was neither pretty nor little. Like Marco, Alaric wished he could have ended it through his negotiations with Claudia. He hoped he had been honest in exactly what he had, or had not, promised. But clearly, the oathstone awaited some further action or clarification, as neither he nor, apparently, Claudia had been smitten. Yet.

"Take Lem, why don't you," he said to Marco, "and see how close you can get to Claudia's camp without being seen. See if you can find out where they're going, and how soon."

Marco smiled grimly. "I'm on it."

Marco and his friend Lem crouched low on a hillside, keeping cover behind the scraggly bushes that comprised the understory of the forest. Below them, half obscured in the dawn mists, the enemy army was busy breaking camp.

Marco wished he could just rush down there, his comrades right with him, brandishing their swords and shouting, and drive the damned soldiers back to Victoria. This spying business was entirely too tedious, but he reminded himself that sometimes he had to suffer through the dull parts to get to the exciting parts. He rubbed his chin, frowning. "Where do you think they're going?"

Lem made a noncommittal grunt and shook his head.

"Not heading closer to our camp, I hope."

"Wish I could see a little better," Lem said. "Damn fog."

"It'll rise in a couple of hours."

"In a couple of hours, they'll be gone."

"True." Marco ached to somehow foresee the right direction and get set up to observe before the army got there. Better yet, if they could provide some actual useful intelligence to Alaric, before it was too late. Surely, there must be some way to use magic to help figure this out. Telepathy, for example. But if that could be done by magic, it was beyond Marco. He sighed. "Let's take a peak over the hill here"—he tilted his head toward his right—"and see if they've sent out an advance patrol. If nothing's happening there, we can check the river road. We still have enough time to do that much."

"Right," Lem said.

Marco set out toward the shoulder of the hill, and Lem followed. For about an hour he scrambled through the underbrush as the hill to their left grew steeper, with Lem not far behind.

There was a sound of branches breaking, and dirt and brush sliding down the hillside. Lem let out a string of curse words, then, "Sorry, I tripped over—Hey, wait. Hey, Marco, look here."

Marco turned, but Lem was nowhere in sight. "Where are you?"

"Here." Lem's voice had a distant, hollow sound. Then he appeared from out of . . . the side of the hill?

"It's a cave of some kind," Lem said. "Back behind those bushes and vines."

Marco squinted, but all he could see beyond the bushes behind Lem was the steep slope. He climbed to Lem's side. "Show me."

They pushed their way through the bushes. A crack in the rock, barely visible even up close, was about ten feet high and just wide enough to squeeze through. Marco raised an eyebrow. "I guess we have enough time just to take a peek inside." He paused to concentrate, willing a small light to appear in his palm. A sharp pain behind his eyes made him wince. "Damn magic," he muttered, then blinked a few times. His palm was shining brightly, and the pain was gone. He slipped through the crack, palm forward, lighting the way.

Lem followed.

Inside, the space opened into a cavern that was almost square in shape, perhaps ten feet on a side. High overhead, the walls slanted together in a peak. The stone on three sides was rough, dark brownish-gray to nearly black. The fourth side, the farthest from the entrance, was as flat as glass, dimly reflecting the light in Marco's hand. He touched the surface. It felt as smooth as it looked, with no cracks or openings from one stone wall to the other. The light he saw was probably a reflection of his own light. He moved the light in his hand up and down, but the reflection didn't move. That was odd. Not a reflection, then. He frowned, then doused his light.

A dim light emanating from the smooth surface lit the cavern.

Marco squinted and looked in. He was pretty sure there was a single source back behind the glassy surface. It looked like it was far away. Maybe he should try to break the glass and get in, and see where the light was coming from.

But no, he'd seen how thick the glass was at the edge where it met the cave walls. It probably couldnt be broken, certainly not with a rock, maybe even not with a sledgehammer. Maybe with magic, but it would have to be more magic than Marco possessed. Maybe Alaric would know what to do with this, but Marco sure didn't.

"Marco?" Lem asked. With a jerk of his head, he indicated the cave entrance. "Time."

They had to go. Marco would report this to Alaric and let his brother decide how to handle it.

Katie sat in a camp chair in one of the back corners of Alaric's tent. She hadn't been in Darimbia long, just a couple of days, but she was restless. She'd left her mother's castle hoping to find adventure, but sitting here inside a tent didn't feel anything like adventure. Who could have imagined that war could be so dull?

"Alaric, can I go outside and walk around the camp?"

He looked up from the candles he was holding. "It's getting dark. I was just going to get these candles lit. How about if you help me?" He raised an eyebrow. "You might like to practice some magic."

Candles. The simplest feat there was. He probably wasn't patronizing her though. Practice was a good idea, but right now she had no heart for it. "I could use some fresh air."

"All right, just don't go far. It'll be night soon."

"I won't go past the sentries." It wasn't much different from being stuck inside her mother's castle, just a bigger area to be stuck inside, and at least the people here treated her kindly.

"Fine." He put one of the candles inside a lamp and flicked his fingers. The candle burst into flame.

Katie stood to leave the tent, but a commotion rose outside just before she reached the door. An instant later, Marco and Lem burst in.

"There's good news," Marco said, still breathing hard.

"And bad," Lem added.

Alaric sighed. "Sit." He gestured toward the chairs that were stacked in one corner of the tent and sat in the one chair next to the table that held a map of the province. He looked over to where Katie still stood near the door. "You're welcome to join us."

This boded to be more interesting than anything going on in the camp outside. Katie pulled up her own chair.

"Now, then," Alaric said with a nod toward the two men, "bad news first."

"Claudia's army is on the move," Marco said.

"What, again? I was hoping she'd stay put for a few days, and we could all catch our breath."

"Yeah." Marco grimaced.

"They're heading past Humpback Mountain toward Shelter Ridge, the one that angles down toward the river," Lem added, pointing to a spot on the map. "Probably hoping to claim the high ground."

"And block us from advancing toward the mines," Marco said.

Katie looked at the map, frowning. "Over there?" She indicated an area beyond where Lem said the enemy troops were.

"Yes." Alaric said.

No one spoke for a few moments. They all studied the map, as the sounds of their own soldiers preparing their dinners, joking and laughing, filled the tent. People who might be dead in a few days if Alaric made the wrong decision here and now.

Katie nibbled at a fingernail.

"We could try to get there first," Marco said at last. "Claim the high ground and give them a little surprise."

"Hmm." Alaric's eyes moved left, right, as he studied the map. "Can we get there before they do?"

Lem cleared his throat. "They're moving their whole army. A lot of people and equipment. They're pretty slow."

Marco's face broadened into a grin as Lem spoke. "But we can move our guerrilla fighters first, probably get there in a day, two tops. The rest of the army can go around here"—he indicated a direction on the map—"which would avoid their army, and hopefully their advance scouts as well."

"That sounds good. It'll be four days before they get there, so that should work." Alaric nodded. "Good. We'll do it. We'll break camp tomorrow. Now, tell me. What's the good news?"

"The good news?" Marco asked. "Oh, right. The good news is, we found a cave."

Alaric frowned. "And that's good news because . . .?"

"It's a really weird cave—"

"Tucked in a hillside behind a thicket of plants," Lem added.

"With some kind of really weird light inside," Marco said.

Katie sat a bit straighter. This was beginning to sound interesting.

Alaric's frown deepened. "You went in?"

Both men nodded.

"And it turned out the light was . . .?"

"That's the thing," Marco said, his voice rising in excitement. "We don't know!"

"We tried to get to it," Lem added, "but there was some kind of barrier. It was like glass, only really thick. We couldn't break it. Never saw anything like it."

"Probably some kind of magical artifact," Marco said. He sat back smiling, feet spread apart, as if he'd just achieved some kind of major accomplishment. "We figured you'd want to know. Maybe you can figure out how to use it somehow."

"Where is it?" Alaric asked.

Both Marco's and Lem's fingers went to a spot on the map.

"It's just one ridge over from where we walloped Queen Claudia's troops last summer. You remember?" Marco said, pointing on the map.

How could he forget? So many dead soldiers on both sides, but the day had been a victory, and the queen's army had retreated. "You're right, that's pretty close. If I open a portal to the ridge, I could get to that cave and back in just a few hours. Might be worth investigating."

Katie's heart leapt. Something even Alaric didn't know about—that would be interesting.

"But I don't know if I want to," Alaric added. "This has 'danger' written all over it."

"Oh, no," Marco and Lem said in unison. "We were both there," Marco added. "We went inside the cave. We hammered at the glass thing. Nothing happened."

"Hmm... but if it is some kind of trap, maybe it's waiting for a magic user to spring it."

"Maybe it's some kind of opportunity, not a trap," Marco said. "Maybe it's exactly the opportunity we've been hoping for."

There was a long silence. Katie hardly dared to breathe.

At last, Alaric sighed. "Why don't I go check it out first thing in the morning," he said, "while you two get our people moving according to the plan?"

Katie's heart was thumping wildly, but this could be exactly the kind of opportunity she'd been hoping for too. "I'll go with you," she said.

Alaric looked at her, brows raised in surprise. "What? It could be dangerous. Are you sure?"

She smiled happily. "Oh, yes. This will be a bit of an adventure, right?"

To Katie's delight, he returned the smile. "Right."

Chapter Eleven

A mystery in a cavern

A laric wanted to see the mysterious cave immediately, but there were command decisions to make, troops and resistance fighters to review, and the enemy's movements to decipher. He was loathe to delegate those tasks, so it wasn't till the day after that he was able to get away. He left with Katie at first light. Lem showed the way, and they arrived before noon.

"Go on back to the camp," Alaric told Lem. "Marco probably needs you. Now that I know the location here, Katie and I can get back on our own."

Lem nodded and turned back.

Alaric ran his hands over the strange smooth surface inside the cavern. It spanned seamlessly from one wall to the other and all the way to the top of the cavern. Whatever it was, it wasn't glass. Glass didn't make his skin tingle, but this—this screamed magic, powerful magic. Yet he could sense none of the bindings and spells that should have been there, that would have been there if he'd created such an object.

Whatever magic had been used to make this artifact was unknown to him.

Alaric ached for knowledge the way people ached for water or air. He needed to know what this was and how it worked.

And if his sense of direction hadn't gone completely askew, the passage beyond the *not-glass* led directly into, not out of the mountain. What was the source of light on the other side?

Katie stood beside him. "What is it?" she asked. There was a resonance in the cavern that gave her voice a bit of an echo—hard to read. But her expression was worried, eyebrows drawn together.

"Probably nothing." Was that true?

She met his gaze, and her frown deepened. "You don't look like it's nothing."

"Nothing I can't handle."

"Are you sure? I know you want to handle everything yourself, and you're really good at it, too. But this—you don't even know what it is, do you?"

He drew in a breath, let it out. The air was cool and smelled chalky. "It's not glass, I know that."

"And I'm betting you want to know what's on the other side."

It wasn't a question. "Of course I do. Knowledge is one of the things that are mightier than magic."

She nodded slowly, her worried expression easing. "And I want to know, too. So let's go find out."

In less than two weeks, Katie had come a long way from the shy person he'd uprooted from her mother's castle. She'd told him, even then, that she wanted to visit new places, find adventures. He'd thought she meant simply to get away, and of course, that had been a large part of it. But the other part was an insatiable thirst for all that life had to offer.

"All right," he said. "Yes, let's. But passing through solid walls is your specialty. Can you take us through this one?"

She let out a breath, scoffing. "Don't humor me. Anyone can do this."

But he couldn't. She worked this particular magic in some way that he couldn't quite follow, though he had tried. It was homegrown and quirky. Or perhaps somehow tied to her femininity.

"Please."

"Very well." She took his hand and walked, without apparent effort, into the transparent material. For a moment, Alaric felt the denseness of it, the tightly packed orderliness of its crystalline structure. Its jagged molecules left no room for his soft flesh, no room even for the air in his lungs. He wanted to cry out with the pain of it.

Then they were through. He staggered and gasped for breath.

Katie shook her head. "You make it look like such a big deal," she said. "Really, it isn't."

"You'll have to show me again when we get back. I'm not used to being this slow, but . . ." He shook his head. "But there's no way I'm going to give up."

She smiled. "Good. Neither will I. Shall we see what's through this tunnel?"

He had to get back. He had to check on his troops, on the resistance fighters, on the enemy movements. But they had a little time, and he loved to watch Katie blossoming. "Yes," he said, "let's."

Once they passed through the invisible seal, the tunnel ahead was dark and rough-hewn from the solid rock. Katie paused to look back. Alaric turned, too, and put his hand on her shoulder. Through some trick of the light, the entrance looked farther away than the one step they had taken. Instinctively, she reached out to touch it. The surface was as smooth as it was on the other side. Glass yet not glass, non-reflective, invisible. Unbreakable.

Katie tugged at Alaric's hand. "I don't like this place. Let's keep moving, or . . . or go back. But let's not just stand here." Her voice sounded dull and distant to her own ears, as if the walls were absorbing the sound.

"No," Alaric said thoughtfully, drawing out the word. His voice sounded as flat and dead as the rustle of last autumn's leaves. "I don't care for this place, either. Do you want to go back? We can, if you'd like."

Katie considered. Going back would be so easy. So safe. But then, she'd always wonder what was here and chide herself for not being bolder. "No, let's just keep moving."

Alaric took her hand, and together they moved down the tunnel. Ahead, it narrowed so much they couldn't walk side by side. Alaric took the lead, still holding Katie's hand, pressing forward. He struggled visibly to take each new step, as if he ached to turn and run but didn't have the energy for it. He lowered his head like a bull, forcing each step onward.

There was a feeling of hopelessness in this place, as if many creatures—perhaps many *people*—had died here, unable to go forward or back. It reeked of some kind of magic, but what? Katie's jaw felt so tight that her teeth might crack. She shivered and pushed on, holding tight to Alaric's hand.

The air was chilly and damp, carrying the smell of rocks and perhaps mold, something cloying and heavy. It felt as if they were walking through some thick viscous fluid much, much heavier than water. It beat down so oppressively that Alaric put his free hand over his head, as if that might somehow hold back the weight of it.

And still, it bore him down. He fell to his knees, hunched over like a caryatid no longer able to carry its burden.

"Alaric!" Katie touched his shoulder. "Get up. Please." She wanted to lift him, but she could barely stay on her feet herself. She pulled at him with all her remaining strength. "Stand up. You can do it."

"Give me . . . a moment." His voice trembled. "It's too far. Too much."

She had never seen him at such a loss. She'd relied on him for courage, but now he needed her. She would not—*could not*—let him down. Her determination gave her strength. "No, we can do this. We must. You just have to get up." She looked around, searching for something that might inspire him. The light at the far end of the tunnel seemed closer—unless she was just imagining it. She tried to make her voice sound confident, more confident than she felt. "Look, we're almost at the end."

He turned his head and looked. Then he swallowed and nodded. "Let me lean on you." He settled his weight on one foot, then the other, and slowly pulled himself to a standing position, still leaning heavily on her shoulder.

Together, they moved forward. The entire mountain bore down on them, too much pressure to bear.

Alaric slipped from her shoulder and sagged against the wall, which seemed to ooze a heaviness that enveloped them both. "Katie, is there space between the molecules here?"

She looked at him blankly.

"Between the atoms? Is there space?" he said.

"Yes." She spoke slowly, forcing the word out against great pressure. "The . . . book . . . says . . ."

"We're almost there. You have to take the lead."

"No, I . . . can't."

"You can. You must. I can't do this anymore, but you can push between the atoms. Just like walking through a wall. You can do this."

"If *you* can't . . . How can I?"

"We'll do it together."

Katie nodded slowly. "The space . . . between." That wasn't so hard. She could do it.

Together, supporting each other, they took a step.

And another.

And a third.

And they were out of the tunnel, as suddenly as if it had never been there. They were in a park of some kind, with trees and grass and, in the distance, a lake. Farther still, the tops of what might have been tall buildings appeared beyond the treetops, faint in the mist.

Katie turned to look behind. The air was clear. Beyond the grassy field where they stood rose a line of trees. There was no sign of the tunnel.

What had they done? How would they ever get back?

She refused to deal with this problem right now. She followed Alaric's gaze as he looked ahead of them, a puzzled expression on his face.

Who was that man sitting on a rock just ahead? Hands on his knees, leaning slightly forward expectantly, the person looked as though . . . but that was impossible. He looked as though he was waiting for someone.

No. He was waiting for *them*.

Chapter Twelve

In Larippia

Alaric had no idea where they were, or what—or whom—the man who sat on the rock was waiting for.

The man was dressed in a long cloak, light brown, of a fabric so tightly woven it was almost shiny, with wide sleeves of the sort that might hide any number of magical objects. His hair was thick and brown, but his short, trimmed beard was streaked with white. He looked like the images of hermit-magicians in ancient paintings. All he needed was a long, crooked wooden staff. Did the man have magical talent, or was he trying to look that way?

The man stood and nodded but did not smile. "Impressive," he said. "I came when the alert sounded, but I didn't expect you to make it through. That was not supposed to be possible for anyone who is not one of us."

Alaric wasn't sure he'd heard the man right. What language had he spoken? To be polite, he returned the nod. Perhaps nodding was a formal greeting of some kind.

"King Alaric Westlander, yes?" the man continued. "And . . ." He peered at Katie as if her name might be written on her face somewhere, in small print. His eyes were as dark as night. "Princess . . . Alicia, is it? Queen Claudia's daughter?"

Katie clutched Alaric's hand tightly and took a step back, half shielding herself behind him.

"But now that you are here," the man continued, "I bid you welcome to Larippia. I am Romulus Orcutt, the Senior Council's Director of Infrastructure. And this security breach is my responsibility."

Larippia. The word in ancient Darimbian for the province of Darimbia. Alaric had studied ancient Darimbian in order to read the ancient classics in their original language, but that had been years ago. He'd never imagined he might one day have to speak it, and he hadn't quite pictured the accents and rhythm of the spoken word. It was almost like poetry. He cleared his throat, giving himself time to search for words. "It wasn't easy."

"It was not supposed to be possible at all," said the stranger. "But now that you're here, I bid you welcome." His eyes flicked to Katie, then back to Alaric. "Please allow me to offer you some refreshment. And when you are ready, I would like to know more about how you did it."

"And I would like to know how you know our names," Alaric said.

The man gave a small smile, the kind that cloaked secrets, and said nothing.

"What language are you two speaking?" Katie asked, still half behind Alaric's back.

Alaric turned to her. "Ancient Darimbian. Our people know it only as a written language. I never thought I'd hear it spoken."

Orcutt made a small bow. "My apologies, Princess," he said in passable modern Darimbian, the language Westland and Victoria shared. "It was rude of me to assume that the royalty, at least, still study the old tongue."

"I . . . wish I had." Katie said, blushing. "But perhaps it's not too late."

"Well spoken, Princess. Indeed, perhaps not."

"Did you call me 'Alicia' just now? It's my first name, but I'd rather go by 'Katie,' if that's all right with you. But . . . how did you know my name?"

"That's what I'd like to know," Alaric said.

"Katie," he said, ignoring their question. "And you may call me Rom."

With an uncomfortable feeling that things were getting entirely out of control, Alaric hastened to say, "And call me Alaric." The last thing he wanted was for the two of them to get intimate in any way that excluded him.

Katie and Alaric followed Romulus along a path leading to the park's edge. It was the strangest place Katie had ever seen. The buildings surrounding the park seemed to grow taller as they approached. They were taller, even, than her mother's castle. Far taller.

As they walked, she became aware of a thrumming noise around them. She looked around nervously to see where it was coming from, but there was no obvious source, and no way to hide from whatever was causing it. She took hold of Alaric's arm.

"What . . . What's that noise?" she asked.

Rom tilted his head, one eye squinted a little. "Noise?"

"Mechanical," Alaric said. "Those, perhaps." He pointed skyward, where Katie now saw that what she'd assumed were birds, were anything but. They seemed to be mechanical, some darting in a straight line at high speeds, others swooping down among the buildings.

"Cars," said Romulus, as if the strange word explained them. He turned left, toward a low building overgrown with vines and surrounded by trees. Not quite hidden from view was a door. Rom approached the door and moved his fingers over one area of its frame. The door disappeared into the wall, and Rom turned to them with a welcoming gesture. "Come on in."

He went inside. A moment later, a light glowed within.

Katie's heart was pounding. "Should we?" she asked Alaric.

He shrugged. "I don't think we have a choice. Not if we intend ever to get back home again."

She'd thought she was frightened before, but the thought of being stuck in this strange place forever terrified her.

On the other hand, she'd wanted to visit new places and try new things—hadn't she?

She took a deep breath and stepped through the doorway, and Alaric followed.

The building wasn't quite a house, but it was more than a storage shed. Shelves lined all but the back wall, shelves filled, not with books but with boxes, bags, containers, and mysterious mechanical-looking objects. The room was spotlessly clean and had a faint, but pungent, chemical smell. To her right, a couch and two soft chairs surrounded a low table. To the left, a desk piled with papers suggested that someone was actively using the space. In the center of the back wall, stretching from the floor almost to the ceiling, a circle of silver or some other metal radiating a faint light dominated the room. Although it was large enough for a person to walk through standing upright, the circle was attached directly to the wall, leaving no place where a person might step.

Katie wondered if Alaric knew what the thing was. He probably did, he knew so much. Would she sound silly if she asked Rom? Maybe it was better just to wait and ask Alaric later, and not seem like a fool in front of the stranger.

No. She had to get used to the idea that sometimes she'd be among strangers and she'd have to ask about things. "What's that on the back wall?" Her voice quavered, but not very much. Maybe he wouldn't notice.

Alaric raised an eyebrow. "It's wild gold, isn't it? But I'm not detecting any spells woven into it."

"Very good," Rom said. "Yes, it is, but the magic woven into it is . . . different from yours." He turned to Katie. "What about you? Do you detect any magic?"

Katie wasn't sure how she'd even go about detecting magic. Between her mother and her three older sisters, it had always been around her. And she'd tried to avoid it—and them.

Avoid it. Did she feel an aversion to the object? She took a step closer, and her heart lurched. This was ridiculous. She took another step. Her heart pounded. "Yes, I think I might."

Rom smiled at her. "Very good, Katie. In your world, can you travel between places?"

In my world? Then where is *this*? "You mean . . . by magic?"

"Yes."

She glanced at Alaric, but he was watching her so intently she wanted to disappear. "Y-yes. We can make portals and go to other places. Or"—again, she looked at Alaric—"at least some of us can. Not me."

"Not yet." Alaric spoke so softly, Katie wasn't sure she'd heard him right.

But Rom heard him and said, "You think she can."

"I think she *will*. In time."

Rom's smile spread wide. "In time. Yes. Good. I believe you may be exactly right."

"What does that mean?" Katie asked. "You think I'll learn in time, or you think I'll go to other places in time?"

"Yes," Rom said. "Just so. In time, you will learn to go to other places in time. And we are going to start right now. Will you come with me?"

"Where?" Katie asked. She felt cold and wrapped her arms around herself. "Or is it . . . when?"

Rom laughed. "Sorry, I didn't mean to be so melodramatic. It's now, and not very far from here. There's going to be a bit of a brouha-ha over your appearance here in Larippia, and we might as well deal with it early on, before things get out of hand."

Alaric felt his chest tighten. He put a protective hand on Katie's shoulder. "What's going to get out of hand? And where exactly are you proposing to take us?"

Rom drew in a deep breath and let it out in an exaggerated sigh. "I was hoping to let the Council explain all this. Please. Humor me for now. Besides, the only gateway back to your world is over by the Council chambers, so in any case, if you are hoping to get back there, you'll have to come with me."

Alaric thought back to their arrival. The opening to that tunnel in the rock had disappeared. Was it still there, somewhere? If so, would they be able to find it by themselves? And if they did, would they have the strength to make the return trip? His jaw was tight with worry, an unfamiliar and unpleasant feeling. But truth, he told himself grimly, is one of those things mightier than magic. And right now, the truth was they had no choice but to trust the man. For now.

Katie was watching him, a questioning eyebrow raised. He gave her shoulder a slight squeeze. "I see," he said to Rom. "Very well, then, lead on."

Rom nodded, once, curtly. "Good decision." He swept the fingers of his right hand over his left wrist, and the circle mounted on the far wall flickered. He then waved his hand in that direction, and the light emitting from it steadied. He closed his right fist, then flung the fingers open, and the thing began emitting a low hum.

Alaric copied the movements as discreetly as he could, but he felt no magic, and there was no effect. He'd have to ask Rom later how the circle worked.

"Are you ready?" Rom asked.

Katie moved closer to Alaric. He took her hand. "Yes."

"Good. Then follow me." Rom walked to the circle. Though it was mounted right on the wall, he took a step through it. His body seemed to . . . flicker. He turned back toward them and made a beckoning gesture. Then he stepped through the circle with the other foot, and he disappeared.

Alaric's heart lurched. He took a breath to calm himself. It worked a bit differently from what he was used to, but still, it was just a portal. He glanced at Katie. She was biting her lip. He needed to show some confidence, or she'd lose her nerve. "Well, then," he said, giving her a bright smile and holding out his hand. "Here we go."

Hand in hand, Alaric and Katie stepped into the unknown.

✤▪────▪▪────▪✤

Rom was waiting for Katie and Alaric as they stepped out of a glowing circle much like the one they'd stepped into. The room they entered, though, was quite different from the one they'd just left. The entire far wall was made of glass. Beyond, the sky was punctuated by a handful of tall buildings in the distance.

In front of this dramatic wall and to one side stood a large counter, behind which sat a neatly dressed woman with dark skin and immaculately coiffed hair. An arrangement of sofas and chairs in muted shades of beige occupied the other side of the room. They were so tidy and clean they might never have been used.

Alaric moved closer to the window. He had traveled enough to have seen tall buildings—six, eight stories tall—but these buildings must be at least thirty stories tall. They stood alone, silhouetted against the sky like a row of exceptionally tall palm trees. He'd seen the like in fanciful drawings of the mighty empire of ancient Darimbia. 'Larippia,' wasn't that how Rom had pronounced it?

He remembered the airborn mechanical vehicles they'd seen in the park. Together with the tall buildings, that would suggest this was ancient Darimbia. Could he see them here, too? He squinted and looked more closely. There were, in fact, mechanical things, possibly vehicles, shuttling among the buildings.

If they had indeed passed through time to ancient Darimbia, how in the fifty names of heaven and earth were they ever going to get back home again?

Rom approached the desk. "Rozlin," he said to the woman sitting there. He spoke to her in the ancient tongue. "These are King Alaric of Westland and Princess Ali—uh, Princess *Katrina* of Victoria. The Council is expecting us."

Rozlin examined the two visitors from tip to toe. She nodded and gestured with her hands. A door opened in the wall to their right. "You may go in now," she said.

Rom gave them an encouraging smile. "Nothing to be afraid of here. In fact, I believe you will find this most interesting." He smiled at Katie and took her elbow, leading her through the doorway and into the room beyond.

Alaric scowled. The man stood a little too close to Katie. He hardly knew her but dared to touch her. This presaged trouble.

He'd have to deal with that, but now was not the time. He schooled his features to careful neutrality and looked around the room they'd just entered. Two men and two women sat at one end of an oval table that dominated the center of the room. They all wore robes like Rom's, and they were all in their seventies, maybe more, old enough to be Alaric's grandparents. A large window filled one wall of the room with the view of tall buildings. Portraits of people lined the other three walls. The people in the portraits also wore robes.

"Colleagues, may we speak in New Darimbian? Everyone here understands it, right?" The people around the table nodded and murmured their assent. "Excellent. Thank you. I would like to introduce King Alaric Westlander and Princess Katrina of Victoria." This time, he didn't stumble over her name. He moved his hand to her shoulder.

Katie took a step away.

Good for her. With an effort, Alaric controlled his expression. He didn't entirely trust Rom, but he had no reason to distrust these others. Not yet, anyway.

Rom turned to Alaric and Katie. "I'd like you to meet Tander."

The man sitting in the leftmost seat, an older gentleman with a neatly trimmed white beard, made a greeting motion with his hand.

"My aunt Morgana."

An elderly woman sitting at the end of the table made a slight movement of her head.

"And my cousins Arden and Ambin."

The remaining two people nodded.

"These people, along with me, comprise Larippia's senior council. I am, as you have no doubt noticed, the youngest member, but I am also the oldest direct lineal descendant of Irinia Orcutt, of blessed memory, which is why I am a member of this group. Together we rule Larippia."

The councilor Tander barked a humorless laugh. "Most generous, Romulus. Truth is, he rules, we advise, and he kindly listens to us—most of the time."

Rom's cheeks reddened.

"Director of Infrastructure, was it, Rom?" Alaric asked.

"We all have our specialties. Mine is, or was, to keep your kind out."

"Our kind?"

Rom waved his hand in a vague gesture. "How long ago was it, in your world, that Irinia Orcutt was assassinated?"

Alaric shrugged. "We don't know exactly. There have been upheavals since then. The best guess is between fifteen hundred and two thousand years ago."

"Yes. Very good. It was one thousand eight hundred and twenty-three years ago—in your world. Ninety-six years ago, here. She was my great-grandmother."

Katie and Alaric exchanged glances, and she moved closer to him.

Alaric had the alarming thought that when they returned to their world, generations would have passed there, and in their absence the war was lost long ago. "So, time moves . . . more slowly here?"

"It's more complicated than that. The seal between your world and ours is complete in both time and space, but we are in different . . . locations in both dimensions."

Alaric frowned. "The seal?"

"Yes. It's a long story, but the gist of it is that shortly after Grandmother Irinia's assassination and the subsequent purging of magic users, we had to leave. To survive, you understand. And so we sealed our world off from yours with magic. It turns out that in the intervening eighteen hundred years, you have evolved some. It was inevitable, I suppose, but now our magic works differently from yours. Your magic can no longer break the seal."

"Then how are we even here?" Katie blurted.

Rom turned to face her and moved closer. "Oh, Katie, my dear." His gaze was soft and so loving that Alaric felt his insides churning.

Alaric put a protective arm over Katie's shoulder. "You overstep," he warned.

"Not at all, Alaric," Rom said. As if emphasizing the point, he shook his head, but he also took a step back. "We'll discuss this later. Soon. But for now, let's just focus on this council meeting. I simply wanted to introduce you to them, and to inform them—"

"To obtain our agreement, Romulus," interjected the silver-haired woman at the far end of the table, Rom's Aunt Morgana. She sat straight, shoulders back and frowning—a formidable woman.

Rom lowered his head and gave a respectful nod. "Yes, of course, to obtain their agreement for you to stay at my country manor, where we will have many things to discuss, and the leisure to discuss them."

"Excuse me," Alaric said, "but don't you need *our* agreement as well?"

A slight smile twitched the woman's lips, and again Rom nodded.

"But there is an issue about time," Alaric continued. "If time here passes more slowly than back in our world, we must return as soon as we can. We are engaged in a war with a neighbor that will have important ramifications for your . . . descendants, are they? In Darimbia."

Rom shrugged. "We left them behind generations ago, Alaric. We do not engage in war."

"But unfortunately, *we* do. People will die if I don't get back to fix this. People Katie and I care about."

"What he hasn't told you," said Morgana, "is that time for you will pass as quickly or slowly here as there, and the location is the same, too. So, the only place and time in your world we can return you to is exactly where and when you left, plus the time you spend here. If you have a day or two, there is no need for you to worry."

Rom shot a look at the older woman that Alaric couldn't interpret. She lifted her chin, staring at him, and sat straighter. Rom's face was flushed. He cleared his throat. "Yes, well. That's true."

Morgana continued to watch Rom, raising an eyebrow slightly. "They are not prisoners, Romulus, are they?"

Despite Rom's having indicated that he was in some way in charge of this council, he wasn't acting that way now. He fidgeted under the woman's steady gaze. The silence was becoming uncomfortable.

Alaric took a step forward. "Madam, I request—"

"Wait," Rom interrupted. "You know we can, we *must* return you to your world shortly after you left it. So why not spend a little time here first? A day or two? You're a man who likes to learn new things, aren't you? There is much here you might want to know."

Alaric met Katie's gaze and cocked an eyebrow. *What would you like?*

She gave a shrug that was so slight he might not have even seen it, had he not been looking for some sign. "I like . . . to learn new things." Her voice was barely audible.

He smiled at her, then said to Rom, "I guess we can stay for one day anyway, as long as it's no trouble for you."

"No, no," Rom said, "not at all." And he smiled, too.

They departed the council's offices as they had entered, through the circle gate. But when they emerged, they were not back in the park building. Rather, they stepped out into a high-ceilinged hallway, obviously part of a home, with a winding stairway and a large chandelier.

"This way," Rom said, leading them through the open archway beyond, to a room dominated by a glass wall overlooking a verdant garden filled with roses and blooming irises, camellias, and other flowers. The windows were open, and the scent of jasmine filled the room. A central fountain among the flowers splashed noisily, and the entire garden faded into an enveloping mist about fifty feet beyond.

Alaric took a deep breath and smiled. Jasmine. It must be late springtime here. He turned to see Katie still looking out a window as if entranced. "Lovely garden, Rom," he said.

Rom tilted his head in acknowledgment. "Always nice to see it through fresh eyes. I wish I could get here more often, particularly at this time of year."

"What's outside, in the fog?" Katie asked.

"Nothing," Rom said.

"Nothing?"

Rom gave her a warm smile. "That's the edge. The outer border of our world. We took the city with us, and enough land to support ourselves, but not much more. Our universe is a small one, but we like it."

Alaric considered this. "You took . . . the whole city?"

"And some of the surrounding countryside, of course. For farming and so on."

"But wouldn't that have left something behind in our world? An empty spot of some kind?"

"Ah, no," Rom said. "We joined it back together afterward."

"A scar," Alaric said. "Some evidence of the joining. A scar, perhaps." Suddenly, he understood. His heart leapt. "Veins of wild gold. They're the remnants of magic strong enough to move cities. Stronger than any magic we're capable of now—in our world. That could explain why we've only ever found wild gold in Darimbia."

"Very good, Alaric. Quite right."

"Our histories are vague on this."

Rom scoffed. "Entirely silent, more likely. The entire community joined our magic together to sever the connection with your world in both space and time. It was the greatest feat of magic ever performed, before or after. We cloaked the entire century and joined together the events right after grandmother's assassination with those of a century later. There would be a scar in time, just as the wild gold is the scar in space. But since no one can travel in time, no one will ever see that scar. Right now, there should be no indication in your world that we even exist." He walked toward the garden wall, where roses climbed, bright yellow and pink and white in the sunlight. He pulled one close to his face and breathed in. "Ah... there's nothing I like better than the smell of roses, but the jasmine can be overpowering."

Alaric and Katie followed him, but Alaric wasn't ready to change the subject. "No . . . But *your* histories would be quite detailed, wouldn't they? You'd have no need to, how did you call it? To 'cloak' any of it, and also, it's quite recent for you."

Rom nodded. "And I suppose that what you're going to say next is that you'd like to visit the Council Library. That can be arranged, but why don't the two of you get settled in first?"

Rom showed Alaric and Katie to spacious rooms, not far from each other. The furniture in Alaric's room was made of a dark wood, almost black and rather too heavy for his taste. But the bed was comfortable, and the view outside the large window was of a lake, with fields beyond that faded into the mist.

The next morning, Alaric was still savoring the rich, dark chocolate drink that had been served with breakfast, when a visitor was announced. Councilor Morgana had come to call, and a servant in Rom's household led her into the room. Morgana was tiny, barely five feet tall, but the servant seemed in awe of her. For that matter, so did Rom, who stood so hastily he knocked into the table, clattering the empty dishes. Following his example, Katie and Alaric stood too.

"Good morning, Romulus."

Rom gave a slight bow from the waist. "Good morning, Aunt Morgana. Please"—he gestured toward the table—"won't you have something to eat?"

"Certainly not," she said, "and I see you're finished as well." She stood erect and wore a stole thickly embroidered with gold thread over her pale blue sorcerer's cloak. Her white hair gleamed against her ochre skin and black eyes. "Alaric, I understand that you are interested in the Council Library. I have come to escort you there."

It sounded more like a command than an offer—the woman *was* formidable—but Alaric didn't want to refuse. He glanced at Katie, whose wide eyes and eager smile were clear enough. "We'd be delighted," he said.

Morgana and Rom exchanged a look, a communication of some kind that passed too quickly to read. "I'm sorry," Morgana said, sounding not the least bit sorry, "but the library allows only one visitor at a time." She turned to Katie. "Of course, I'll be glad to bring you there as well. Tomorrow, shall we?"

"Thank you," Katie said. Her voice came out in a whisper, and she gave Alaric a beseeching look.

Alaric didn't want to leave Katie any more than she seemed to want him to go. In particular, he didn't want to leave her alone with Rom. He didn't quite trust the man. More worrisome, he didn't exactly know why. Rom had been a generous host and had behaved properly since that one unwanted touch in the council chamber yesterday. "I . . . We could make an exception to that rule, just this once, couldn't we?"

The elderly councilor drew herself up. "No, we cannot. Surely your companion can find some way to entertain herself for a few hours. A tour of the gardens, perhaps. Would you like that, young lady?"

Katie's face lit up. "Yes, I would, if it's not too much trouble."

"It would be my pleasure," Rom said, smiling at her.

Alaric felt completely outmaneuvered. That didn't happen to him often, and he didn't like the feeling. Yesterday, a visit to the library would have been the most desirable thing in the world. But today, somehow, it felt like a trap.

CHAPTER THIRTEEN

Katie gets to know Rom

Katie had been sorry not to be included in the visit to the library, but Rom was a charming host, eager to share his knowledge of horticulture. They spent a pleasant hour touring the garden, but when the sun grew uncomfortably hot, they retired to the shade of a birch tree near the fountain, enjoying the sound of splashing water.

Rom sat back, his limbs spread out and relaxed. "You know, I visit your world from time to time. More seldom, though, I will confess, as time goes on." He shook his head. "Your world is very confusing."

Katie laughed. "*My* world is confusing? It seems straightforward to me, compared to this one."

"Maybe 'confusing' is the wrong word. Violent. I never knew when I was doing the right thing, or what the consequences might be for doing something wrong. It was very stressful. Your world seems so dangerous."

She could relate to that. She gave a small, self-conscious laugh. "Not just 'seems,' Rom. I think it *is* dangerous. Maybe I'd like to visit it a little less often, myself."

Rom studied her appraisingly, but his smile was warm and genuine. "You're a lovely young lady. Claudia is your mother, right?"

Katie felt a sudden chill and drew back.

He bit his lip. "Did I say the wrong thing? I meant that she seems to have raised you well."

"Oh." She'd have to think about that. If her mother had raised her well, then was it good to be so shy? Even though her mother didn't like it? "All right."

"And your father?" He still had that appraising look in his eyes, but now he wasn't smiling.

"I don't have a father."

"Oh, Katie. Everyone has a father, even if they've never met them."

Katie stood up and walked closer to the fountain. She glanced back at Rom, who was now sitting forward, no longer relaxed. "I'm sorry, Rom, I only meant that I don't know anything about my father."

"Your mother never told you anything." It didn't sound like a question. His expression seemed sad, somehow. Or maybe serious, as if this were a difficult or painful matter.

She shook her head.

"Well, you have a right to know—if you want to. Do you?"

"You're asking, do I want to know about my father?"

He nodded.

All through her childhood, Katie had wanted to know. She'd asked her mother more than once, but had always been cut off and pushed away, until her mother forbade her to ask any more. Even as recently as two weeks ago, if someone had asked this question, she would have answered yes without a second thought. But now, seeing the intent way he was studying her, she wasn't so sure. What if her father was a wastrel or a scoundrel, like her sisters said? Worse, what if he was dead?

No, she had to face her fears. She wouldn't be able to live with herself if she left here not knowing whatever Rom had to tell her. She straightened her back. "Yes. I do."

Rom gazed into the distance. On the other side of the fountain, a camellia was starting to bloom, and behind it, jasmine vines draped over a fence, filling the air with their sweetness. "I have said that I visit your world occasionally. When I was younger, I was fascinated by it. Your wild and warlike and beautiful people." He shivered. "There was one time, it must be almost twenty years ago, when I was a younger man, and foolish, and I indulged in an affair with a most seductive woman." He turned now to Katie. "Your mother."

Katie felt suddenly short of breath and a bit dizzy. She put a hand on the lip of the fountain to steady herself. "W-what are you saying?"

"I loved her, I really did." He spoke more quickly now. "Or at least I thought I did. But she asked for things I was sworn not to give, and I . . . I couldn't. We quarreled. She made it clear that I was no longer welcome there, and I returned here. She warded her castle against me, but my magic isn't the same as hers. I have ways to see. I can bypass her wards, but I respected her decision not to let me stay. I still do. A few years later, I learned that she'd had a daughter. The timing was right, so it seemed probable I was your father. Even though I kept my distance, I watched you grow."

"So . . . you're not sure, but you think maybe . . ."

"Oh, Katie, no, I wasn't sure. Not until you came here," Rom said. "But now I am. There's no way that a person of your world could pass through that gate, much less manage to bring someone else with you. The magic in your world doesn't match the magic binding the gate shut. *You* passed through the gate because your magic is like mine, and that's because I'm your father."

Katie's heart was pounding. She considered her experience in the tunnel. The 'gate,' as he called it. Now that she thought about it, the tunnel had been very odd. The farther they went, the weaker Alaric had become, but she had not. If anything, she had become stronger. "That doesn't prove—"

"Also, there's this." Rom held out his hand. "Give me your hand."

Katie shrank away from him. He made a gesture of encouragement, and she walked back to the bench. Reluctantly, she put out her hand.

"Look at your little finger," he said. "See how it isn't straight? It curves in the middle and doesn't lay flat against the others. Look." He held his hand up and rotated it. The little finger curved outward in the middle like hers. "It's an Orcutt family trait. We all have it. Grandmother Irinia did, too."

Katie looked at her own hands as if they were alien organisms, not part of her. As if she was seeing them for the first time. "You're my father?"

"Yes," Rom said, "I believe I am."

Katie pulled away from Rom. She rubbed her hands on her dress—her traitor hands. Who was this man? How dare he, after all her years of suffering alone in her mother's castle, just waltz right up and say he's her father, and not even apologize for abandoning her?

She clenched her fists, forced them open, clenched them again.

How dare he!

Rom watched her, his eyebrows tilted up. With a question? An apology? He remained silent.

"How do you want me to react to that?" she asked, the tension in her voice obvious even to her.

He sighed. "I don't know. I suppose you have every right to be angry with me. I haven't been much of a father. But I was pretty young—probably not much older than you. I wasn't ready for fatherhood, but your mother was, well . . . She can be pretty irresistible when she wants to be."

Katie tried to imagine her mother as irresistible. She herself generally wanted to avoid her mother whenever possible. But then, she was not a person her mother cared to impress. Would Rom have been, back then?

She sat down on the bench, her anger fading. "Tell me. Tell me about her. How did you meet?"

"Ah." He let out a long sigh and sat beside her. "She was so beautiful." He looked out, away, back into time. "Oh, to be young again."

He smiled wistfully. "Anyway, there I was, yearning for adventure, and it happened that your mother was in Darimbia at the time. She rode out with her army to oversee tax collection, or something like that. Some government business, I forget what. She rode on her white horse in her golden armor, and her red hair shone like the sun." He touched Katie's arm. "You look a lot like her, you know."

Katie's face felt suddenly warm. "Oh, no, then that wasn't *my* mother you saw."

"Oh, yes, it was. I don't mean your coloring. That's a lot more like mine. But your features—the shape of your face . . . Anyway, I was so struck with her, that I didn't think about it at the time, but now I understand that she must have recognized my magical ability as soon as we met. She was so charming. So *interested* in me. One thing led to another, and, well . . ." He turned away, his face flushed. "She's a hard woman to resist."

Katie touched his shoulder. "That's all right, I understand." She did. She'd seen her mother pour on the charm for certain visitors, if they had something she wanted. "But Rom, if it's true that you had a relationship with my mother, why wouldn't she have mentioned you to me? Even when I asked about my father, she never said a word. Could she have been with another man, too?"

Rom frowned. "I don't know. I really didn't know her that well."

Katie mulled his words over in her mind. "You and I do have the same coloring, but it's not an unusual coloring. We have the same crooked finger, but maybe that's not so unusual either."

"I know how you came here," he said. "We have the same magic."

"But are you sure it's the same?"

"Hmm." His brow furrowed. "It certainly seemed to be the same when you arrived here. But we could do some experiments if you want. If our magic is the same, there's a lot I could teach you that no one over there"—he gestured with his head, as if modern Darimbia were just beyond the mist—"would know. And if it turns out to be different, well, maybe by that time, we'll have some other way to know the truth of it."

"All right," Katie said. "Maybe Alaric and I can stay for a little while, and I'll study your magic with you. But until we know for sure, let's not announce our relationship to everyone. Our assumed relationship. I don't want to set the wrong expectations while we're still not sure."

Rom gave her a warm smile. "As you wish, Princess."

❖▪━━━━▪▪━━━━▪❖

The door to the house opened. Katie looked up to see a servant bow, then step aside. Morgana strode in, with Alaric at her heels. Rom stood and took Katie's hand so that she stood, too.

Alaric clutched a large book, holding it close to his chest, as if it were a fragile treasure. He looked excited, grinning like a child. "I can't thank you enough," he said. "This book—" He broke off, staring at Rom's and Katie's hands.

Katie quickly took her hand from Rom's.

"It was entirely my pleasure," Morgana said. "I can't remember when I've enjoyed visiting the library as much as this time with you." She touched his arm and smiled up at him. "And that lovely little glass of wine afterward didn't hurt, either."

Alaric turned toward her. "No, it didn't. Your stories of your childhood were fascinating. I would love to hear more, sometime." To Katie, he said, "Morgana's parents knew Irinia Orcutt personally."

Morgana gave a little laugh. "Of course they did. My father was her husband's brother."

"And she's heard all the stories."

Morgana laughed again. "A thousand times," she said. Her eyes crinkled when she laughed. Katie thought she'd like to have an aunt like that. "But everyone here has heard them from me so many times, they have no patience anymore. Isn't that right, Romulus?"

Rom gave a start. "Auntie?"

She ignored him and continued, looking up at Alaric again. "It's a pleasure to have someone brand new to tell them to. And I hope you'll find that biography of Aunt Irinia interesting."

"I'm sure I will," Alaric said.

"Well, Romulus," Morgana said, "tell me, have you been treating our princess well?"

Rom gave a slight bow. "Yes, Auntie, of course." He turned to Katie. "I hope you'd say the same—?"

Katie looked from Rom, all hopeful, to Morgana, stern, then to Alaric, who was frowning. Was something bothering him? She didn't want him to have anything to worry about. "Yes, thank you, quite well. It's been an . . . interesting morning. But I do hope you'll let me visit the library with you sometime."

"Perhaps tomorrow morning," Rom said. "I'll show you around myself."

"Oh, good," she said. "And what will you do tomorrow, Alaric?"

The last thing Alaric wanted was for Katie to spend more time alone with this stranger who had suddenly become his rival. He scowled. "It's been most interesting here," he said. He was speaking to Morgana, but he glanced at Katie, noting how close she stood to Rom. His jaw felt tight. "But we really do need to get back to our own world. There's a war going on, and we are fighting for the descendants of your people."

"Of course." Morgana dipped her head in acknowledgment. "Any time you want to go, you may. And please, take that book with you." She gestured at the book in Alaric's hands and gave him a smile.

Rom cleared his throat.

Morgana's smile vanished. "Nephew?"

"Auntie, I—" He shifted his weight from one foot to the other. "If Alaric is going back right away, I wonder whether Katie might stay a bit longer here with me—?"

Katie stiffened and her eyes widened for a moment, as if Rom's offer was unexpected. Or as if she hadn't expected him to try to separate the two of them. Was the man manipulating her in some way?

She looked from Rom to Alaric, then back again. She drew in a breath. "I have to go back too, of course." She turned to Alaric. "But please, could we both stay maybe just another day or two? I'd like to see the library, and I'm sure Rom could show both of us a lot of interesting, um, magical things."

Magical things! Alaric scowled. It seemed the fellow had already started weaving some kind of magic around Katie. He had to get her out of here, and the sooner, the better. "Absolutely not. Marco is already going to be worried about us. Maybe Rom could visit us sometime"—*or better yet, never*—"and show us his *magical things* then." He gave the phrase the cynical twist it deserved.

Katie opened her mouth, but no words came out. She looked to Rom, as if hoping for his assistance.

"Perhaps just one day, Alaric?" Rom offered.

Katie leapt on his words. "Oh, yes, just one day. That wouldn't hurt, would it?"

Clearly, she had no sense of the critical situation the war was in at the moment. Alaric couldn't blame her for that. What did she know of war, anyway? For that matter, what did she know of life? Of course she couldn't see how the man was manipulating her. "I'm sorry, but no," he said to Rom. "This has been a most interesting stay, but we really do have to get back right away."

Katie drew in a deep breath and let it out. "I'm not—" Her voice came out with a bit of a squeak, and she cleared her throat. "I'm not as important to the war effort as you are. I understand you have to get back. But perhaps I could stay a day or two more? That would be all right, wouldn't it, Alaric?"

It was certainly not all right. Not even close. He ached to say no. He could probably get her to return with him by command or by argument, but that would be unfair to her. She was an adult and had the right to make her own decisions. Yet he couldn't bring himself to say yes.

"Just a short time," she pleaded. She turned to Morgana. "That is, if it's no trouble."

"As you wish, dear," Morgana said. "There's no rush, and I can bring you to your world whenever you're ready." She glanced at Rom, then back to Katie. "Or show you how to do it for yourself, whatever you prefer."

Alaric didn't like how this conversation was going. He liked it even less when Rom put his hand on Katie's shoulder and she didn't move away. It was hard to keep his voice civil. "Katie came with me, and I'd like to bring her back with me as well." He held out his free hand. "Katie."

She didn't move away from Rom, didn't come to him.

His heart sank.

She shook her head ever so slightly, looking close to tears. "I really would like to stay a little while longer. Just a day or two. I haven't even seen the library yet."

Alaric felt like he'd been slapped in the face. He hadn't expected her to refuse his direct request. He took a step back, suddenly aware that he was holding the book a little too tightly. "As you wish, Katie." His voice came out stiff.

Katie gave him an apologetic look. "I'll come back later, I promise." She turned to Rom, then Morgana. "I can do that, right? I can go back any time, right?"

"Of course. No one will keep you here any longer than you want to stay." Morgana smiled at her, then said to Rom, "That's right, isn't it?" There was a stern edge to her voice.

"Yes, Aunt Morgana," he said. "Of course."

Katie looked up at Rom, who smiled at her. "It's just that there's so much for me to learn here. Rom says that my magic is like his, and he says that he'll teach me." She turned her gaze back to Alaric. "Wouldn't that be good? Then I'd be able to help you in the war even more."

Alaric swallowed, trying to relieve the tightness in his throat.

She must have seen something on his face, for she added, "Besides, I can hardly do any magic, so I'm not very important to the war effort, not like you are. I could stay for a few days, couldn't I?"

No, you can't stay. Not for one instant without me. "Of course." He plastered a smile onto his lips and hoped she wouldn't see through his lie.

CHAPTER FOURTEEN

Return to Darimbia

T he trip back to Alaric's own time was far easier than the passage into Larippia. He followed Morgana through one of the circular portals and found himself in a cavern. Behind him was the smooth, transparent wall that Katie had brought him through, and he was outside of it. In front, sunlight streamed through the cave's opening. He stumbled as he took a step on the cave's uneven floor.

Morgana gave his arm a squeeze, then let go as he regained his footing. She handed him the precious book. "May the heavens favor you," she said. "And don't worry about the princess, she'll be safe enough. I'll keep an eye on her."

Alaric was relieved to know that Morgana would be looking in on Katie. He doubted Katie's physical safety was the problem, but that was between Katie and Romulus, not Morgana. He put the thought aside. "Thank you," he said, "for everything." He smiled at her, then drew her into a hug. He wished he'd grown up with an aunt like

Morgana—stern, smart, witty, and loving. "I'll do what I can for your people here."

She gave him a curt nod, turned, and stepped into the transparent wall. The instant she was all the way through it, she disappeared.

For a few moments Alaric looked at the blank wall where she'd been, missing Katie. The loss pressed on him so heavily he could hardly breathe. Could he have done more to bring her back with him? Maybe he should have insisted more strongly. Or maybe he should have agreed to stay, at least one more day. But he hadn't, and there was no going back now. He forced himself to draw a deep breath and found strength in it. She'd said she would return. He hoped she would. Meanwhile, he had work to do. He walked toward the cave's entrance, clutching the book to his chest. It did nothing to alleviate his heart's heaviness. He felt like he'd aged ten years.

It would be a long walk back to the Darimbian camp.

Marco was waiting for him just outside. He sat on a log before the charred remnants of a campfire, staring into the ashes as if he might divine his fortune there. He looked up as Alaric approached, leaping to his feet when he saw who it was. "Alaric! Thank the heavens you're back."

Alaric embraced his younger brother. "It's good to be home again." With a pang in his heart, he thought again of Katie, who had not come back with him, then pushed the thought aside. "Have you been waiting here for me since I left?"

"It's only been two days, and besides, we took turns." Marco looked down with a barely noticeably shake of his head. "We moved our camp and wanted to make sure you got back okay."

"I trust you've held everything together while I was gone."

"Barely." Marco grimaced. "A little bit more magic than I possess would have helped."

"Tell me." Alaric gestured toward the log, and they both sat.

"Well, you know the queen's army was breaking camp and about to move. What we didn't expect is that they were also about to attack."

Alaric felt his heart lurch. He frowned. "What? I thought they were four days away. I've been gone only two." He scrutinized Marco from head to toe. "You look fine. You beat them off?"

Marco wiped his hands over his face. "I wish. No, we didn't. They brought only some kind of elite units that moved more quickly than the whole army could have. The queen came with them. She cast some kind of magical cloud or something. It was daytime, but the world went black as night. We couldn't see anything, but her troops didn't seem to have that problem. Luckily, there were thick woods, and it was familiar territory. We managed to escape, but we've had to retreat. We're now that much closer to the Westland border, and of course the queen's army is preparing to press its advantage. That's when Lem and I and the others decided to wait for you here, to bring you back as soon as possible."

Gone just two days, and all this had happened. Alaric could have countered the darkness spell, or cast one of his own. Even Katie could probably cast one, it wasn't that hard. Katie—he had to stop thinking about her. He had to focus. "Where is our army now?"

"It's a bit far. I . . . I tried to get through that freaky barrier you and Katie went through, but I couldn't even make a scratch in it, much less break it. So all I could do was wait here, hoping you'd come back."

"Thanks for your faith in me."

"In you, yeah, naturally, but . . . where's Katie?"

Alaric looked away and sighed. "She stayed there. I'll tell you later. But now, let's go join our army and see if we can throw a few surprises back at Claudia for a change."

To save time, Alaric fashioned a portal that led to an area he and Marco were familiar with, not far from where the Darimbian resistance was camped. It was already mid-afternoon by the time they joined their people, and Alaric was exhausted. He blamed the use of magic to make the portal, but at the same time he knew that wasn't entirely true. Yes, the magic had taken a lot out of him, but it had also saved them a day of travel.

More than the magic, leaving Katie behind in Larippia hung like a weight in his heart, sapping his energy. She had abandoned him, but somehow, he felt he was the one who had failed her. No, worse. He felt he'd failed himself in some much deeper way.

He told himself that the situation in Darimbia was exactly the same as if he'd never met Katie, never brought her here. But nothing was the same. He had to focus on the war effort, but it seemed impossible. The gloom sapping his energy had nothing to do with Darimbia and everything to do with the emptiness of his life when Katie wasn't in it.

Katie missed Alaric more than she wanted to admit. She went over their parting argument in her mind again and again. Could she have said or done something differently? Something that would have erased the hurt look in his eyes, or the loneliness she felt now, without him? She reminded herself she'd get back as soon as she could—only a day or two—but she didn't want to cut short her time in Larippia, time to get to know her father a little better. After all, who knew when she'd ever manage to see him again?

When she joined Rom for breakfast the next morning, she put on a cheerful face.

"How about a little magic?" he asked, eyes wide and happy with anticipation.

Her heart lurched. "Magic?"

"Yes, I said I'd show you how we do it here, and I'm willing to bet you'll find it easy, and maybe even a little fun."

Oh, great. Just what I need. 'Fun' was not even remotely how Katie would describe the practice of magic. She couldn't help thinking about the last time she'd tried to practice magic under Alaric's tutelage. That hadn't gone well, not even a little. What a disappointment she'd been to him. She didn't want to disappoint Rom, too. The only thing that would be worse than trying to do magic his way and failing would be to refuse to try at all.

She swallowed hard. "All right. When do we start?"

Rom looked at her with concern. "Are you feeling well?"

Was she? Maybe she could avoid this if she was sick. There was certainly a large, tangled knot in her stomach. Alaric would have known how to put her at ease, but he wasn't here, and what did she know about Rom, really? She was alone among strangers, and now that she was here, she wished she could just disappear. But she couldn't do that, not anymore. The one thing that always worked for her in this kind of circumstance, the response she was really good at—hiding—was the one thing she mustn't do.

She steeled herself. "Yes, I'm fine. Let's do some fun magic."

Katie gazed in wonder at the city around her. Rom had assured her he knew of a most delightful way to learn magic, and now the two of them stood on the rooftop of one of the taller buildings, preparing for a trip in one of Larippia's strange flying cars. A light mist covered the buildings below, golden in the hazy sunlight. One of the flying cars approached in a slow, elegant curve, and then settled onto a rectangle painted in white on the roof. "What kind of magic is this?" she asked. "Are the cars made of wild gold?"

Rom laughed. "That's a good guess. There's a talisman embedded in each of them that's been charmed to enable it to fly, yes. But the talisman is actually quite small. You could hold one in your hand. It creates the scientific conditions under which a solid object like this car can fly."

Katie turned her gaze from the car to Rom. "What do you mean?"

"All magic must be grounded in science," he said. "At least, our kind of magic. The scientific principle in operation here is that of lift."

"Lift?"

"Yes. As a solid object passes through a liquid or a gas such as air, a partial vacuum is created by the displaced air molecules, and since something has to fill that space, the car rises. Lift pulls a vehicle up, perpendicular to its direction of travel. Without magic, a vehicle must be moving forward to create lift, but the talisman in the car moves the air molecules above the car aside so that lift can occur."

Katie brightened. "Oh! Like Brownian motion! I know about that."

"Yes, it's kind of like that."

"But then, if that's true, how does the car ever go down again?"

"The same way. It's completely under the driver's control. Get in. I'll show you."

Rom opened one of the car doors, and Katie sat inside. Rom closed the door, then went around to the other side and got in. They were surrounded by wide glass windows. Below the glass in front, a shining silvery circle was etched onto the car's interior surface.

"Put your hand over mine," Rom said. "I want you to feel what this is like."

Katie did so, and he touched the circle with his fingertips.

A thrill shivered up her arm and down into her heart. Something about the car changed, too. It was almost as if the car woke up. As if it became more *real*.

She gasped.

"Are you all right?" Rom asked.

"Yes, I just—"

"You sense it, then. That's good, it means your magic and mine are aligned. The same kind of magic."

"Is that good?"

Rom looked at her. "I don't know if I'd say 'good.' It's just different, like being right-handed or being left-handed. But I will say this: You'll probably have fewer limitations when you do magic our way. This should come very easily to you now that we've started."

Katie drew a breath and let it out. Apparently, she was doomed to exercise magic one way or another. It might as well be the easier way. "In that case, let's get on with it."

He indicated the silver circle in front of them. "By touching this circle, I have connected with the vehicle. Now, we're going to rise." But he sat, looking at her, and waited until she nodded. Then he moved his fingertips upward a few inches.

The car rose, hovering several feet above the building's rooftop.

"Gestures aren't necessary, but they help with the control, especially for beginners," Rom said in a matter-of-fact tone. "More experienced people don't use them, though, since many people talk with their hands. It can confuse the car."

Katie looked out her window. "Will it hover this way forever if you don't move?"

"As long as I'm still in the vehicle and still intending for it to hover, yes. Basically. There are some exceptions related to safety."

"And if you . . . I'm sorry, Rom, but if you die while traveling?"

"The vehicle will land itself safely. Same if I fall asleep or lose focus. It's connected to me until it lands, or until another driver takes over. Now, shall we go for a ride?"

Katie's heart thumped with excitement. Maybe a touch of fear, too. She leaned forward, looking all around. "Oh, yes!"

Keeping just within the wall of mist that surrounded the city, they flew in a lazy circle all around the city. It was far larger than either Westland's or Victoria's capital city, extending almost beyond sight over the horizon. Abundantly laced with parks and gardens, it was also surrounded by agricultural land that extended into the mist.

Rom gave her a smile, his eyes aglow with anticipation. "Now you try."

Katie gasped, and her hand went to her heart. "Me? I'm . . . I'm not . . ."

"Believe me, there's absolutely no danger. The vehicle has plenty of safeguards, and I'm here, too. Just touch the circle, think about where you want to go, and decide to go there."

She swallowed and eyed the circle. It suddenly seemed ominous. She looked back at Rom, who nodded, then back at the circle.

She touched it.

A thrill ran through her, shivery but not unpleasant.

The vehicle slowed. "Give it a direction," Rom said.

She studied the cityscape out the windows and picked a building that stood tall on the farthest horizon, shining in the sunlight. *Go there.* She packed the thought with as much intention as she could muster.

The vehicle veered in the opposite direction, into the mist.

Katie's heart leapt into her throat, pulsing rapidly. "Rom! Where—?"

He put a hand on her arm. "It's okay. Just wait a minute."

Before she could frame her question, they emerged again from the mist. They were almost on top of the building that had been, just a moment ago, so far away. She stared, voiceless, then finally managed to ask, "What happened?"

"Do you remember, I told you that when we separated from your world, we took only the city and its farmland?"

She nodded. "Yes, but . . . we were going that way"—she pointed toward the city ahead of them—"and now we came from here." She pointed back toward the mist. "How?"

"It's a closed geometry, our world. You can go in any direction, and after a while, you come back around to where you started."

Katie considered this. "Is that true in my world, too?"

"Perhaps." Rom smiled. "But you'd have to go far out into the stars and beyond before that happened. Your world is a lot bigger than ours."

She tried to imagine living in a world that was as closed in and bounded as Larippia. She didn't think she'd like it, going around in circles all the time. "Don't you ever feel kind of trapped here? Wouldn't you rather live in a big world like ours?"

Rom tilted his head, as if he was listening to a distant voice. "Oh . . . I used to, when I was younger. We're not supposed to go there, but of course we have the ability, just like you do. I was as rambunctious as the next young man that age, so I sneaked out one day." He took his gaze from her and looked out the window. The vehicle was hovering over the building. "Why don't you land, just there on the building's rooftop, and I'll tell you."

Katie willed the vehicle to land, and it floated slowly to the building, touching down on the roof without even a slight bump. She grinned at Rom. "It looks like my magic is just like yours. I could be a great magician here."

"You could be a great magician anywhere."

"Now you sound like Alaric." She wondered how Alaric was doing and what was happening in Darimbia. He'd been gone only a day, and already she missed him. She shouldn't stay here too long.

"Oh, I doubt he knows the half of it," Rom said.

Rom showed Katie how to open the door of the vehicle, and they stepped out onto the building's rooftop. A light breeze was blowing from the mist, carrying a fresh, pleasant odor. Katie breathed in deeply, then let out a sigh. "The air here smells wonderful."

"Newly mown hay."

She walked over to the parapet at the edge of the roof, and Rom followed. "So, tell me about your great adventure in my world," she said. She crossed her arms. "I know you said the other day that's how you met my mother. But I want to hear more."

Rom faltered and half turned, as if he wanted to head back to the car. "Maybe this isn't the place . . . Maybe somewhere else, another time."

Katie had to laugh. "Oh no, you aren't going to get off that easily."

He gave her an apologetic smile, then joined her at the parapet. "Fine. I guess you should know." He looked out over the view and was silent for a moment, gathering his thoughts. "When I went into your Darimbia. I knew what to expect, of course, the fighting and all. We do try to keep track of what's going on over there. At the time, your mother's army was not far from the spot where I entered, and I decided I wanted to see the army more closely."

"What? You might have been mistaken for one of the Darimbian fighters and . . . and been killed. Weren't you afraid?"

"I probably should have been," he admitted, "but I was young and bold and foolish. I got pretty close to the camp, and there was your mother, riding out of the camp along with some of her soldiers." He let out a long sigh. "She was so beautiful."

It sounded like something out of a romance novel. Katie echoed his sigh. "Love at first sight," she said. "But how did you actually meet?"

"Embarrassingly, I just walked into the camp, and of course, I was taken prisoner. But I was unarmed and protested my innocence vigorously. Most likely, they would have sent me away with a warning, I clearly wasn't a threat. But I also kept demanding to see the queen."

Katie's heart tumbled. "Oh . . . you were very brave. I'd like to have someone love me like that, someday."

He raised a questioning eyebrow.

Don't ask me about Alaric. He doesn't love me. She didn't say the words out loud, but she looked away from him.

He must have gotten the message. He cleared his throat. "Yes. Well, I'm sure you will, someday."

"So, did she come see you?"

With a smile, he said, "Oh, no. I don't think Claudia would ever 'come see' anyone. She had me brought to her, and she was as beautiful close up as she'd been on horseback from a distance. Maybe more." He looked up and away, remembering. "Yes, definitely more." He turned his gaze back to her. "So now you know how your mother and I met." He started walking back to the flying vehicle. "Let's go back to my place now, shall we, and get some lunch."

"Oh, no, Rom." Katie tugged at his sleeve. "Tell me, did she fall in love with you at once? How long were you together? Why did you leave?"

He laughed. "So many questions!"

She crossed her arms and frowned at him, leaning back against the parapet wall.

"Oh, all right." He returned to the wall. "As I remember—this was a long time ago, mind you—I stuttered out something pretty incoherent, offered to help her if I could, anything, if only I could stay."

He must have really been smitten. "That's pretty bold," Katie said.

He sighed, and the look of sorrow on his face was unmistakable. "Maybe so, but it worked. Somehow the conversation got around to magic, and I told her I could work magic. And then she really got interested in me. One thing led to another, and after a short time, all that led to . . . Well, she got pregnant with you. I didn't know that, but still, I wanted to marry her. I wanted to bring her back here with me, but she wasn't interested. I must have become rather tedious and over-insistent. We quarreled. A lot, I'm sorry to say. After a few increasingly uncomfortable weeks, she sent me away. Just away. Didn't care where. She worked some of her kind of magic and put a perimeter up around her camp that I couldn't cross."

"You couldn't? Even with your own magic?"

"I wasn't going to use my magic against her, Katie. I'd never do that. I . . . went home."

"But don't you want to see her again?"

Rom looked away, discreetly wiping the corner of his eye. "We'd better get back," he said. "I promised Auntie Morgana we'd join her for tea."

Chapter Fifteen

A reintroduction

Queen Claudia's army attacked at dawn.

The Darimbian resistance fighters weren't ready. They were in a bad location. Not imagining an attack would come so soon, they thought they might have a day to recover. They'd camped in a clearing by a lake, where the water was clean and plentiful, and they could tend to their wounded.

Alaric wasn't ready, either. He was still weak from creating the portal yesterday. He would have liked to weave a large portal all around his army's encampment, a portal that Claudia's troops would enter, thinking they were going into the camp, but exit in some place far, far away. But this was a fantasy. A portal of such a size was beyond his powers even if he was in prime health. Which he wasn't.

He did what he could. With Marco, Lem, and two others protecting him, Alaric focused his magic to weave a wall of haze around his people's encampment. It was pure illusion—a weaving similar to making a portal but with no connection to any other place. Easier to make, and easier to maintain.

But Claudia or one of her daughters was advancing with her army. They broke holes in Alaric's misty wall. A shout went up, and a couple of the resistance fighters pointed to a spot where the area beyond had become visible and enemy troops in their brown uniforms were running through.

Marco waved a small band of fighters to engage the enemy, and Alaric, frowning, repaired the hole. Mist protected them again.

But a hole appeared at another point in Alaric's wall. He barely had time to do the repair when a third hole started to appear. Alaric felt a headache starting, but there was no time to ease off. The magic he needed to repel the queen took all his concentration.

Another shout went up again among his soldiers, louder this time. Two men ran toward him, calling him and pointing.

Alaric pulled his attention back from the webs of magic he held in his hands. He had missed the spot where the Victorian army had clambered over his magical wall of haze, not using magic at all, simply by climbing.

Alaric's camp was overrun by the queen's superior force.

Alaric let his wall vanish and gathered his magic into a rain of rocks and boulders that dropped from the sky onto the enemy. He fell to his knees, exhausted, but managed to hold back the attackers while the resistance force retreated into the forest.

He couldn't keep this barrage up much longer. His strength was waning.

As sunset turned to dusk, the resistance regrouped as best it could within the forest. They watched as Claudia's army lit fires and camped in the clearing where they had been only that morning. They couldn't stay here. It was too close to the enemy.

A Darimbian who knew this part of the province guided them by moonlight to a safer location, bounded by a shallow river on one side, where they could occupy a hilltop and prepare to defend themselves.

The next morning, Katie woke early and went out to Rom's garden. The sun was just rising, glittering through the mist and splashing the leaves and flowers with golden light. She sat on a bench near the fountain and rubbed her eyes. She'd hardly slept. The water in the fountain burbled softly, almost like a lullaby, but sleep was not on Katie's mind.

She couldn't imagine her mother in any kind of love relationship. And yet . . . Was she reading Rom right? It almost seemed as though . . . Did he love her still? The unanswered question circled around and around in her mind like a prisoner yearning to be free.

The sound of footsteps interrupted her reverie, and Rom's voice said, "That's fine, just set it up right there."

Katie turned.

Rom had had breakfast brought out to his garden. As a kitchen maid set their places at a small table, he walked over to Katie and sat by her side on the bench. "I've been thinking a lot about our conversation yesterday," he said.

"So have I." She took a breath, steeling herself.

"I want to apologize. I shouldn't have shared all that with you," Rom said. "I'm sorry if I troubled you."

"No," she said quickly, "it's not that." She searched his face. He looked worried. Did she look that way to him, too?

Finished with the table, the kitchen maid glanced at them, then lowered her eyes. She took her tray and wordlessly headed back to the house.

Katie waited until the maid was gone. "I . . . Rom, are you . . ." Her words faded, unable to escape her lips.

He cocked an eyebrow, eager to hear the question.

She choked out a few more words. "Do you think maybe you're . . ." Her throat was suddenly dry. She swallowed.

Rom took her hand and patted it encouragingly. "Maybe I'm . . . what?" He looked deeply into her eyes, his head tilted questioningly.

Maybe this was a really bad mistake. *He has no idea what I'm about to ask.* But she couldn't hold back the words any longer. "Are you still in love with her?"

Rom's hand went to his heart, and he seemed to stop breathing. Birds rustled in the bushes, calling loudly to one another. A slight breeze rustled the leaves of the trees.

He stood. "Forgive me, Katie, I don't think I want breakfast after all." He took a step back to the house, not looking at her.

Katie's throat was suddenly tight. She reached out a hand, but he was already too far away. He must have suffered all these years. *He's still suffering.*

She swallowed. "Wait, Rom. Maybe I can help you."

He shook his head, not speaking. But he stopped walking.

Katie stood and went to him and touched his shoulder. "Maybe it's not too late. Please. Let me try."

When he turned back to face her, his eyes glistened with tears. "I really shouldn't involve you. It's not your problem, it's my own lack of courage. When I left your mother all those years ago, I was angry at her. I thought I'd go home and just forget about her."

"But . . ."

He gave her a wan smile. "I didn't know about *you* then, of course, or maybe things would have gone differently. I'd like to think so. But back then, I thought I'd find someone else once I returned here, and I'd marry and settle down. Soon I'd forget your mother, and that would be that. I have a life here, after all." He drew a deep breath and sighed it out. "Such as it is."

"'Such as it is?'" she echoed with a laugh. "Look at you! You're a member of the ruling council. You have this fine home, this beautiful garden." She looked toward the doorway to the house, where the kitchen maid had brought their breakfast, now growing cold. "Servants."

He flushed. "I don't mean to sound ungrateful for what I have, but it's not all it seems. I never married—never found anyone here who could compare with Claudia. I'm kind of a joke on the governance council. You've seen how Auntie Morgana treats me. I may as well not even be here." He shrugged. "All the gifts I've been given, and still I've never made much of anything of my life. I wish now I might have been a father you'd be proud to have, but all I can give you is an illustrious name. Whatever that's worth."

Katie felt her heart might break. "You're . . . a fine father. Much better than anyone I might have imagined. I only wish I could have known you sooner."

Rom's shoulders slumped, and he trudged back to his seat on the bench. "For what it's worth, I did go back to your world from time to time, as often as I could. I spied on your mother and learned about you, but I never worked up the courage to approach her. After a while, I guess I gave up. I stopped going there and just"—he shrugged—"stayed here."

He looked around at the garden and back to the house. "It's not a bad life, really. I know I disappointed Aunt Morgana when I never married, disappointed a lot of people, really, since I'm the most direct living descendant of Irinia Orcutt. But—"

"But I can help you!" Katie exclaimed. Her heart felt it might burst with pent-up desire. "Please, I really want to."

Rom studied her for a long time. It was as if he might be looking through her skin at her bones, how she was built, the arrangement of her blood vessels. She lifted her chin and said nothing. She waited.

"All right," he said. "Let's talk about how."

Katie remembered how easy it had been to return to her mother's library via Alaric's scrying pool. How easy, and how terrifying. Then, a part of her had still been Mouse, wishing not to be noticed in any way. She gave a small, involuntary shudder. If her mother had discovered her there . . .

But now, it was different. She was going to see her mother on purpose.

Was she ready for this? The knot forming in her stomach argued that she wasn't.

No, if she wasn't ready now, when would she be? She'd worked magic with Alaric and even more magic with Rom. And she was the most direct lineal descendant of the great Irinia Orcutt. She had to get over being Mouse and stand up on her own. She owed it to her forebears and to Alaric, who believed in her, and most of all to herself, to try.

Rom didn't seem nearly as certain as she was. It took two days for him to make his plans and his excuses, and most of all, to steel his courage. Two days in which Katie worried about Alaric, about how he was managing and how the war was going. About whether he missed her anywhere near as much as she missed him.

But on the third morning, Rom met her in the garden, drew a great shaking breath, and announced that he was ready. He fidgeted with his new, dressy clothing, pulling at the thin ruffles at the cuff, and straightening, over and over again, his jaunty cravat.

They left Larippia through a passage near the border between Darimbia and Victoria, a place of towering mountains and dizzying chasms. A thread of mist wound through the mountains, suggesting a river far below, and the breeze that blew up the steep hill carried humidity and the fresh scent of conifers. It was bitingly cold.

Looking out on the scene, Katie shivered and rubbed her arms to warm them. "It's beautiful," she said. "But I don't see how my mother could possibly have brought an army across here."

Rom laughed. "Not without some powerful magic, she couldn't. And I don't think anyone in your world has that much magic. She'd have brought them to Darimbia much farther west, nearer the coast. My people placed this gateway here precisely because it's so rugged and impassable. Not likely to be discovered."

Impassable? "Then how do you—"

"Trust me, I am quite familiar with the jump from here to your mother's castle. I've done it many times."

Katie remembered how Alaric had woven his gateways. It was beyond her, at least for now. But Rom's magic already seemed so familiar, so easy. "Oh, I wasn't doubting that you can, I was just wondering how?"

He took her arm. "You have to know the place where you're planning to emerge, right?"

She nodded.

"Good. Now, this is pure quantum physics. When it comes to the tiniest particles of matter, distance means nothing. You know that when they are attuned, two particles halfway across the world can vibrate together. Across the universe. Space and time don't matter, only affinity does. This is no different. You too can travel back to any place that has significant meaning to you."

Katie continued to nod thoughtfully. "That makes sense, I guess. But how?"

"By sheer will, Katie. Because at some very deep level, you never left. And the place has never left you."

Katie mulled this over. *Never left.* She wasn't sure she liked the idea that she'd never left home. Then she realized that as long as she thought of it as 'home,' Rom was probably right. She shivered. It was getting colder. "But then, what about you? You said my mother set up some kind of barrier you couldn't cross."

He sighed. "That's true. Couldn't, or *wouldn't*, if I'm going to be completely truthful about it. I experienced what you might call a permanent failure of will. But if *you* bring me across, I believe that won't be a problem."

She felt dizzy, almost as if the ground under her feet had just given way and she was now tumbling into the chasm below them.

"Katie? Are you all right?" Rom's voice seemed to come from a distance.

She wanted to say yes, she was fine, nothing to worry about—but somehow, the words wouldn't come out. She shook her head, then managed to say, "I don't know how."

"Oh." He looked abashed. "I see. Tell you what. Let me take you to the spot I used to go to, where her army was camped at the time, and I'll show you how it's done. Once we do it together, it should be pretty obvious. Like the car, right? Once you experience it, you'll know."

Katie brightened. "Like the car? I can do that."

Katie followed Rom's technique without difficulty. It seemed almost natural, like walking. Not that babies don't work hard to learn to walk, of course. She'd watched the servants' children at her mother's castle try again and again to lift their bodies up onto wobbly legs. Every one of them eventually succeeded—and Katie was no baby. She was ready to learn. More than ready.

The effort was surprisingly easy. Katie thought of the complex spell Alaric used to travel from place to place. This was so much simpler, she couldn't wait to show him. She drew in a breath and thinking of Alaric, let it out in a long sigh. She'd go back as soon as she could. But there were things to be done first.

She sequestered Rom in the library, the least used place in her mother's castle. The hard part was next.

Katie would have to see her mother. If her plans were going to succeed, there was no escaping it.

Rom bit his lip and swallowed hard. He looked as anxious as she felt. Maybe more.

She'd have to be strong enough for both of them. She squared her shoulders and gave him what she hoped would look like a confident smile. "Just wait here," she said, "You'll be perfectly safe, people hardly ever come here. I'll be back soon." At least, she hoped she would.

She left the library and paused. How best to approach her mother? She couldn't just barge in, unannounced, into the queen's chambers. The only way she ever went there was if the queen sent for her.

What if her mother wasn't even here? What if she'd gone to Darimbia to check in with her generals?

Darimbia. Katie thought of Alaric and wondered again how he was faring. She really did have to get back to him. She had promised—and she wanted to. She'd do it as soon as she took care of this one thing. Hopefully, her mother was not in Darimbia now.

Katie decided that she'd go to her own chamber, then send one of the servants to request an audience with her mother. But what if her mother wasn't glad to see her? Her breath came faster at the thought.

She forced herself to stay calm. Her mother was the queen, and she had a temper—but she was still her mother. Katie found a maid in the hallway leading to the royal quarters and asked the young woman to notify the queen of her return. She left the door of her room open and paced the length of the room and back, waiting to be summoned.

"Hello, Princess Mouse."

Katie jumped; a moment of pure terror set her heart pounding. She took a deep breath to calm herself and turned.

A freckle-faced page grinned at her. He was probably about fourteen years old. She remembered him; his name was . . . what? Sheldon? No, Shelley. And his smile was not unfriendly. Why had she never noticed this before? Hesitantly, she returned the smile. "Hello. I was just . . . I wanted to see my mother. Is she in her chambers?"

If anything, his smile grew broader. "That's a coincidence. Your mother wants to see you too. I mean"—he looked furtively to his left and right—"her majesty the queen. In the throne room. She said I was to bring you."

So that I don't run away, Katie thought ruefully. *And I might have, once, but I can manage this now.* She checked her dress; it was slightly wrinkled but no more than usual. It would probably pass her mother's inspection. She ran a hand over her hair to smooth it. "All right. Lead on, Shelley."

They walked through a columned arcade and down a flight of stairs, then through a wide hallway ornamented with tapestries and ancient portraits. Katie noted the one tapestry that hung almost to the floor, and that covered an alcove she had hidden in more than once. She thought of her older sisters and wondered whether she'd ever need to hide like that again. She allowed herself a small smile. No, her days of being bullied by them were over.

At the door to the throne room, the page asked her to wait, and he went inside. A moment later, he reappeared and with a wide smile, gestured her in.

Her mother stood by the window, gowned in emerald green silk that was trimmed with a narrow band of pure white fur. Her red hair glistened in a shaft of sunlight, and she wore diamonds that flashed rainbows with her every slight movement.

Katie smoothed her skirt, which now seemed impossibly rumpled, and tucked a stray wisp of hair behind her ear.

"Welcome back, my dear," her mother said. "I hope that horrible man didn't treat you cruelly."

Who, Rom? Cruel? But that couldn't be right, the queen didn't know about Rom yet. She must mean Alaric. "N-no."

"Of course he did," the queen said. "I can't blame you for not wanting to talk about it, but I know." She swept over to Katie and pulled her close into a hug. "My poor darling. I'm so glad you've come home again." She drew back and looked closely at Katie. Katie worried that her hair might be out of place.

"I found the torque I'd locked around his neck," the queen continued, "and the two of you gone. He couldn't have unlocked it himself. So, you must have done it, which means he must have managed to teach you a bit of magic."

"Well, yes, but—"

"But of course he must have been a real trial for you. I'm glad you realized your mistake in time." She drew back from the hug and took Katie's hand. "Come, now, show me what you can do."

"Mother, please, listen. I've brought someone back with me. Some-one with quite a bit of magic, someone you know."

The queen lifted a perfectly arched eyebrow. "Yes? Who?"

"Romulus Orcutt."

Katie's mother turned as pale as the alabaster columns in the throne room. She put a hand to her heart and reached out with the other hand as if looking for something to steady herself. "Who, did you say?"

CHAPTER SIXTEEN

The fighting intensifies

For a moment, Katie was terrified that she'd done something horribly wrong by bringing Rom here without at least asking first. Her heart fluttered. Would her mother punish her? Worse, would she hurt Rom?

But the queen regained her composure and gave Katie a warm smile. "Did you say Romulus Orcutt? How in the world did you ever meet him?"

Katie breathed a sigh of relief. "It's a long story, but, Mother, would you be willing to see him? He's in the library."

The queen paused and looked away, frowning. For a moment, Katie forgot to breathe. Then her mother turned back to Katie, her face painted with a too-perfect smile. "Yes, of course." Her voice was plastered with affection, and she ran her hand along the side of her head, as if adjusting her perfect coiffure. "Really, child, we mustn't leave him in the library a moment longer. What kind of hosts will he think we are?" She hooked her hand behind Katie's elbow, leading her from the throne room.

Two sentries fell into step behind them.

"So, I assume you know about him and . . . me?" the queen asked as they navigated a long hallway. The library was as far from the throne room as it could be, short of being in the private quarters of the castle.

Two more sentries came to attention and saluted as they walked by the formal dining room. Katie peered inside. It was being set up for some kind of dinner, and a distant sweet odor wafting in the air currents from the kitchen beyond hinted at an enticing dessert.

She probably shouldn't be the first to mention her parentage. "Yes, he said he'd had a . . . relationship with you a while ago, but"—how to say this in a neutral way?—"it didn't last. I think he still misses you."

Her mother stopped walking and turned so that they faced each other. "He's your father, Katie." She looked Katie up and down as if seeing her for the first time. "You do resemble him, you know."

And there it was. Her parentage acknowledged at last. Her blood rushed to her face. She opened her mouth to say she knew, then thought better of it. She closed her mouth, speechless.

The queen tilted her head. "Has he . . . asked anything about your magical ability?" She was using that tone she reserved for questions when there was a particular answer she wanted to hear.

Katie grimaced. She didn't relish the detailed questioning she feared might lie ahead, but she wasn't going to lie to her mother. "Yes, we've talked about it."

"And—?"

"And it appears I do magic in the same way he does."

Her mother nodded and resumed walking toward the library. "Good," she said over her shoulder. "Is he teaching you?"

Katie rushed to catch up. She thought about the air car and smiled. "Yes. It's so easy with him."

Her mother's eyes narrowed, and her expression hardened with purposefulness. "I've always loved him, you know. I'm glad you brought him back." She didn't sound the least bit loving—but her mother was a hard woman. Just because she never sounded loving didn't necessarily mean she never loved, somewhere deep down.

They turned the corner, and the door to the library was straight ahead.

Katie opened the door for her mother, then entered the library, closing the door after her.

Rom stood as the women entered. His eyes were wide, his mouth slightly agape, as if the hinges of his jaw weren't quite working right. "Claudia." His voice came out in a whisper, vocal chords forgotten, the word intelligible only by the movement of his lips.

The queen swept over to where he stood and reached out as if to touch him, pausing just short of the actual contact. "Oh, Romulus, I've missed you so much, you can hardly imagine. I'm glad you've returned."

Standing behind her, Katie wished she could see her mother's expression. Rom appeared a bit overwhelmed. A croaking "But . . ." escaped his lips. He raised his arms toward her, and then the two of them were in an embrace.

They kissed.

Katie turned away, thinking of Alaric, wondering where he was. Wondering if he would ever hold her and kiss her in a love that endured as her parents love seemed to have done.

But, no. Alaric didn't love her. She had to remember that, even if she did ache to see him again.

"Katie," her mother said.

Katie looked back at them, her vision slightly clouded with tears.

"Your father and I want to thank you for bringing us back together again. And now, we're all here, one reunited happy family." The queen held out her arm in a welcoming gesture. "Come here, and let me give you a hug."

This was so unlike the mother Katie had fled that she didn't know whether it was the happy ending she'd always dreamed of, or the start of some new and terrible horror story.

Later that afternoon, Katie, Rom, and Claudia sat at a small table that had been set up in the queen's private reception room. They were just finishing a small afternoon snack of duck confit and truffle crackers. Just to hold them over, the queen had said, until the "regrettable" late-night dinner she'd planned to honor one of her generals. Apparently, they would be celebrating some kind of victory in Darimbia—not a final victory, but an important one nevertheless.

Katie hoped that Alaric was all right. More than just *all right*. Though she didn't dare to say it here, she hoped that Alaric might recover from whatever this setback was and win in Darimbia.

Her mother led the conversation with Rom, asking him questions about his life and his interests, hanging on every word. Eventually, she turned to the subject of his magical abilities and laughed sympathetically at his stories of his various adventures and mishaps. "What about traveling to a place where you've never been?" she asked him. "Have you ever done that?"

Rom pulled at his cravat and loosened it, then took another sip of his wine. He coughed, and his face reddened. He cleared his throat.

"Well, not without some kind of link to the place, no," he said. He cleared his throat again.

"Did something go down the wrong way, darling?" Claudia leaned over and stroked him on the back, letting her hand linger. "What kind of a link?"

"Having been to the place is the best, of course. By far the easiest. But if someone is there, someone whom you know quite well, then it might be possible to travel to the place even if you've never been there. Because, you see, you'd really be traveling to that person, and . . . well, yes, it can be done." He gave his throat a final cough and wiped his lips. "That is, *I* can do it. What about you?"

Claudia drew her hand away. "I'm sure . . . with practice . . ."

He gave her a sad look. "Perhaps not. Magical ability travels through the bloodlines, and ours are not the same."

Katie wondered if she could, as Rom said, travel to a place she didn't know simply because she knew well a person who was there. Then she might travel to Alaric and stay with him while her mother and Rom sorted things out. She had promised Alaric she'd return quickly, and it looked like her parents didn't need her around anymore.

"But maybe I can," Katie said. "Can you teach me?"

Her mother gave her an appraising look.

Rom nibbled at his lower lip, a slight frown creasing his brow. Thinking. Considering. Finally, he spoke. "I doubt it."

Katie's shoulders slumped. "I thought . . . I thought I had magic like yours and could learn from you. Why do you think—"

"Oh, no, Katie, it's not that. It's just that I don't know anyone well enough in this world to do it with. Present company excepted, of course."

Alaric? No, probably not. Rom hadn't been with him for very long.

"Is there anything like that you think any of us *can* do?" the queen asked Rom. Was there a hint of anger and frustration in her tone? If there was, Rom appeared not to notice.

Rom looked up and to the side, rubbing his chin. "Well . . ."

Katie and her mother waited, barely breathing.

"There's spirit travel," he said.

"What?" They spoke in unison.

Rom looked abashed. "I haven't done this, haven't even thought about it, in a long time. I'm not sure I still can."

"Of course you can," Claudia said. She sounded annoyed. "Honestly, Romulus, sometimes you are a bit too timid about things."

He shrank back into himself, and Claudia reached out to touch his hand. "I'm sorry, darling. I just meant that it must be like riding a horse. Once you learn how, you never really forget. Do you?"

He took a gulp of his wine. "No, I suppose not."

"What's spirit travel?" Katie asked.

Rom pushed his chair back. "Delicious," he said with a nod toward Claudia. To Katie, he said, "It's a way to travel—in spirit—to a place or person or even to an object with which or whom you have a special connection. But you cannot transport your entire body. You visit like a, well, like a ghost. The person will be unaware of you."

"How do you do that?" Katie asked.

"What's the point of that?" Claudia said at the same time.

Rom looked from one to the other. "No point, I guess. Though you might reach out to the person, or object, you traveled to, and affect it in some small way."

Katie thought about reaching out and touching Alaric, and he'd never know. Or maybe he would have a slight sense of her being near. She smiled. "Can you teach me?"

"Yes, of course," Rom said, returning Katie's smile.

"And me?" said the queen.

Rom looked at her sadly, and with a minute sideways motion of his head said, "I can try, but—"

Claudia pushed back from the table with such force that her chair clattered over backwards. "Never mind," she said, "It sounds worthless anyway."

Dinner that evening was an elaborate affair, formal attire required. The general who had driven the Darimbian rebels back almost to Westland's border, wore his full-dress uniform, replete with medals and ribbons. He sat, as appropriate for a guest of honor, at Claudia's right, with two of his commanders next to him. Rom sat at her left, and Claudia had insisted that Katie sit next to Rom, at the head of the table.

Katie wasn't comfortable there, particularly as her sisters, farther down one of the sides, seemed to alternate between glaring at her, pointing at her, and giggling. It looked like they were making jokes at her expense.

But the food was good—appetizers of pheasant rolls with wild mushrooms and trout with capers and lemon. And Rom seemed happy. That was the important thing.

Claudia paused in her conversation with the general and turned to Rom. "I'm so glad you're back here at last," she said. She lifted her glass—not the expansive public gesture she'd made earlier when she'd toasted the general, but a smaller, more private gesture. "To you, my darling," she said. "I only wish you'd come back years ago."

"So do I," Rom said. He clinked glasses with her, and they both sipped. "I should have tried harder, much sooner. So much of our lives have gone by alone, when we could have been together."

Claudia smiled at him.

Katie wondered if her story with Alaric would unfold the same way. He'd asked her to marry him, but she'd said no. Had she been wrong to reject him? She didn't think so. He'd only asked her because of his oath with her mother, not out of love. And besides, she wanted to see more of the world. What better time to do that than now, when she was still unattached?

But what if she returned to Alaric after a few years of travel, only to find he'd fallen in love with someone else? Married, perhaps. He'd told Katie she was the only one of her mother's daughters he would marry—but if she went away? Given his oath, he might have to marry one of her sisters. Maybe he'd see them with a more open mind. He might be dazzled by Stefania, for example. Katie looked over at Stefania, who was looking at her and, with a hand concealing her mouth from Katie's view, leaning toward Mercuria, whispering something that made the two of them giggle. They might already be planning some way to steal Alaric's affections.

The bite of pheasant Katie was eating suddenly tasted like ash, and she couldn't swallow it. Her stomach felt like it was full of clay, not food.

All she needed was to throw up now in front of her mother and Rom and her sisters. Katie hurriedly excused herself and left the room, her appetite gone.

The day after the battle, Alaric had moved his forces to a more defensible location. The following day, he'd worked with them to shore up their defenses. The resistance fighters were clever and resourceful. They'd come up with several inventive ideas that didn't involve magic, some of which were quite good, so the situation was far from hopeless. The river patrol, for example, extended the security of their encampment while involving only a few extra sentries. But much of the defense work involved magic—devising illusions of walls and barriers where none existed, for example, and creating small portals through which an enemy soldier might fall, only to reappear in a nearby prison area. Marco tried to help with the magic as much as he could, but there was only so much he could do.

In the early morning of the next day, mist hung over the river, dulling the sound of water flowing by, and coating the far bank in gentle gray. Alaric's head still ached from his extensive use of magic, and he rubbed his hand across his forehead in a vain attempt to relieve the pain. He couldn't tell whether the mist was the remnant of yesterday's magic or a simple weather phenomenon.

I've been working too hard, doing too much. At this rate, it won't be long until I'm burned out. But Alaric couldn't pull back.

Katie could have helped, of course, if she were here. But she had chosen not to return with him, and Alaric knew it would be wrong of him to try to influence her decisions. He hoped she was doing well, wherever she was. Still in Larippia probably, with that scoundrel Romulus. With every passing day, it seemed increasingly likely the Larippian had wooed and won Katie's affections. Alaric grimaced, then forced himself to put the thought aside. No time for that now.

He focused on the terrain. The mist was starting to thin, and he wanted to investigate a location that the river scouts had identified as a potential hiding spot for a surprise-attack force.

At a bend in the river, Alaric stopped. The place looked familiar. It seemed to grab hold of his heart, and twist. A wave of sorrow swept over him.

He paused to collect himself, then moved aside some low-hanging branches and entered a small clearing bounded by woods on three sides and the river on the other. A rock almost as large as a person stood in the river near the bank, and the water gurgled as it meandered around it, a pleasant counterpoint to the rushing sound of the river's flow.

The rock.

Without doubt, this was the place where, six years ago, Alaric's father had died.

The memory of that day came rushing back, vivid and fresh. Alaric would normally have been in the palace with his advisors, handling the routine issues of governance. But he'd gone to see his father in Darimbia the previous evening, when his father had revealed a risky plan and made other arrangements with him. In the morning, they'd been camped in a relatively advantageous position, facing Claudia's army. They'd been there for two weeks, at a stalemate in which the two forces engaged almost daily, the results inconclusive. This day boded to be another of the same.

"I don't want to do this anymore," his father had told him. "Too many people have died already. Too many innocent people. This fight is between Claudia and me, and that's the way we should decide it."

The king had sent a proposal to Claudia: a one-on-one battle of magic against magic. The defeated mage's army would surrender the position. Just the position, the king had assured his advisors and his son Alaric, not the war. And Claudia had accepted.

Neither Alaric nor the queen's daughters had been allowed to witness the battle, but when his father lost, the moan that went up throughout his army and the Darimbian volunteers that fought with them was unmistakable. His father had been brought back to camp on a litter, his body a mass of sores.

Still alive, the king had ordered a retreat to this spot, perilously near the Westland border, the war all but lost.

Along with the doctors who traveled with the army, Alaric had done what he could to try to heal his father's wounds. But they were magical in nature, and Alaric could not unravel the knots of the spell that had caused the festering sores.

Two days later, his father was dead, and Alaric, only twenty years old, was the king.

Now, his forces had been pushed back again to the river's edge, with Westland only a few kilometers away. Should he try the same daring move as his father had done? Six years older now, Claudia might be weaker. But the last few days had been grueling, and Alaric was not back to his full strength. Was he willing to pay the price of failure?

He thought of Katie. He would never consider asking her to risk herself in a battle against her mother, but her presence here would be a comfort to him, and a source of strength. He didn't want to put her in direct danger, but he wished he could see her again. He wasn't ready to die.

No, he decided. He would not challenge Claudia directly. There were a few other stratagems he could try first. The situation wasn't desperate enough for a one-on-one challenge. Not yet.

He'd find some other way.

CHAPTER SEVENTEEN

Katie learns more magic

The next morning, Rom sat with Katie in one of the queen's smaller receiving rooms, their two chairs pulled side by side. She nervously wiped her hands on her skirt, then straightened the fabric, afraid she might have wrinkled it. "How was the dinner—the rest of it?" she asked Rom.

He looked away. "I don't know. I can't figure your mother out."

You and me both.

"She was so loving to me early in the evening," Rom said. He pulled at his cravat to loosen it. "But by the time dessert came around, she was ignoring me completely, absorbed in talking with General Shoken. It was like I wasn't even there."

"Well, the dinner *was* in his honor," Katie offered.

"Of course, yes, but . . ." Rom shook his head. "That must be it. Never mind, Katie, it's not your problem. Are we still on for this lesson in spirit travel?"

Katie brightened. Learning magic from Rom was so easy, as if she'd always been meant to learn it this way. "Oh, yes!"

"So, is there anyone in particular you'd want to . . . visit?" Rom asked.

Katie took a deep breath. "Alaric?" She wanted to do more than visit. She wanted to go back to him as she'd promised, but how could she? She was the one who had brought Rom here, and now it sounded like he might still need her help. Her mother had been so angry at him yesterday afternoon, and what he had just said about last night worried her.

"Alaric?" Rom echoed. "But I thought you wanted to learn spirit travel. You know Alaric well enough to go to him in person, don't you?"

"Oh, no, I mean, yes. I suppose I might." She'd watched Alaric weave a portal a couple of times, but the process was still mysterious. She wasn't at all sure she was capable of it. Then again, if Rom had a different way of traveling in person, she wanted to learn it. Only not right now. "But for now let's just do spirit travel, all right? So that I can learn it." *Besides, if I go there in person, I might not come back here, and I'm not ready to leave yet. I brought you here, so it's my job to make sure everything's all right between you and my mother before I go.*

"All right." He gave her an affectionate smile. "In that case, we'll need something of his, something that can serve as a focus for the travel."

Katie didn't understand. "A focus?"

"Yes. It would be something that has enough . . . enough of *him* in it that it will still resonate with him, in the way I told you about earlier."

"I don't know, I don't really have anything of his. I still have the clothes he gave me when I went to his home a while ago. I could go and get those."

"His clothes?"

"No, I think they belonged to one of the Darimbian fighters."

Alaric frowned, then shook his head slowly. "Not good enough."

Katie fell silent for a moment. Then she had an idea. "What about the room where he lived . . . where he was imprisoned when he was here? That might still have some of his clothes in it."

Rom's smile was almost radiant. "That's perfect. More of him will be there than just his clothes. Do you think we might do this in that room?"

Katie jumped up, eager to visit the place where Alaric had lived, to experience him again, even vicariously. "Yes, of course. Let's go."

Rom stood. "Perhaps we ought to ask your mother—"

Katie's heart gave a little skip of alarm. The less her mother was involved in anything to do with Alaric, the better. "Oh, no, no, no. Itll be fine." She certainly hoped it would.

Rom followed her down the corridor and up three flights of stairs to the small tower room.

She paused on the top landing. No guard sat in the chair by the door, and there were no empty bottles of her mother's wine to indicate anything amiss. But when she looked closely, the floorboards seemed to be stained a bit darker near the chair, perhaps spilled wine not cleaned up soon enough.

She opened the door to the room. It was unchanged, except, of course, for its missing occupant. Katie breathed in the air, which was a bit stale but still smelled faintly of Alaric's presence, spices with a distant hint of ocean breeze. She felt a pang of loneliness.

"He lived here, did he?" Rom asked, then added without waiting for an answer, "Very modest quarters."

"My mother was holding him prisoner," she retorted with a flash of anger. "He has a whole palace of his own back in Westland."

Rom gave her a conciliatory smile. "Of course. I meant only . . . well, no matter. Shall we get started?"

Katie ran her hands through her hair, then suddenly aware she was only tangling it up, she smoothed it. "Yes, let's."

"Is there anything here that's particularly Alaric's?"

The book he'd had here would be best. The man did love books. But of course, he'd brought that book out with him, the one thing he'd taken. She looked around and found a small pile of clothing neatly folded and stored under the bed. She pulled out a dark blue tunic with stars and comets embroidered on it in silver and gold thread. This made her smile. How like Alaric! "Will this do?"

"Perfect," Rom said. "Now, sit here beside me"—he sat on the narrow bed and patted the place next to him—"and let's begin."

Katie took the indicated seat, her heart quickening its pace.

Rom cleared his throat. "The thing that makes this particular magic work is the resonance of all particles in the universe with all other particles, though in some cases that resonance is very weak and indirect." He blushed. "But of course, I've told you that before. Now, the trick is to find the resonance that is uniquely Alaric's, and lock onto it." He took the tunic from her, crushing the fabric between his two hands. He closed his eyes and breathed deeply, letting out the breath in a long "Ahhh . . ."

Katie could feel Rom searching, but Rom hadn't known Alaric for very long, and so his search lacked a certain definition. It was too vague. She, on the other hand, could almost picture Alaric, could almost reach out and touch him. She took hold of the tunic and breathed in. There was a hint of Alaric's masculine smell, vanilla and myrrh, a slight hint of the sea. Time and distance no longer separated Alaric's presence here from wherever he was.

And then she could almost see him. In a tent somewhere. Not a lot of light crept in, and Alaric stood, his back to her, looking at a map spread out on a table. A lamp lit the table a bit more than the rest of the tent. He was hunched over, perhaps trying to make out some detail in the map. How handsome he was, his brow furrowed, deep in thought. But he looked so tired.

Katie reached out to him, then saw that her own hand was nearly transparent. She gasped and turned to Rom. He stood beside her, as transparent as she was. "Are we really here?"

"Yes," Rom said. "And no."

Alaric did not turn at the sound of their voices, but continued scrutinizing the map.

"Then is this a . . . a vision?"

"A true one, yes," he said. "What we are seeing is real, but he cannot see or hear us."

Alaric rubbed his eyes and stared at the map. Though hidden by the deep woods, the place where they were camped was still not as secure as he would have liked, and much too close to his own border. But how to turn this situation around?

The hair on the back of his neck prickled. It felt almost as if someone had come into the tent behind him. But the entry flap was in front of him, not behind. They'd have to have crawled under . . . He turned to look.

No one was there, of course. How could there be? But for some reason he thought of Katie. How pleasant it would be if she were there, in the tent with him. Perhaps she'd have a different way of looking at the location problem he was trying to unravel. Or at least, she'd be a good sounding board. More than that. Katie was such a kind and generous spirit. The truth was that Alaric wanted her near him just because he wanted her.

Could this be love?

He reached out a hand, pretending she was there, pretending he could touch her. And he almost felt as if he could.

When Alaric extended his hand, Katie could almost feel his touch. She reached out and took his hand in hers.

Tried to take it, that is, for her ghost-hand went right through his.

Then Rom was by her side, pulling her, bringing her back to herself. "No, he said, "that's too much. You have to be careful how much of a presence you're creating. Let's back away." Suddenly, they were sitting together in her mother's castle.

"You almost materialized there," he said. "I didn't think you wanted to do that."

Katie brushed a tear from her eye, hoping Rom didn't notice. "Not yet," she said, relieved that her voice didn't waver. Then she realized what he'd said. "Materialize? I could do that, this way?"

"Not normally," he said. "Not unless you're extremely drawn to the person or place you're visiting. Are you and Alaric . . ." He searched her face intently. Whatever he saw there made him drop his question.

She suddenly felt an almost overwhelming need to get out of this room, away from everything that reminded her so much of Alaric. Loving this man who didn't love her could only lead to trouble. "Please don't tell my mother," she said.

✦⊷————⊶———⊷✦

Once again, Katie and Rom shared a late-afternoon drink with her mother. They sat on a small terrace overlooking the castle courtyard, just off one of the queen's private reception rooms. And once again, her mother was all honey and sugar.

"How are you feeling, darling?" her mother asked. "I was so devastated that you had to leave the banquet early, before the accolades began."

Katie didn't know whether she'd rather her mother call her "darling," or just go back to calling her "Mouse." At least "Mouse" seemed an honest expression of her mother's feelings. "I feel better now," she said. "Thank you. I don't know what came over me last night."

"Perhaps something you ate disagreed with you?"

Perhaps it wasn't something she ate, but rather something she had thought, that had disagreed with her, but she wasn't going to get into that. "Yes, that must be it," she said. "But at least Rom was able to stay."

The queen eyed Rom, considering. "Yes, at least that. Romulus, dear, I hope you didn't feel I was neglecting you."

Rom cleared his throat, coughed, and took a sip of his wine. "No, no, not at all. Of course you had to pay attention to the general. Quite understandable." He glanced at Katie and gave her a surreptitious wink.

It took a bit of effort for her to hold back a smile.

Claudia swirled the wine in her glass, studying the color. "I was looking for one of the bottles of my most special wine for this occasion, but apparently, it's already been used, or . . . perhaps misplaced. I hope this is satisfactory."

Missing bottles of a special wine? Katie thought about the guard she'd given a few bottles of wine to, it seemed so long ago now. Alaric had said it was very good wine. It was probably best not to say anything about that now. Besides, Katie was no wine expert, but this wine seemed excellent to her.

Rom nodded. "Oh yes, quite satisfactory."

"So, did you two do that spirit travel thing you were talking about yesterday?"

"Yes, we did," Rom said. Katie nodded.

"And how did it go?"

"Quite well," Rom said, before Katie could intervene.

"You were successful?"

"Oh, yes," he said, "beyond our—"

Katie kicked him under the table. "We managed it for a short time, but then we were pulled back here."

Claudia studied her daughter for a moment, then turned her attention back to Rom. She took his hand. "A short time may be all we need."

"For *what*?" Katie asked.

"To prevent that villain Alaric from taking over Darimbia, of course." She gave Katie a narrow-eyed look, then stood and walked behind Rom, and began to massage his neck and shoulders.

Rom moaned with pleasure.

"He's not a villain, Mother," Katie said. She wasn't sure she'd have dared stand up to her mother like this before she left. Was that only a few weeks ago? "He has as much a claim to Darimbia as you do. I mean, as we do."

"But darling, that's not true at all. Darimbia was mine when I first became queen. Alaric's father stole it from me. I'm only trying to reclaim what is legitimately mine." Claudia gave Katie a warm, almost pitying smile. "I should have seen to your education better. Fortunately, you're still young. It's never too late to learn."

Confused, Katie looked at Rom, hoping he might clarify the situation. But he sat with his eyes closed, a soft moan occasionally escaping his slightly open mouth as the queen continued to stroke his back.

"But the Darimbian freedom fighters—"

"Besides," her mother continued, pressing hard at the spot where Rom's neck joined his back, "he has forsworn his oath to me, and so now fate and the oathstone are on my side." She moved her thumbs outward and pressed again. "You're with me in this, Romulus dear, aren't you? He ran off with your daughter—with *our* daughter—but refused to marry her."

Rom gave an unintelligible groan.

"Mother, no, that's not what happened. He *did* ask me to marry him. I was the one who refused."

"But darling, in that you only displayed good sense. Of course you refused, he's so much older than you."

Eight years didn't seem like that much. Not between her and Alaric.

"Besides," her mother continued, digging her thumbs into each joint of Rom's spine as she moved her hands down his back, "he was supposed to marry one of the older girls, closer to his age."

"Only because they had magic at the time, and I didn't," Katie persisted. She'd never stood up to her mother for this long, and her stomach was beginning to clench tight.

Claudia relaxed her grip on Rom's back and drew herself up. "There, then. You see, he is forsworn, and so it is our right and duty to defeat him."

Katie felt close to tears at the idea of anything happening to Alaric. "I . . . I don't want to hurt him."

Claudia walked over to Katie and put her hand on her shoulder. "Of course not, darling. We'll only disable him a little bit. Right, Romulus? Just long enough for our army to claim the territory."

Rom looked uncertain. "I don't see how we can disable him without hurting him in some way. Or worse."

Katie's heart began racing. She stood abruptly. "No! No hurting him."

"Now, darling," the queen said, pulling Katie into an embrace, "of course we won't hurt him any more than absolutely necessary. In fact, you can come along and see for yourself. Maybe even help out a little, if it means less pain for him. Fair enough?"

Rom cleared his throat. "Of course we will not kill him, and we will not permanently disable him. I cannot. We Larippians do not kill. When we severed ourselves from this world, we disabled that part of the magic for good and forever. Can you imagine the chaos in a closed world like ours, full of magicians, if there was ever a feud?" He shuddered. "No, I won't kill him—but I can slow him down."

Katie looked from one of them to the other. They were both watching her. Her mother had a good point about Darimbia being hers to begin with. How could she, Katie, be so selfish as to sacrifice her mother's happiness for her own childish desires? But what about the starvation and deaths in Darimbia when her mother had been in control? This was a complicated issue. She wished she could discuss it with Alaric.

Alaric! They'd talked about disabling him. That suggested they might hurt him if it was necessary. Perhaps she should come along so that she could make sure Alaric would be all right. She didn't owe him more than that, did she? It wasn't as if they were in love and were going to marry. "You did say you don't want to hurt him, right?"

"Absolutely," the queen said. "No more than necessary. We're not out for vengeance. Romulus and I are only going to work together to win back what's rightfully mine. Ours. Besides, this will be a good opportunity for you to learn some more of Romulus's magic."

Katie couldn't argue with that.

"We will win in Darimbia," the queen said, "and Romulus will be my consort. He will rule Darimbia on my behalf, and this is as it should be. Right, Romulus darling?"

He looked uncertain. "Your consort, you say?"

Claudia looked down and tucked her hands behind her back, suddenly the soul of modesty. "If you will have me."

Katie stared wide-eyed at the two of them. Her parents united!

Rom stood transfixed, his jaw hanging open. Not a sound came out. Then he said, "Yes, yes, of course. I've dreamed of nothing else."

"We can figure out how to kill that villain Alaric later," said the queen.

"No!" Katie cried out. "I don't want you killing him, not now, and not later."

Her mother gave her a beatific smile.

The next morning, Katie and Rom and Claudia climbed the stairs to the tower room that had served as Alaric's prison. "I still don't see why we have to come up here to look for Alaric," Claudia complained. "There are so many more comfortable places in the palace."

"But this place is full of Alaric's presence, so if you want to look for him, this is the best place to do it," Rom explained. "We could take some of his clothing and go somewhere else and give it a try, but here is where we'll most likely succeed." He sat down on the narrow bed and patted the place beside him to indicate a seat for Claudia.

He was being exceedingly patient, almost more than Katie could stand. She rolled her eyes and sat with a definitive thud. Why couldn't her mother just accept the explanation and get on with it?

"Go on, then," the queen said to Rom. She pulled her skirts smooth and sat with an expression of distaste, crossing her arms over her chest.

Rom cleared his throat. "Very well." He handed Katie the shirt she'd held yesterday, the one with the stars and comets. She bunched the shirt up and held it close to her heart. How dear Alaric was! She could hardly wait to see him again.

Rom took another shirt and held one side of it out to Claudia. "We'll share this," he said. "I don't think—that is, I'm not sure your magic is the kind that will do this trick, but if we both hold onto it together, perhaps we'll stay connected, and you'll be able to see or hear some of what happens."

"Don't underestimate me," Claudia said with a warning glare. But she took hold of the shirt's sleeve.

"Now, feel his presence," Rom said. He closed his eyes and lowered his chin. He took a deep breath. "Follow the linkage in every particle of this shirt, and you will find him there."

It took Katie less than a moment. She'd been aching to see Alaric again.

Alaric was no longer in his tent. He was outside by the bank of a river, and a dozen resistance fighters were gathered around him, two of them out of breath and disheveled, all of them agitated, talking over one another. Alaric was a little more stooped than Katie remembered. He gestured them to silence, then spoke slowly, with long pauses as he gave commands. He looked old and tired.

Katie's heart went out to him. She wished she could be there to help him, but what was about to happen could only make things worse. Hopefully, not too much worse, and then she'd come back and help him, as she'd promised. "They promised not to hurt you," she whispered. He didn't seem to hear her.

A moment later, Rom appeared beside her. He was so transparent that, in the sunlight, it was hard to see him. Katie looked at her own arms, and she too was nearly invisible. She scanned the area nearby. "Where's my mother?" she asked Rom.

He glanced around. "Not here . . . exactly. As I suspected, she can't make the jump."

"I can hear you, Romulus," said the queen's voice, "but I can't see you. Where are you?"

"We are close to Alaric," Rom said.

"I can't *see*," the queen complained. "Bring me along like you promised."

Katie and Rom looked at each other. He shrugged. "Dearest Claudia," he said, "I am bringing as much of you as I can, but my magic is different from yours. Just close your eyes and listen in."

The queen muttered a curse word, then said, "Very well. Proceed."

Rom loosened his cravat and took a step forward.

Alaric turned to go back to his tent. His spies had returned with the unwelcome news that the queen's forces were on full alert and planning to attack, probably the following day. He'd gone over the options both with his army commanders and with the leaders of the Darimbian resistance. The options were few. Some were worse than others, and none were good.

From a strong position in Darimbia, they'd been driven back nearly to the Westland border. Preventing the Victorian army from entering Westland had therefore become the top priority for the commanders of Alaric's regular army. The Darimbian resistance fighters were disgruntled, Marco chief among them. They had argued, and then, under pressure, they'd brainstormed a few quite wild ideas.

The strategy they'd settled on combined a daring defense of Darimbia by the resistance, fighting from treetops and marshes and bogs, along with an attempt by Alaric's army to lure Claudia's army across the river into Westland. There, reinforcements would be hidden and waiting, and would be brought in to surround the invaders.

The odds of success weren't high, but it was the best they could come up with. Alaric smiled to himself. His fighters were good people, all of them. He only wished there was a way to spare them the inevitable injuries and deaths.

If only he weren't so tired. Surely, he must be recovered by now from his magical exertions two days ago. He shook his head to clear it, pulled back the flap of his tent, and went in.

In the dim light, Katie stood, along with that lowlife Romulus, and . . . someone else he couldn't make out very clearly.

He blinked, and they were gone. An illusion, perhaps caused by the sudden change in lighting combined with his own weakened state.

Not gone, no. They were gone from sight, but something here in the tent was far from normal. He felt Katie too strongly for this to be an illusion.

And yet—he couldn't see her. The tent was empty.

"Katie?"

He hoped she wasn't in danger.

Rom waved his not-quite-transparent hand, and a scarf appeared in it. It looked like the cravat he was wearing, only fainter.

Katie mirrored his motion, trying to learn it. She, too, held a scarf. It was like gossamer, so fine and delicate it hardly seemed to exist at all, so weightless it almost floated in the air. If she let go of it, she was sure it would vanish.

"Let's see how this works," Rom said, moving around behind Alaric.

"What?" asked the queen's voice. "What works?"

"I'm going to weaken him a bit, as we said."

"How?"

Rom heaved a sigh. "By reducing his air supply, with a simulacrum of my cravat around his neck."

"What?" Katie cried out. "Don't hurt him. You said you wouldn't."

"Just a little . . . temporarily," Rom said. "Watch what I'm doing. You can learn how to influence the material world, even in spirit form." He wound the cravat around Alaric's neck and began to tighten it.

Alaric gagged. His hands went to his throat. He tried to wrap his fingers under the cravat, but they went right through it. He took a rasping breath.

Katie almost let go of the scarf she was holding. "Rom, no," she cried out. "That's enough."

"I heard him choking," Claudia's voice said. "That's good. Do it more. Harder."

Rom tightened his chokehold.

"No!" Katie said, her alarm growing. She put her hands over Rom's, her scarf all but forgotten. This time she wasn't copying him. She tried her best to pull him away.

Nothing happened.

Alaric fell to his knees.

Alaric couldn't breathe. His lungs struggled against the blockage, but not a thimbleful of air came in. *Is this what it feels like to die?* Instinctively, he reached to work his fingers around whatever was blocking his throat.

Nothing was there.

It could only be magic—but there was no one here powerful enough to do this to him, unless . . . unless . . .

It had to be Claudia. He looked around but could see no trace of her. He'd always considered invisibility to be impossible, but could she have somehow mastered it?

In the dim light of the tent, though, someone did seem to be there. He squinted, but the image didn't sharpen. He turned his head and used his peripheral vision.

Katie? Could it be Katie? He had sensed her presence in the tent just moments ago.

No, surely Katie would not wish to harm him. Not Katie.

But the faint image of Katie had her hands on some kind of band around his neck, and she was pulling. He had to face facts. He had taken Katie into his heart and into his home, only to be betrayed. Only to have given her the means to destroy him.

Worse—if Katie wanted him to die this badly, he wasn't sure he wanted to live.

Chapter Eighteen

The truth will out

"What's happening there?" Claudia demanded. "Have you ki—disabled him yet?"

"Not... yet..." Rom struggled against Katie's hold on him, but he continued to tighten his scarf around Alaric's neck. "But soon. Katie, let go of me."

"Katie," said her mother, "what are you doing?"

Tears stung at Katie's eyes, equal parts anger and frustration. "You said you wouldn't hurt him!"

"Not"—Rom's teeth were gritted with his effort—"permanently."

"There, dear, see? Once you and Romulus get rid o—I mean, once you *temporarily* disable Alaric, my army will deal with the rest of the traitors. And the war will end. Isn't that the best thing in the long run?"

In the room where the three of them physically sat, Katie's mother must have leaned close to her, for her voice came out as a barely audible whisper. "Men are not to be trusted. When you master Romulus's magic, we won't need *him* anymore, either. With magic like his, you shall be my heir."

Katie was aghast. Had her mother never intended to marry Rom, only to use him? She tightened her grip on Rom's arm. As soon as Rom disabled Alaric, or worse, would he be her mother's next target?

How could she, Katie, live with the deaths of these two men on her conscience—her father and the man she loved.

The man she loved. Yes, she now saw clearly, she did love Alaric, even if he didn't love her. Even if he never forgave her for her role in this attack.

She would not, would *not* continue to participate in destroying him. "Rom, stop!" She pulled Rom's arm as hard as she could, forcing his chokehold loose.

"Ignore her, Romulus, dear," said Claudia's voice.

With a thrust of his elbow, Rom dislodged Katie's hand from his arm.

Katie gasped and stumbled backwards. She watched in horror as Alaric slumped to his knees. *This is my fault. I wanted to help him, but instead I've brought him to harm. He would be better off if we'd never met.* She stifled a sob. *It doesn't matter that he doesn't love me. I love him, and he needs me now. I'm going to help him even if I die trying. But how?*

Whatever magic she had learned from Rom was probably much less than he himself possessed. Anything she did, he would no doubt be able to counter. But she couldn't just stand there and do nothing. She looked at the gauzy scarf in her hand, then at Rom, still pulling on the scarf he'd wound around Alaric's throat. Then back at the scarf she held. She took a deep breath and willed herself to be strong. She made a loop of the scarf, and threw it around Rom's neck. And she pulled.

Rom staggered back. He loosened his grip on the scarf around Alaric's neck to free his hand, then clawed at the scarf around his own neck.

Katie felt tears flowing down her cheeks, and her breath came in sobs, but she kept pulling. "Leave him alone," she cried.

"Katie, stop," came Claudia's voice.

Rom made a grunting noise but seemed unable to form words. Then he was gone, his connection between the two locations broken. Katie's spirit remained in the tent, staring helplessly at Alaric's form slumped on the ground.

In the room in her mother's castle where the three of them sat, someone started shaking Katie. It jostled her connection with Alaric's tent, which vibrated unsteadily.

Alaric was alive. Still on the floor, he shook his head and struggled to get to his feet. He looked right at her.

"I'm sorry," Katie whispered.

Someone slapped her face painfully, and in that instant, Alaric's tent vanished. Katie was back in the room with her mother and Rom. The room seemed to wobble, and the edges of her vision grew dark. She fainted.

"We had him!"

It was Claudia's voice, cold and angry.

Katie blinked and then opened her eyes.

Her mother stood over her, arms akimbo, frowning. "That's right, don't pretend you fainted. We had him, and you ruined it. What kind of daughter are you?"

Rom sat more upright. "Now, Claudia, please—"

Claudia ignored him. "You could have inherited all of Victoria and Darimbia too, but no. You had to ruin it all. I swear, Katie, if you keep giving in to this useless sentimentality, you'll never amount to anything."

Katie flinched and covered her eyes. At this point in a monologue like this, she would normally be crying—but somehow, she wasn't. The vision of Alaric, weak and slumped on the floor swam before her eyes. "You were going to kill him."

"Now, now," Rom said. "Your mother wasn't even there."

Katie turned on him. "She was using you to do it. That comes to the same thing." Turning back to her mother, she straightened her spine. "I will not let you kill him," she said, amazed at her own firmness.

"What?" The queen's face flushed red, and she fisted her hands. "You won't—let—me? I'll show you who won't let whom do what. Romulus and I will take care of this matter. And what will you do to stop us? You don't have a fraction of our power—of either one of us, much less both of us together."

Her mother was right, of course. As always. Katie wanted to scream. To cry. No, what she really wanted was to hide, just melt into the wall and disappear. But that wasn't possible anymore because if she went away and didn't try her best, however inadequate, to help Alaric, then he would die.

"You are banished to your room," her mother continued. She raised her hands and shook back her sleeves as if in preparation for a magic spell.

Katie knew what was coming. She'd been the victim of it before, growing up. In a moment, she'd feel a compulsion to go to her room, a need too strong to resist. But if she did resist it somehow, her mother would have one of the sentries escort her there and stand by the door to make sure she didn't leave.

And while Katie was in her room, her mother and Rom would try their best to finish Alaric off. More than try. Alaric was seriously weakened. The two of them were highly likely to succeed.

Katie couldn't let that happen. It was her fault Alaric was in this danger, and she was the only one who could protect him now. Against Rom's kind of magic, she was his only hope. She stood, tense, fists clenched, refusing to cry. "Yes, Mother."

Hadn't Rom said that she could use the sympathetic properties of particles of matter to travel between places? She'd done it now in spirit, but hadn't he said her attachment was so strong she could go there in person?

She needed a safe place where she could focus without interruption.

Katie turned and strode to her room.

Of course a sentry followed, no doubt to make sure she was doing as her mother had ordered. Down the stairway she raced, and along the arcade facing the residential courtyard. The sentry's footsteps were loud, no time to turn and look. Katie opened her door, entered her room, and slammed the door shut.

She took a deep breath, then another. The soldier's footsteps stopped outside the door. He would remain right there in front of the threshold to prevent her from leaving.

Katie smiled with grim satisfaction. She would not stay inside, not if she could help it. Maybe she had lost Alaric forever, but that wasn't important now. Since he didn't love her, she'd never had him to lose. Regardless, she was going to help him because it was the right thing to do. She'd gotten him into this mess, so she would do whatever she could to get him out of it. And, as Alaric himself would no doubt say, doing the right thing is mightier than magic.

She was going to Alaric, going to help him stand up to her mother. She sat on her bed, and the blanket chest caught her eye. Dolly! The doll was still at Alaric's palace. She felt a pang, a desire to hold the doll close, to feel protected against the entire world of magic. To be young and innocent, to be taken care of and sheltered. But Dolly was not what she needed, not now. Now Katie needed to use her more of her magic than she'd ever used before. She turned away from the chest.

She reached inside herself to feel her connection with Alaric, to feel it in every particle of her being. From her fingertips to her heart, she wanted to be with him. Oh, how she wanted him! She imagined his touch, fingertips on her cheek, his grey eyes ablaze with the silver of magic and of desire. His kiss.

And, between one heartbeat and the next, she was in his tent with him.

Weakened, Alaric struggled to stand. He made it to his knees but barely had the strength to pull enough air into his lungs. He stopped to catch his breath. What had just happened?

He looked around. No one was there. But hadn't he seen Katie just a moment ago? Not Katie herself in person, but a phantasm that looked like her. Katie and . . . maybe . . . someone else. Had that been real, or had it been an illusion of some kind?

Katie and that other person had tried to kill him—Katie or . . . or what? Or who?

Yet, how could that be? The evidence was strong: his throat was still sore, and he felt dizzy and disoriented. He was having so much trouble breathing that he couldn't quite manage to stand. He sat back on the ground.

He'd never be able to weave any kind of magic in this condition, and without that magic, his people would be sore pressed to hold their ground against the enemy forces. He needed help. "Marco!" The word came out raspy, and no louder than a whisper.

Of course Marco didn't come. No one outside the tent could have heard that weak cry. Alaric gathered his breath to call again. His throat was sore, tangible evidence of that intangible attack. Gingerly, he rubbed his fingers over his throat, half expecting them to come away bloody. But his throat didn't hurt to the touch, and his fingers remained clean.

In a burst of air quite different from that in his tent—air that smelled of faint perfume and old leather and cedar—Katie appeared.

The real Katie, not at all like the dim phantasm he'd just seen.

"Alaric?" she said. "Are you all right?" She looked worried, almost on the edge of tears.

If she'd just tried to kill him, why would she be worried about him now? None of this made any sense. "I . . ." he said, but then couldn't think of what to say next. He ran his hand over his face and tried again to stand. He made it to his knees before he stumbled.

She came closer and reached out to him. "Let me help you." A single tear ran down her cheek. "I am so sorry."

His heart lurched. For a bare instant, he shrank from her touch, then made himself stop. She looked anything but violent. She looked so loving and so hurt that he wanted to fold her into his arms. "You're sorry? You were here just before, weren't you? You—" *Tried to kill me.* He couldn't say it. "What happened, exactly?"

Emotions flitted across her face too fast to read. "You saw me? Here?"

Alaric nodded. He reached for, and found, the closest camp chair and lifted himself far enough to sit in it. "I saw you."

She shook her head. "No, that's not supposed to happen. He said it wasn't possible. He said we were only here in spirit, and you wouldn't know."

This statement raised entirely too many questions, some of them decidedly unpleasant. Alaric started with the easiest and most obvious one. "Who's 'he'?"

"Rom."

He must have given her a blank look, for she added, "Romulus Orcutt."

Alaric felt the mention of the man's name like a stab wound to his heart, a wound that was fresh and still bleeding. "Rom from Larippia. Your . . ." He almost said, "Lover," but he couldn't. It was as if voicing the thought would give it power. "The man you left me for."

A look of pure anguish crossed her face. "No! I mean, yes, Rom Orcutt, but no, I never left you for him. I told you I'd come back, and I did."

"With him."

She studied him. "What are you thinking, Alaric? That I turned against you and brought him back to help me kill you?"

Yes, exactly. That had been what he'd thought—but was it true?

Tears were running down her cheeks. She bit her lip as if to force herself to remain silent, to give him time to answer. As if his answer might demolish her.

He considered the idea again. She had been there, she admitted as much. But could she have been the instigator of the harm he'd suffered? No, he didn't believe that. "No, I don't think you have an evil bone in your body or a harmful wish in your heart. I'm glad you came back, but I can't say the same about Orcutt."

She sighed and pulled up another of the camp chairs beside his. "I guess that's about right. I'm afraid it's my fault. I may have enabled his attack before, but I didn't mean to. I tried to stop him. I don't want to hurt you, and I don't want him to hurt you, either. I'm here because I think you're in danger, and I want to help."

"And Romulus Orcutt is the cause of the danger." His worst fears about the man, confirmed. His hands had fisted so tight, they hurt. He made himself relax them.

"It's my mother who's behind it, but yes. I think Rom will try to hurt you." She stiffened and looked all around, peering into the dark corners of the tent. "And now that I think about it, maybe you'd better get out of this tent because if he was here once, he can probably get back here again. And he'll be with her, too, and he'll do whatever she tells him. But she doesn't love him, and, oh, Alaric, I've made a mess of everything, and I have to help straighten it out."

He wasn't quite following all of this, but there was one thing he heard clearly enough: there was danger. "Are you in danger too?"

"No! Yes, maybe." She frowned, thinking. "I don't know. But *you* are, and we have to get you out of this tent because that's where they're going to show up. Please."

Alaric studied her. Her expression was full of concern for him. He believed her. It was the kind of belief he knew was mightier than magic. "All right."

Pushing down with both arms, he raised himself from the chair. He wasn't as dizzy as he had been. His throat didn't hurt as much anymore either, and he was breathing more easily. "Let's get Marco involved. Then you can tell the whole story, and we'll figure out the best thing to do." He held out his hand to her and smiled. And when she took his hand and returned the smile, he felt like the whole world lay sunlit and new before him.

By all the magic on Earth and in the heavens, he had missed her. More than he'd ever dreamed possible.

Katie walked through the resistance fighters' camp with Alaric and Marco. Men and women moved about, folding and stowing tents, preparing and eating quick meals, tending to their horses. Katie had never seen such a swirl of activity. It seemed everyone knew just what to do and was doing it quickly and professionally. In an odd way, the camp reminded Katie of her mother's kitchen. A smile twitched at Katie's lips. But of course there was a key difference. Her smile faded. The purpose of the activity in her mother's kitchen was a good meal. Here, the end result would be death.

They watched several young men pile stones to make a wall on the downhill slope. "If they come from this direction, they'll be coming up the hill," Alaric said to Katie. "That's a disadvantage to begin with, but if we can finish this wall before they get here, we should be well protected on this side."

"We could use a few more days for that," Marco said. He gave Katie a questioning look.

She bit her lip, then said, "I don't think we have that much time."

Alaric grimaced. "All right. What can we do now? Where do you think is the greatest danger?"

She surveyed the encampment. Everywhere, people were busy. Two young women sat nearby, rolling bandages and arranging them into medical kits. A boy no older than eight stacked the bags neatly into the back of a wagon. What was a child doing in the camp? How could they possibly protect him? The responsibility felt like a weight pressing on Katie's chest. Did Alaric feel this way all the time? Did Marco? "I . . . I don't know," she said.

"We have secured the entire hilltop, but it's hard to patrol the wooded side," Marco said. "Maybe you could do some magic to shore up the defenses over there?"

Alaric drew a breath, then let it out in a sigh, running his hand over his throat. "I'll do what I can, of course. It would be good to make that wall look a lot higher from the outside, but I'm not sure…"

"Can I help?" Katie asked.

Alaric turned to her, eyebrows raised.

Though she had been hesitant before to use whatever magic she possessed, now that she had inadvertently brought danger right into Alaric's stronghold, she had to do whatever she could to make the situation right. She met his gaze and held it.

Alaric almost seemed to be following her thoughts. "I can show you how I do it," he said, "then let's see if you can do the same thing."

Marco's expression was decidedly skeptical.

Katie glared at him. "What? You think I can't?"

He waved his hands dismissively. "No, no, no. Far be it from me."

Alaric scowled at his brother, then turned to Katie with a smile. "Well, *I* think you can," he said. "I'm sure of it." He looked almost as happy as he had when she had taken her mother's torque off him in that cave almost three weeks ago.

Katie had possessed magic even back then, when she thought she hadn't. But in the whirlwind of events since she and Alaric had fled her mother's castle, she had learned she had magic powers perhaps even beyond Alaric's own. Alaric would show her how, and then she would do this. She returned Alaric's smile, and her heart swelled with emotion too large to contain.

She did love this man—whether he loved her or not.

Marco headed toward their left, toward the section of the wall where he wanted the illusion placed. Katie turned to follow. As she turned, she glimpsed a shadowy figure in the doorway to Alaric's tent—a figure that was somehow both there and not-quite-there. Rom.

She reached to touch Alaric's arm. "Do you see him?"

Alaric followed her gaze. He frowned. "I'm not sure."

Katie's face felt suddenly warm. She would not let Rom harm Alaric. Would *not*. "Go help Marco," she said. "Rom is there, now. I'll deal with this."

"No. If there's danger, I want to help y—"

"No, you can't. His magic is not like yours. But I know him. I won't let him hurt you. I know how to do this."

Alaric's jaw was a tight line, his hands fisted. He didn't move.

"Alaric, please. If you trust me at all, hurry. Go."

He hesitated another moment, then nodded, turned, and followed Marco down the hill.

The faint vision of Rom turned his head, watching Alaric and Marco depart. In his hand, he clutched the cravat he'd used to strangle Alaric.

Katie approached him. "Is my mother with you?"

Rom glanced over his shoulder, as if checking to be sure. "In the physical room, yes," he said. "But not here. Why did you send Alaric away? I'm trying to help her with this war of hers the easiest and quickest way possible, with the fewest deaths. Don't you see? If we just get rid of Alaric, that'll be the end of it."

Katie looked around the camp. Partisans and soldiers alike were preparing for battle. For victory or for death. The energy in the camp was high, determined. "Is that what my mother told you? She's wrong, you know. Even if Alaric dies, these people will keep fighting. Marco will lead them, and if he dies, someone else will. Alaric is fighting for what's right here, for these people. These are *your* people, Rom. You mustn't harm him."

Rom peered right, left, right again, for all the world as if his answer might be written on the walls of the tent. He scratched his head. "I'm only trying to help."

"Well, you're not. You're making it worse. Go away. Go back."

"What'll I tell *her*? She's going to be very upset, and when she gets upset . . ." He gave his head a hard shake as if trying to dislodge the image of Claudia being upset. "And if she finds out you're here and not in your room—"

How timid could one person be? Katie could hardly believe she too had been like that once. Had she inherited the trait from him? But no more. "Then don't tell her," she said. "Make up some story."

"What?" He wrung his hands as if the task was impossible.

Suddenly, Katie saw with great clarity how it could work. "Tell her you tried to get here. That's true, right? You tried, but Alaric wasn't in the tent." She wanted to make sure Alaric was not still around, but she forced herself not to glance in the direction he'd gone. "That's true, too, right? So, tell her he was nowhere to be seen, and you couldn't stay in the tent because there was nothing or no one to hold onto to keep you here."

He bit his lower lip and looked so miserable he might start crying. "But that's not true. You're here. I can stay here because I can stay with you."

She put her fists on her hips, her anger so strong it was hard to keep in control. "That's the part you mustn't mention. No matter what. She thinks I'm in my room. If she finds out I'm here, who knows what she'll do, but it won't be good for any of us. Just tell her you got here, Alaric was gone, and you couldn't stay. That's all true. You don't have to mention me."

Slowly, he nodded.

Then he disappeared.

Alaric's heart was in turmoil as he followed Marco down the hill to the ridge. Had he done the right thing, leaving Katie alone with that man? Was Orcutt going to attempt to harm her? Or to get her to take her mother's side against him? The thought that Katie might ally against him turned Alaric's stomach sour.

Worse. He had prided himself on his ability to avoid entanglements of the heart. After what had happened to his father . . . Alaric shivered. He never wanted to experience that. But the thought of Katie leaving him—of her working against him—was almost too much to bear. He wanted to turn around, to tear her out of Orcutt's clutches. Is this what love felt like?

He considered. Clearly Orcutt had some kind of power over Katie—but he wasn't her lover, she'd said that much. And Alaric believed her. Her open truthfulness was one of the things he . . . loved . . . about her.

If he turned back now, it would essentially be telling Katie that he didn't trust her. Didn't trust her to stand up for him, or didn't trust that she had the power to handle a situation she'd assured him she could. Either way, it would not be an act of love.

At the bottom of all his fears, Alaric knew now, without a doubt, that he did love Katie. And he trusted her.

He took a deep breath to steady himself, then turned his attention to the problem at hand. A platoon of young soldiers was building a wall at the crest of the hill. Other soldiers brought carts full of stones, salvaged or quarried from somewhere nearby. Marco called to them, and one of them, clearly the sergeant in charge, stopped working and came toward them.

"How's it going?" Marco said. "It's a bit higher than yesterday, I see."

The sergeant grimaced, then acknowledged Alaric with a gesture that was a bit more than a nod, a bit less than a bow. "Your Majesty," he said. "We're working as hard as we can, built it up another foot or so, and we're extending it from the cliff over there"—he gestured off to his left, Alaric's right—"as far as we can in this direction. "We'll be okay if we have enough time, maybe about a week. You think we do?"

Marco grimaced. "Probably not. One of our spies says Claudia's troops are on their way, or will be soon."

"I'm here to help," Alaric said, hoping he had the energy to create an illusion of solid rocks running hundreds of feet across the hill. It was a task that would drain him even if he were totally recovered—and he was far from that.

"Alaric!" Katie's voice came to him through the general camp noisiness.

He turned and saw her running toward him, her hair flying free behind her, a vision of loveliness. He held out his arms to embrace her, then decided that was probably not the right action in front of all these soldiers. He turned the gesture into taking her hands.

"He's gone," Katie said, a bit breathlessly, smiling.

"Does that mean we have more time?"

Katie frowned, considering. "I'd say that's unlikely. He'll tell her he didn't find you in the tent, and she'll be angry. So, if anything, she'll attack sooner and harder. Let me help you with this wall. Show me how you do it."

Alaric nodded. If Katie could help, maybe they had a chance. "I do it by weaving the air into the form of a rock. Making it denser makes it appear more solid. In fact, it actually does become more solid under those conditions, for as long as I can hold the illusion together. Not as solid as rock, but Claudia's soldiers will feel something in front of them. Their eyes will tell them it's solid rock, and they won't advance because no one can walk through walls. Except you, of course."

"But if someone pushes them, they might walk into it. Would that stop them?"

Alaric chuckled at the image. "Depends on how hard the push is. Now, watch." He began moving his hands through the air.

Katie watched, moving her hands to mimic his movements.

Alaric felt for the air molecules, allowed the slight breeze to push them into threads. He stroked the threads to make them firmer, then gathered them to weave together into the form of rocks, the illusion of a wall.

It was tiring work, and the sun beating down was uncomfortably hot. Sweating, Alaric reached for the warmest air molecules and folded them into his weaving.

The wall grew longer foot by foot as he worked his way across the hill.

He looked back at Katie and almost lost hold of the threads he was weaving. She was moving her hands in motions a lot like his, and following behind, she made the wall about two feet higher.

Nearby soldiers had stopped what they were doing and gathered to watch.

Alaric caught Katie's eye and smiled. The pride he felt in her accomplishment renewed his energy and determination. The wall was only an illusion, and Claudia would have the power to dispel it. But there were two of them now, and only one of her. Not counting Orcutt, of course, but Alaric refused to think about that now.

Katie returned the smile. Sweat gleamed on her forehead and arms. She must be tired, maybe even more tired than he was, but she was gamely working alongside him without complaint.

Alaric felt his heart blossom with pride. But he wanted to make sure she didn't work herself into complete exhaustion. He had to take care of her. With surprise, he realized he wanted to care for her more than he'd ever wanted anything. He tied off his section of the illusion and said, "Let's take a short break. It's hot, and there's a lot more to do. We need to pace ourselves. Let's get some water, and maybe a bite to eat."

She nodded gratefully, tied off one last knot in the air, and a rock appeared in the wall.

As they walked toward the shade of the nearest tree, Alaric took Katie's hand. She gave his a squeeze and said, "That's tiring work. The way Rom does magic is much easier."

Romulus Orcutt. Why did she have to bring *him* up? "He taught you?" he said, keeping his tone carefully neutral. "How did that go?"

She gave a small laugh. "Oh, Alaric, it was so easy. I must have inherited my magic from him, not my mother. Magic was hard to learn here, but once Rom showed me, I just had a sense of it."

Alaric stared at her, his mind blank as he tried to absorb what she'd just said. "Rom is . . . your father?"

"Yes, of course," she said, "you knew—Wait. You didn't know?"

"No. When you stayed in Larippia instead of coming back with me, I thought . . ." He trailed off. Should he tell her?

She raised a questioning eyebrow. "You thought what? That maybe I'd chosen him over you?"

That was exactly what he'd thought. He swallowed, remembering the despair he'd felt. "I was afraid . . ."

Katie looked at his anguished face and pulled him into a hug. "I would never choose anyone over you. Never. I know you don't love me, and that's all right, you have to be true to your own feelings, but I love you. I'll travel and build my own life, but I'll never forget you."

He pulled back to look at her. "You know I . . . What? Don't love you? Katie, I asked you to marry me. Do you think I would ask you that, if I didn't—"

"No, really, I understand. You swore an oath, and maybe you preferred to marry me instead of one of my sisters. You don't have to pretend you love me."

Still crying, she was beautiful, even with tears sliding down her cheeks. He gently wiped a tear away with his finger. "Don't cry, Katie. Dearest. I do love you. Only you. And my offer of marriage still stands. Travel if you want, of course you must, but marry me, and I'll come with you if I can."

She sniffed and wiped her other cheek. "You . . . love me?"

He couldn't even remember how it felt when he'd resolved never to fall in love. "By all the heavens, Katie, I swear I do."

"Then yes. Yes!" She was positively glowing.

Never had a woman been so beautiful, never had his heart felt so much like it would burst. Never had a moment been this perfect. How could he resist? He leaned over and kissed her on the lips.

After a while, a distant sound drew his attention.

All the nearby soldiers were cheering.

CHAPTER NINETEEN

The oathstone has its way

The next day, Claudia stood in her scrying pool with Rom. From high in the air above the enemy's encampment, she could see the wall that Alaric had woven from the air, and she tore a hole in it. It was surprisingly hard work tearing that hole, much more than it should have been. She couldn't quite see all the magic that went into that wall. In fact, some sections of it were entirely opaque to her. She grudgingly had to admit he'd done a good job—but the small hole she managed to create was sufficient. Claudia's soldiers, who had been blocked from advancing all morning, now slipped into the encampment in a steady stream.

"Oh, darling, isnt this just ever so exciting?" she asked Rom, her heart aglow with the anticipation of winning. She rubbed her hands together. There was hardly anything she liked more than winning.

Rom's face reflected the light from the water in the scrying pool below. He should have been smiling in delight—but he wasn't.

Claudia took his input seriously. In the few days they'd been to-gether, he'd already shown his value to her, both in the way he had of seeing things, and more important, in the way he performed magic. Plus, he was generally so eager to please. "What is it?" she asked.

"All my life," he said slowly, choosing his words with care, "I've been taught to avoid conflict and to do no harm. You understand I live in a closed world, so it could hardly be any other way. What goes around, comes around—literally. This fight you and Alaric are having … I don't know, I found it exhilarating at first, but I'm more and more uncertain about it."

He was not mentioning something, Claudia was sure of that, but she couldn't figure out what. She frowned. "What changed?"

"N-nothing." He shook his head as if to clear it and gave her a warm smile. "I'm happy to see you so excited, anyway."

Claudia turned back to the image in the scrying pool, her heart leaping to see the progress her soldiers had made. "Look how they're getting through. Alaric doesn't know I've gotten past his wall, or if he knows, he doesn't have the strength to fix it." She put her arm around Rom and gave his shoulder a squeeze. "I always knew I was stronger than he is. Help me widen this hole a bit, would you, dear?"

A ringing tone wormed its way into her consciousness. It was grow-ing louder.

In fact, it was annoyingly loud already.

"I'm not sure—" Rom began, then stopped and shook his head as if to clear it.

In just a few seconds, the ringing had become more insistent, an unharmonious clanging. She could hardly hear herself think and couldn't maintain the concentration necessary for active scrying. "What's that?" she said. They weren't floating above the battle any longer, but standing, wet to the ankles, in the clear water of the scrying pool. She shouted to the sentries that stood by the door of the room. "Whoever is making that noise, get them to stop it at once."

But the soldiers stood hunched over, hands pressed against their ears.

Rom stumbled out of the pool, then gave Claudia a hand. They dried their feet using the towels nearby. "I've heard a sound like this somewhere before," he said, "but I can't remember where." He looked like he was feeling the same pain that she was. "I can barely think."

The pain was drumming at her temples. It felt like her eardrums might explode. "What *is* that?" Claudia repeated, frowning. "I'll kill whoever is responsible for this interruption."

Rom looked deep in thought. Or in pain, maybe both. Then he drew in a sharp breath, his eyes lighting up. "I know what it is. Do you have an oathstone here?"

What, did he think this was some kind of primitive society? She looked at him, scornful. "Yes, of course. We are not savages."

"Let me see it."

"Now? Really, Romulus? My head is bursting, I have no time for this. I'll just send someone to . . . to follow the sound and find its source and shut it off. I'm sure it must be possible."

"Not if it's your oathstone, it won't be," he said. "In Larippia, we use oathstones to swear all our important agreements, and I have been witness before, when one was broken."

"We'll just have to leave the castle," Claudia replied. "Temporarily."

"That would solve the problem for your soldiers who come with you, and for me. But not for you, if it's your oath the stone is protesting." Rom put on a confident and determined expression. It looked a bit frightening—a side of him she didn't know. "The sound will follow you everywhere," he continued, "and it will get louder. You'll have to deal with it. Come on, let's just go check out that oathstone." He held out his hand to her.

"Can you turn it off?" she asked. "If we go there in person, I mean."

Rom grimaced. "Maybe. But not if you've broken some oath, not until you make it right. In any case, the next step is to go there and see it for ourselves."

Claudia groaned, the sound barely audible now above the ringing and pounding in her head. She looked right, then left. Surely there must be some other way. But nothing occurred to her, nothing suggested the magic she might use to get away from the problem. She'd have to give Rom's suggestion a try. In a voice that was almost a growl, she said, "Fine."

She led the way to the door of the oathstone chamber and then down the narrow stairs. The sound was more insistent here, deeper, more demanding. Claudia put her hands over her ears and continued down the stairs.

The oathstone glowed an eldritch green, not at all pleasant to look at. The glow was intense, pulsing slightly in time with its clanging.

"This is amazing," Rom said, his eyes wide. "That's the largest oathstone I've ever seen, and it's still functional. I had no idea any of these survived in this world. Do you see how it's pulsing? There's no doubt it's responding to a broken oath."

She managed a small laugh. "Most of the sovereign rulers have one."

"And they all still work?"

"Apparently." She grimaced. This was no time for such chatter. "Can you shut it off?"

"It's protesting a broken oath," he said, as if that explained the hammering in their heads.

"Romulus. Can. You. Shut. It. Off?" she said through clenched teeth. "Now. Please."

He took a deep breath and put a hand to his heart. He stood a bit straighter, as if steeling himself. "I'm afraid not. The only way to shut this off is to keep the oath that's been broken. And it will get worse—louder—until whoever broke the oath makes it right." He hesitated. "Or dies. Have you"—he stared intently at her, as if expecting the answer to appear on her forehead—"broken any oaths lately? Or has someone else broken an oath made here?"

Claudia paced back and forth, fists clenched. "I made an oath with Alaric, weeks ago now. He agreed to marry one of my daughters with magical ability and pay me tribute from Darimbia, and I agreed to cease fighting."

"But you're still fighting," Rom pointed out. He could be dense sometimes. And annoying.

"Well, he hasn't married any of my daughters with magic, either, so either we're both forsworn or neither of us is."

"Katie?" Rom asked. "She has magic."

Claudia was getting angry. If only this damned clanging would stop. If only Rom weren't being so tedious. "She didn't have it at the time the oath was sworn, so she doesn't count."

But Rom didn't give up. "This may depend on exactly the wording he and you used, and exactly the intent of both parties."

"Whose side are you on, anyway?" she shouted. Her head was splitting, and her patience was at an end.

He seemed to be at wit's end, just like she was. "I am on whoever's side will turn off this damned racket."

Claudia stared at the oathstone. It was easier to face than what she suspected was coming. "Maybe I can break the stone."

"Best case, you will fail," Rom said, dashing this last hope. "Worst case, you'll have a dozen little oathstones chiming at you with a complete lack of harmony, and they'll all continue to get louder. They'll kill you, and at the rate things are going, they'll kill me and your sentries as collateral damage. Claudia, you have to stop this thing. Call a truce. Talk with Alaric. If he doesn't hear it, that will mean the oathstone has accepted whatever action he's taken, and it's up to you to do your part."

And there it was—the one thing she didn't want to hear. "Never! I'm not going to call a truce. I'm in the best position I've ever been to win this war."

Rom put his arms around her. She stiffened. It was a useless gesture, but the embrace was oddly comforting. She didn't move away. He held her until she relaxed a bit in his arms. "A truce is temporary, dearest. Only temporary. You can make it happen. Talk with Alaric."

Claudia scowled. "All right," she said, "but just a short one. Then, I'll make him pay."

Rom appeared to Katie in a vision.

She understood now, how he could be there, and yet not there. "Are you with my mother?"

He said something, but she couldn't make out what. She could barely make out from the vague impression of his presence, that he was trying to speak. She shook her head and cupped her ear. This time, Rom nodded vigorously as he shouted a faint "Yes."

"We're kind of busy right now," she told him.

She and Alaric were more than *kind of* busy. She was using all her concentration to hold together the wall that Alaric had built, and he looked strained with the effort to repair the hole Claudia had gouged in one of its sections. A hole where the enemy troops were climbing through and engaging in ever-increasing numbers with Marco's forces on the ground. They were both stretched as thin as they could be.

Again, Rom said something.

It almost sounded like *truce*, but that couldn't be right. "What?"

"A truce," he shouted, the words barely audible. "Claudia wants to talk with Alaric."

"Who are you talking to?" Alaric said.

"Rom. I think he's saying that my mother wants a truce. She wants to talk with you."

Alaric narrowed his eyes skeptically. "Why? Nothing has changed here in the last couple of hours. She's in a strong position."

"Maybe she's getting tired."

"We can hope. But then, why should I grant it?"

"Because we're getting tired too?"

Alaric sighed. "I suppose there's no harm in everyone getting a bit of a rest while we talk, but I need to know this is no trick." He looked up, right to left, thinking. "A truce for the rest of the day, a one-hour talk on neutral ground away from both encampments, and guaranteed safety for all parties while the truce is in effect. I want her to swear it on her oathstone. Can I trust her to do that, Katie?"

Katie shook her head. "I'm not sure. Maybe not. But I think you can trust Rom, if he promises."

Alaric paused, his head slightly tilted as he looked away, thinking. "All right, then," he said, "but I want Rom's promise and personal guarantee as your father when she has sworn."

"I heard," Rom said, his voice like a whisper in the breeze, "and I'll get back to you in a few minutes."

Claudia crossed her arms and set her jaw tight. Ringing in her ears or not, she'd be damned if that upstart two-penny king was going to dictate terms to her.

"Did you hear him?" Romulus asked.

She lifted her chin. "Yes, but I'm not going back anywhere near that oathstone." With these words, the ringing grew, maybe not so much louder as deeper inside her skull.

Romulus looked at her sorrowfully. "I'm afraid you'll have to."

"I said no." She shook her head, then was immediately sorry she had. The ringing made her dizzy. "Absolutely not. Find some other way."

"No, my love. His request is not unreasonable, given the current state of hostilities. And I have agreed to witness."

Claudia arched an eyebrow. "Then you can agree with me now that it's okay to, shall we say, stretch the truth a little bit in that regard."

"Regrettably, no. Anything involving an oath sworn on an oathstone is a serious matter. I will not be forsworn, and neither shall you." He turned back toward the door of the oathstone chamber and held out his hand. "Now come."

She'd always found Romulus easy to manipulate, that was one of the things she liked about him. But this was some new man speaking—a man to be reckoned with. An attractive man. She nodded and allowed him to lead her back to the stairway.

Once she acceded to Romulus's request, Claudia found that approaching the oathstone was surprisingly easy. She let him lead her.

Bad as it was, the stone's mind-numbing ringing was no worse as they grew closer than it had been elsewhere in the castle. She looked at Romulus, not sure exactly what was needed, hoping she didn't have to tell him of her ignorance.

To her relief, the man seemed to intuit her need for him to take the lead, and to spare her the embarrassment of her weakness. The desire to please him rose within her as a kind of release from the relentless pressure of holding her world together all alone.

The oathstone glowed with a pulsating green light, throwing ominous shadows on the stone walls and ceiling of the crypt. Its magic pressed against them, reflected from the walls all around them, ancient undecipherable spells bound into the rock.

"Say the words," Romulus said.

She took a deep breath. "What I say—" Her voice broke, and she started over. "What I say here binds me."

"I am your sworn witness," he intoned. When she remained silent, he said, "You know the terms. You must swear them on the stone."

"I hate this," she said, "but . . ." She couldn't bring herself to touch the monstrous thing, to swear another oath with consequences like this.

He raised an eyebrow, an unvoiced *Go ahead now, do it*.

But Claudia was having second thoughts. "Maybe I shouldn't swear to a truce. It would be a very good time to attack while they're unsuspecting."

The ringing in her ears seemed to grow louder, pushing her brain hard against her skull.

Romulus put his hands over his ears, shaking his head. "No, I know you, and you are not a dishonorable person."

He didn't say, *Besides, the oathstone would kill you*. Claudia was grateful for his restraint and, if she was going to be perfectly honest with herself, for his praise. She put her hand on the stone. It was surprisingly cold. Chill energy shot through her body. She shook but did not—could not—remove her hand. "I agree to a truce for the rest of the day. This afternoon I shall conduct a one-hour discussion with that bast—with King Alaric. It will be on neutral ground. I will have my soldiers lay down their arms and conduct no warfare while the truce is in effect. However, this oath is void if I am attacked first. I do so swear."

The room rumbled with the sound of distant thunder.

Romulus touched the stone as well. He shook visibly, but spoke in a firm voice. "I so witness."

A flash brighter than lightning flared in the chamber. Both of them stumbled backward, a moment of imbalance as their hands were freed from the stone with perceptible force.

Despite the cold, sweat beaded on Claudia's forehead, but the ringing in her head started to subside. It seemed the stone was giving them the rest of the day off, time enough to honor the oath she'd sworn with Alaric. She was going to loathe every minute of it.

CHAPTER TWENTY

The end of the beginning

Katie couldn't believe that her mother had agreed to Alaric's terms. But she believed Rom when he told her about the oath that her mother had sworn, and he had witnessed, on the oathstone. She consulted with Alaric, who proposed a location. Two hours later, they walked beside the river to the designated meeting spot.

Alaric seemed pensive. He touched a tree trunk almost caressingly as he walked to the river's edge. He picked up a stone, rubbed it in his fingers, then threw it into the water. "My father died here," he said. "He died fighting *her*. This truce is hard for me—the whole agreement we've sworn is hard for me, but it's the right thing for Darimbia."

Katie put her hand on his sleeve, but before she could find the words to comfort him, her mother and Rom appeared. Of course they'd used magic, but it looked like they'd just walked out from behind the trees, as if they'd always been there.

"Hello, Katie dear," her mother said. She held out her arms as if for a hug, but she wasn't smiling.

The combination made Katie nervous, and she drew back. Alaric put an arm around her.

With a barely noticeable nod and a visibly tight jaw, the queen said, "Alaric."

"Claudia," he replied, his voice as frigid as hers. "You requested this truce, so you start."

The queen looked at Rom. She had an almost desperate look on her face, the kind that might be hoping he would offer her a way out of this. Rom moved closer to her and touched her shoulder with an encouraging smile. She cleared her throat. "I would like to propose that we reinstate our oa—our agreement."

Alaric frowned. "Reinstate? That oath was sworn on an oathstone. It remains in effect. And I have honored my initial part of it."

"You were going to marry one of my older daughters." Claudia's voice was heated, and it rose in pitch. "You were not going to marry Katie. One of my *magical* daughters, Alaric."

To her own surprise, Katie spoke up. "Oh, but I *am* magical, Mother. I always have been—just with Rom's kind of magic, not yours. And Alaric *is* going to marry me. I have accepted his offer."

Alaric's frown turned into a smile, and he drew Katie close.

Rom leaned toward her mother and spoke quietly in her ear. Katie couldn't make out all the words, but she did hear something about the oathstone.

Her mother glared at Rom, then at Alaric and Katie, then back at Rom. "Must I, Romulus? Truly?"

"It's your agreement," he said. "It must be, or the oathstone—"

Claudia cut him off. "Very well." What was she not letting him say about the oathstone?

"We shall stop fighting," Claudia continued, "but we shall leave our forces in their respective positions for now. I shall arrange the details of the wedding, and it will be the most splendid one imaginable, as befits a princess and a king. It will be a long and impressive guest list, Katie, and *you* will be the center of attention."

If her mother was hoping for a rise out of her, Katie wasn't about to provide it. "Of course," she said. "I would expect no less from you."

Claudia continued, speaking to Alaric. "I shall cede Darimbia to you on the day you marry Katie, not a moment before. Naturally, it will take months to arrange an appropriate wedding celebration, and there must be no violation of the ceasefire during that time, or this agreement is over."

"That's too long," Alaric said. He sounded angry enough to break the ceasefire on the spot.

He was right. Katie was worried, too. It would be too easy for a months-long ceasefire to be broken. Any small accident might do it. The more she thought about it, the more likely the possibility seemed. "We're getting married this afternoon," she said.

Alaric shook his head. "Katie, your mother is right to want a royal marriage celebration. But it must happen more quickly."

"Yes, of course she's right." Katie gave her mother a smile that she hoped was convincing. "She always is." Then her heart melted—just a bit. Her poor mother, always needing to be right. "And the celebration will be as regal as any in history. Can you help with that, Rom? We'll invite people from your realm, too. Your aunt, and the others. It will be wonderful. People will talk about it for decades to come."

Rom's eyes grew wide. With a nearly imperceptible shake of his head, he opened his mouth to respond, but before he could, Katie cut him off.

"But we'll be secretly married before then," she said. "We can't wait months while the perfect arrangements are being made, all the while hoping the truce won't be broken. Isn't that so, Alaric?"

Alaric's eyes crinkled into a smile, and he gave Katie's shoulder a squeeze. To Rom and the queen, he said, "Of course you two will be present. As is appropriate for the parents of the bride. And you will be witnesses."

"Oh, to see my daughter married," Rom said. "I never imagined such good fortune."

Glaring, Claudia gave him a slight shove.

"It would be a privilege," Rom said. He pulled Claudia closer.

Some indecipherable conversation seemed to occur in the looks they gave each other.

"Agreed," Claudia said. "Maybe a small wedding, with just a hundred people or so. Maybe we could arrange that in a month."

But Katie was certain even a month's truce would be too dangerous. "Oh, no, Mother," she said, "I definitely want that dazzling wedding celebration with our people, and Alaric's, and Rom's. A celebration that will be remembered for centuries. Let's not give up on that. But let's not wait. We can get married quietly"—she glanced at Alaric then plunged ahead—"today."

"What?" Claudia and Alaric spoke simultaneously.

Katie's breath came too quickly, too shallowly. She wanted Alaric and her mother to get along together, but not by opposing her. "Help me here, Rom."

He gave her a look that seemed full of meaning, but which was indecipherable to her. "She does have a point," he said. "It would be good for all of us, and for Darimbia too, if the military conflict could be ended as soon as possible." He tilted his head toward Claudia. "Less expense, and your revenues will start coming in sooner." To Alaric, he said, "Freedom for Darimbia. We both want that."

Alaric nodded. "Agreed. We will adjourn to my palace and marry today."

"Oh no," Claudia countered. "You will marry at my place or not at all."

Katie and Alaric spoke at the same time.

"All right," Katie said.

"Never," said Alaric.

Katie touched Alaric's arm. "It's what we want," she said. "Sometimes you have to compromise a little."

Rom stood a bit straighter. "Of course! You will be married the Larippian way. That will favor neither side. Agreed?"

"Very well," Alaric mumbled, while Claudia spoke a bit too loud, "Fine."

Rom beamed. "It will be done on Claudia's oathstone."

Alaric glared at them both. "Since when do Larippians get married at Claudia's palace?"

Rom met his gaze. "They marry on an oathstone. Do you have one, too?"

"Unfortunately, no."

"Well, then." Rom shrugged.

Katie touched Alaric's arm. "Sometimes we have to give in a little."

Mouth in a tight line, Alaric gave a slow nod. "Very well."

Claudia moaned. "I never want to see that oathstone again. I'm going to have it removed from my palace."

"Of course you may, dear," Rom said, squeezing her shoulder, "just as soon as the marriage vows are spoken."

"I'll be glad to take it off your hands," Alaric muttered under his breath.

Rom ignored him. "Their marriage is the best way to fulfill this oath of yours," he said to Claudia. "You want that, right? And the sooner the better."

"She'll be sorry she ever married that man," she said, her voice loud enough for Katie and Alaric to hear.

She's trying to intimidate me, talking about me as if I weren't right here. Katie lifted her chin and looked her mother in the eye. "No," she said, "I won't be."

Rom leaned closer to whisper to Claudia, but his voice carried enough for Katie to hear. "Go ahead and do it. Put an oath on Alaric and Katie's backs instead of yours. That's what they want, so let's see how they manage with it. Maybe you'll have the last word after all." He gave Claudia a wink.

A wink! Katie couldnt imagine how he had the nerve to do that.

But the queen actually smiled. "Very well."

It was not the kind of wedding Katie had imagined. There was no priest or officiant, no procession, not even a ring.

Alaric held Katie's elbow, steadying her as they climbed down the stairs to the oathstone chamber. The stairs were steep and slightly uneven, the natural bedrock they were cut from still evident. But the stairs were wide enough to descend firmly. Katie had never seen her mother's oathstone chamber. Suddenly uncertain, she looked up at Alaric.

He gave her a smile of encouragement.

Behind them came Claudia and Rom, and behind them, an escort of half a dozen soldiers, three from each side. Eight people to witness an oath that could never be broken.

A strange light, greenish and flickering, lit the chamber from below. At the bottom of the stairway, Katie paused and took a deep breath. All this was so sudden, so fast. So permanent.

Alaric squeezed her elbow, then moved her to the side to make room for the others.

Claudia and Rom reached the bottom of the stairway and moved to the other side. The soldiers remained on the steps.

"Are you all right?" Alaric whispered.

Katie's heart beat rapidly. It seemed to echo in the stone chamber. This was her last chance. Her last possibility of freedom. Her last opportunity to travel where she wanted, when she wanted, beholden to no one, without the need to compromise with Alaric's schedules and duties.

Katie took a deep breath and looked into the eyes of the man who loved her. Compared to being with him, none of that seemed to matter. They would work it out. "I've never been better," she said. "And you?"

His smile lit the chamber brighter than the light from the oathstone. "Never better," he said.

Rom cleared his throat. "Are you ready?" Since he was the only one among them who had witnessed an oathstone wedding, they had all agreed he would lead.

"Yes," Katie and Alaric chorused in unison.

Claudia grimaced. "Make it brief," she said, shifting from one foot to the other. Her eyes darted around the chamber as if ghosts might be haunting its corners. "Let's get out of this place as soon as we can, and save the longwinded speeches for the celebration later."

Rom gave her a nod of acknowledgment, then turned to Alaric. "Alaric Westlander, do you swear on this oathstone and by all you hold dear that you will love and honor and protect this woman, Alicia Aurelia Margreta Katrina Emilia for all of your days, and remain true and faithful to her?"

"I do," Alaric said.

"Alicia Aurelia Margreta Katrina Emilia, do you swear on this oath-stone and by all you hold dear that you will love and honor and obey this man, Alaric Westlander for all—"

"No, wait," Alaric said. "I didn't swear to obey her, and she should not have to swear to obey me. She should be free to do as she feels right." He took Katie's hand and gave it a gentle squeeze. "Though of course I would hope you would obey me." He smiled at her. "If you feel I'm right. And correct me if you think I'm wrong."

She considered. Would she have the strength to stand up to him if she felt he was wrong? She hoped it would never happen, but if it did—she would have to, for both of them. "Please, Rom, make both oaths the same."

Rom cleared his throat. "Alicia Aurelia Margreta Katrina Emilia, do you swear on this oathstone and by all you hold dear that you will love and honor and protect this man, Alaric Westlander, for all of your days, and remain true and faithful to him?"

"I do," she said.

"Now, place your hands on the oathstone and swear."

They both touched the oathstone. A frisson of electricity ran through Katie. She gasped. Alaric's expression wore the same rough shock. His voice came out with a harsh rasp. "I do so swear."

Katie found her voice and repeated the words. "I do so swear."

Rom put his own hand on the stone beside theirs. He shuddered with a vibration whose reflection Katie felt. Then he drew in a sharp breath. "These two people are joined forever in marriage. I do so witness."

A thunderclap rang out, and the light in the chamber flashed brighter than lightning.

The deed was done.

It didn't take three months for Claudia to organize the wedding reception. Two months and a week were enough, and she'd done a wonderful job of it. Garlands of flowers festooned every street of the capitol city, and a holiday was declared.

Visitors from many countries poured into Victoria's eponymous capital city. Every inn in town was full, and estates in the countryside also hosted visitors, some for family obligations, others for money. For the week leading up to the wedding celebration, carefully coordinated receptions were held at various inns and on some of the surrounding estates. Katie and Alaric visited all of them, sometimes only to say hello and accept congratulations, as their busy schedule allowed no time to dally.

Rom returned to Larippia, carrying invitations to his relatives.

On the final day of the celebration, a dinner for the closest fifty family members and most powerful allies was served in the castle's banquet hall.

When all the guests were seated, a trumpet sounded, and a servant with a stentorian voice announced, "Your Highness, ladies and gentlemen, I present the bride and the groom."

Katie glanced at Alaric. He looked so handsome in a white satin vest and half-cape, embroidered with silver thread and white seed pearls in patterns of stars and moons and comets. Her own dress was made of the same fabric, with delicate lace over its low neckline and a long, full skirt. It was the fanciest dress she'd ever worn. When Alaric first saw her in it, his eyes had gone wide and he'd barely found the voice to say, "Katie, by all the heavens, you are beautiful—inside and out." He'd given her a soft kiss on her cheek and added, "I'm a lucky man."

Hand in hand, Katie and Alaric stepped into the hall.

A terrifyingly loud noise swelled up.

Katie froze, her free hand clutching the fabric of her skirt.

All the years she'd lived here, entering this hall had never been pleasant. Too many people in clothing entirely too fancy, too ready to make fun of her. Was it happening again? She bit her lip, her eyes darting around, looking for cover.

But there was no cover wide enough to hide her bejeweled white dress. No place to hide from every staring, shouting, smiling, cheering person in the room. Her heart pounded, and her breathing was rapid and shallow.

Alaric squeezed her hand and leaned toward her to speak quietly. "It's only applause, Katie. They're applauding us. Look, dearest, look around. They're all happy for us."

Katie looked around. It was true. Marco pushed back his chair and stood, clapping and yelling "Huzzah!" so loudly she could hear him over the general noise. A gentleman with gray hair and a black goatee was the second to stand, still applauding. He was grinning. Soon another person stood, then a fourth, and then everyone in the hall stood, clapping and smiling.

Katie's sisters each had an escort. The two princes from Bonaveria sat next to Jocasta and Mercuria, the eldest two, and poor Stephania was left sitting next to wealthy Lord Tobey. They too applauded, and they stood when everyone else did. But the sisters' smiles looked decidedly forced.

Rom stood next to the queen, and beside him was Auntie Morgana. Both applauded vigorously, and Morgana leaned toward Rom, saying something into his ear. Rom's grin widened, and he nodded. Then he stopped applauding just long enough to give his aunt's shoulder a brief squeeze.

Katie took a deep breath, and her fear subsided. The past two months with Alaric had been the happiest of her life. "This is certainly different from the first time we were together in this hall," she said to Alaric, managing a smile of her own.

He gave her hand another squeeze, his face radiant. "When I first saw you here, I never imagined how different it would be. Are you ready?"

She nodded, and he led her into the room.

They had reached the head of the table. Claudia, still standing, reached over to give her daughter an obligatory hug. "Not shy anymore, are you?"

Given her moment of panic, Katie wasn't sure how to respond. But there was no need. Claudia moved by her to shake Alaric's hand. "I suppose I have you to thank for that. Well, I'm grateful, but don't assume that makes us friends."

"Maybe we can settle for acting friendly now. Who knows, maybe some kind of real friendship will come in time." He gave his mother-in-law a smile. She didn't return it.

Alaric shrugged, then held the chair for Katie.

But Katie didn't sit. Instead, she said, "They say things change after the baby comes."

Her mother staggered, and Rom reached out to steady her. Claudia brushed his hand away. "How soon?" she asked.

Katie touched her still-flat abdomen. It felt the same from the outside, but inside she could sense the life that was growing there. She met Alaric's eyes, and saw her own love reflected in them. "Not soon," she said to her mother. "Maybe eight months. Yes, I think things will change." She tried her best to give her mother a smile, but there was a quiver in her lips.

"Oh, not as much as you may think," Claudia said. "You probably think the two of you won this little war, but don't forget the terms of the agreement. Baby or not, I'll be expecting regular payments from you, or—"

Alaric moved closer, into Claudia's personal space. "We'll be making them, of course."

The queen pulled herself up to her full, rigid height. "And as for you, Alaric, perhaps you think you're rid of me, but you'll soon discover that Katie is a lot like me. More than you imagine. And after she has a child, or children, you'll see more and more resemblance. You'll never be rid of me."

The idea was horrifying. "I'm nothing like you, Mother, and I never will be."

But Claudia smiled enigmatically. "You're strong-willed and stubborn, and you don't quit until you get your way. Just like me. And remember, I too was a shy child, but I got over it. Never say never."

Katie and Alaric exchanged a glance. He gave her a barely visible shake of his head, just enough to bolster her courage.

Katie gave her mother a large and completely genuine smile. "Oh, Mother, you're not that old. There's plenty of time to change. You suffered when you were a child because your father was abusive, but Alaric isn't like that. If I'm like you, then maybe you're like me, too. You'll have a baby grandchild, and you'll visit us often, and Alaric will always make you feel welcome. Won't you, Alaric?" She looked at him long enough to make him nod. "We're going to put all this conflict behind us. I can feel it in my heart."

Her mother took a breath and let it out. "Sit. Our company is getting restless, and it's time for the toasts."

They sat, and chairs up and down the hall scraped the wooden floor as the guests took their seats.

When the noise in the room had died down, Claudia said quietly, "No one can foresee the future. It will play out as it will."

Katie smiled and shook her head. Her mother might think things wouldn't change, but anyone could see that Rom was already beginning to have an effect on her. "Yes, of course," Katie said, "and it will be glorious."

D ear Reader,

  Thank you for reading *Mightier Than Magic*. I know your time is limited, and I hope you enjoyed spending some of it with Katie as she struggled to realize her destiny as a powerful magician, and with Alaric, who needed to learn to love.

To be notified of upcoming releases and to receive special content that's available only for newsletter subscribers, you can sign up for my more-or-less monthly newsletter on my website . Here, too, you can follow my travels in our own world.

If you enjoyed *Mightier Than Magic*, perhaps you might also want to check out my science fiction novels. One place to start might be the book *Saving Aran*, where a young city boy named Cort rises to the challenge of saving a planet that is, in some ways, magical in its own right.

I greatly appreciate your help in spreading the word about *Mightier Than Magic*, including telling your friends and fellow readers. And remember, reviews also help readers find books they will enjoy. Please consider posting a review on Amazon, Goodreads, Bookbub, or your blog or website.

To follow me on Facebook:
https://www.facebook.com/gskenneyauthor
To follow me on Instagram:
https://www.instagram.com/gskenneyauthor

And now, here's an excerpt from *Saving Aran* . . .

Saving Aran

By G. S. Kenney

The cry of pain echoed in the alley and flowed out into the street like a liquid. Like blood. Cort drew in a sharp breath and touched the scar on his arm. "That's a child! He's in trouble!"

"None of our business," his friend Lor advised. His voice carried a warning.

Cort jogged a few steps to look into the alley, and his heart fell. It was Karl, the biggest bully in the school, with some of his gang. No friends of Cort, and a lot bigger than he was. Two of Karl's cronies were holding a struggling child while Karl was trying to cut the boy's arm. "No!" the child screamed. "No, stop!"

"Just cutting my initials." Karl said. There was a sneer in his voice. "Hold still."

Cort's friends had caught up with him at the mouth of the alley. "Four of them," Tark said. And three of us, he didn't have to say. "Leave it." Four fifteen-year-olds against three thirteen-year-olds were bad odds.

Cort touched the scar on his arm again, his breath coming more quickly. He'd been only eight when a gang of bigger bullies, teasing him about his father, had gotten nasty when he'd fought back. One of them had drawn a knife, and if a teacher hadn't intervened just then, he probably wouldn't have survived to help this child today. "Can't," he said.

He drew a deep breath, let it out in a whoosh, and stepped into the alley to rescue the child that Karl and his gang were tormenting. He waved his arms and trying to appear bigger than he was. "Hold off!" he shouted. "Soldiers coming!"

The gang members looked up, loosening their hold on the child, who ran off crying.

Of course, no soldiers came. It took Karl only a moment to grasp the situation. "You all alone, Street Scum," he said. "Now I cut you instead." He swept his knife in a broad, threatening gesture.

Cort drew back.

"Savage!" Karl's leering, singsong taunt cut the air like his knife.

"Not!" Cort retorted. His heart pounded so loud the sound seemed to fill the alley. He breathed shallowly and too fast, looking from right to left and back again. His friends were gone. No blame for that, but he sure wished that one or both of them had his back now. At least the poor kid had gotten away. Good.

But there was no escape for Cort. If he turned and ran, he was as good as dead. His back would provide too easy a target for four knife-wielding fifteen-year-olds.

Cort stood his ground.

"Where's your knife, Savage?" Karl passed his own knife from his right hand to his left, then back again. He made a mocking jab at Cort, who jumped back to avoid being cut.

Karl's three friends were moving around to block his escape.

"Yeah, where's your *bone* knife?" teased the boy at his left.

It had been a mistake last year when Cort had mentioned that knife—the only possession his father had left him. The school bullies never forgot. Cort clenched his fists, then forced them to unclench. If only he had a stunner or, even better, one of the starmen's lasers! He'd blast all of them, especially Karl.

By Earth, he just wanted to survive the next five minutes.

He didn't have much of a chance. The older boy was fast and mean, and, unlike Cort, he had a knife. But the odds were better against Karl alone than against Karl and his three friends. "So why does it take four of you to blast one person half your size?" he taunted back. "You afraid of me, Karl?" He tried to keep an eye on the three boys to his sides and rear. "You afraid I can beat you one-on-one?"

Karl snorted a contemptuous laugh. "I can take you, Savage," he sneered, his eyes narrowing. "I can blast you to Earth without a ship."

"Then get your friends off my tail."

Karl signaled with a jerk of his head, and the three other boys moved to the side of the dead-end alley where they had trapped Cort. Karl slashed at Cort, hard and vicious, not mocking this time.

Cort scraped against the wall as he ducked. "I'm going to cut you into little pieces and jettison them like garbage out the hatch. No one going to find the body." Again he jabbed forward.

Cort grabbed his arm and pulled. Off balance from the extended thrust, Karl fell to his knees. In an instant Cort was on the older boy's back, fighting for possession of the knife.

But Karl was bigger and stronger. He rolled over so that Cort was locked underneath him. Still, Cort refused to let go of his knife-wrist. Karl twisted so that he faced down toward Cort, now pinned to the street under the bigger boy's bulk. And he began driving the knife toward Cort's chest.

With every fiber of his strength, Cort fought to keep the knife away, but centimeter by centimeter Karl pushed the knife downward.

Cort's arms burned with the effort. When they started trembling, Karl's sneer turned to a grin.

Cort could hold Karl away no longer. Just before his arms gave way, he squirmed hard to his right. The knife meant for his heart plunged into his left arm. The cut seared like fire.

Cort forced himself to pull away, ripping muscle and skin.

Someone yelled, "Karl! Soldiers!"

In an instant, Karl jumped up, and he and his friends were gone.

Cort sat, pressing his right hand over the wound. Blood ran through his fingers and down his arm.

A squad of six soldiers ran down the deserted street toward him. Not aliens, of course. The starmen seldom visited the city, not even the few alien soldiers. Judging by the uniforms, these were in a private army, working for some rich kingpin who could afford to hire his own protection. Maybe even Sleb's, the kingpin who owned the block Cort lived in. It was a job requiring little education, and Cort and his schoolmates usually scorned it—but right now he was thrilled to see them. Behind the soldiers were two boys—Cort's friends.

Breathing a sigh of relief, Cort tried to stand. He felt faint and stumbled.

"Bad wound you got, boy," said the first soldier to reach him. The soldier supported Cort as he stood.

"Babies playing with knives!" another soldier said. "It makes me want to puke."

"Easy, Osk," said the first, "we all played with knives when we were little. You aim to fly a ship, you need a practice run or three."

"Osk was probably one of the worst," added a third soldier.

Lor said, "He was trying to save a little kid."

"Were you, now?" the third soldier asked Cort, studying him as intently as if his face might reveal how to save, not just a little boy, but all the khena trees of Aran.

Cort drew a breath and straightened up. If the soldier laughed at him, he would have no regrets. He'd do it again if he had to. By Earth, he'd save all the khena trees of Aran, too, if it came to that.

But the soldier just nodded, then fumbled at his pouch and withdrew something. To Cort, he said, "Hold still, boy. This is a starman bandage. It'll stop the bleeding and prevent infection, too." He started to wrap the bandage around Cort's bleeding arm.

"What're you doing, Garn?" Osk said. "Sleb'll blast you to Earth if he finds out you wasted one of his expensive bandages on this street rat."

"Weren't you ever a child once, Osk? The boy did a good deed, so we'll do one for him, too. Sleb isn't going to find out, now, is he?"

Osk was silent.

Garn finished wrapping the bandage, then patted Cort on the shoulder. "Get out of here, boy, before those thugs come back."

"Thanks," Cort breathed. "You saved my life. I won't forget."

The soldier laughed and said, "Save someone else's life sometime."

"Hey, think big," Osk muttered. "Save the whole buggin' planet." He turned to leave, and the other soldiers followed.

Cort made a vow to himself that he wouldn't forget. He wouldn't forget the kind soldier, and he'd save other lives, too, if he ever had the chance. More immediately, he wouldn't forget Karl, either. He intended to repay both.

The house was small, only one room, with one door, one window, one worktable, and one shelf for storing cooking utensils, but Dilia was grateful to have any kind of home at all. In the lawless nighttime people died out on the street, or went missing, which amounted to the same thing.

She was kneading dough for the bread that would be their dinner when she heard the door open. Preparing dinner was her responsibility, since Cort went to school, and his mother Mara had to work. Dilia turned to see Cort silhouetted against the glare of daylight. He was thirteen, the same age as her, but taller. Someday soon, if he kept growing, his head might almost reach the top of the doorway. She put a hand up to shield her eyes while he, uncharacteristically awkward, took off his pack and closed the door.

Dilia caught sight of a fresh white bandage on Cort's arm, and her heart leapt in fear. Had he been in a fight? How badly was he wounded? Might he... Dilia had trouble even thinking this...die? An injury could easily mean death in the city, where infections were not unusual, and the medications the aliens used were hard for the city people to come by, even on the black market.

She covered the dough with a damp cloth and came over to look at his arm more closely. The bandage was shiny and unusually white. "Is that an alien bandage?"

He nodded and looked at his arm, as if he too was still marveling over the exotic dressing. And maybe he was.

Dilia felt a wave of relief. With one of the aliens' bandages, whatever wound was underneath it would heal quickly, and it wouldn't get infected.

She turned his arm one way and another, examining the shining white bandage as if she might by sheer intensity see the cut underneath. "Is it bad? Does it hurt?" she asked in a shaky voice. Dilia loved Cort as something like a brother and a best friend, rolled into one. His death would be devastating, as bad as losing her father, as bad as then losing her mother. Cort was a bright flashing danger sign that said, "Don't dare love him too much. You could lose him, too."

Cort shrugged. "No, it's nothing. I'm fine—really." But he winced when she turned his arm a certain way, and Dilia now understood that he'd been awkward with the door because he was favoring that arm.

"What happened?" she asked. "Are you in a gang?"

"No," Cort said, looking away.

Maybe he wasn't, yet. But in another year or so, he and his school friends would all be in gangs, making trouble and getting hurt. There must be a hundred gangs ranging from school children to adults, city-born to newcomers newly arrived from the forest. Everyone was out to get what he could, however he could. Anyone not out making trouble was bound, sooner or later, to be a victim. Someday, Cort would be seriously hurt. And there was nothing she could do to prevent it.

Dilia had to stop thinking about this. She took Cort's school tablet out of his pack and sat against the wall with it, using her bedroll as a cushion. "We're really getting your money's worth out of your tuition—two for the price of one."

Cort flopped down to sit next to her, rearranging the bedroll so that it would pillow both of them. He smiled at her. "I learn more, too, when we go over it together."

Instead of attending school, Dilia worked in a shop near the gate to the base. Her meager earnings barely paid for her food; anything left over was added to Cort's mother's earnings and to whatever Cort managed to steal so that they could pay the tuition to keep sending Cort to school. But Dilia had no complaints. She was grateful to Mara for taking her in, and she loved being part of this family. Besides, she was learning so much just by sharing Cort's homework.

Turning to today's Mechanics lesson, she hunched over the tablet as if it contained all the riches they owned, her long auburn braid falling over her shoulder. But the lesson might have been written in a code for which she had no key. She couldn't concentrate. All she could think was that Cort was going to get himself killed.

Read more of Saving Aran at https://www.amazon.com/dp/B0B 46X6RJ/.

Acknowledgments

J ohn Donne famously said that no man is an island. This is certainly true of writers. I would like to acknowledge the other people who contributed to this book.

My husband Daniel Kenney, above all others in my life, has supported my writing career even when, sometimes, it meant sacrificing his own time with me. I know it hasn't always been easy. Sweetie, I hope this book, and my others, make it feel worthwhile.

My children, now grown, were my first beta readers way back when. They encouraged me to publish my stories long before I felt ready, and they encourage me still. These books are their legacies too.

James Frenkel, editor of this and all my other books, has also become a good friend. He goes beyond constantly encouraging me. He has always had or made the time to answer my questions and point me in encouraging (though not always easy) directions.

Thanks, too, to the talented people at Deranged Doctor Design, who created this wonderful cover, and to Laurie Cooper of Pub-Craft, my marketing guru and mentor, and now also a friend.

One of the best things that ever happened to my writing career was becoming a finalist in the 2018 Golden Heart contest of the Romance Writers of America. A lot has happened to the Golden Heart and to RWA in the interim, but my cohort of Golden Heart finalists, the Persisters, are some of the most generous and supportive people I've ever known anywhere—as well as an incredibly talented group of writers.

Other writers are crucial to any writer for support and feedback. My critique partners have conscientiously helped make my books better, and they've also kept me writing to a schedule when sometimes it was the hardest thing in the world to do. And Jeanne Estridge, a fellow Persister, writing partner, and friend, helps me remember to show up at the computer, even when I can do no more than staring at the screen.

And you, gentle reader, thank you for opening your heart and mind to these books. I hope to see you again in this journey.

With warmth and gratitude,

G. S. Kenney